He didn't notice the Rundii at first. It was standing more or less where the corridor twisted out of sight and the light was weak. When he saw the shape standing there watching him, he froze.

It was the same creature that had so recently attacked him, of that he was almost sure. There was a difference in the native's attitude, however. It seemed hesitant, unsure.

Zeitman realized, as he acted, that the time between becoming aware of the Rundii, and drawing his vaze to shoot it down as it leapt at him, was less than a heart's beat. He shot, and the Rundii screeched loud and long as it lay on the floor, and pumped its body fluid on to the hard rock...

Zeitman left him lying there, and began his pursuit of Kristina, knowing neither where she had gone, nor what else she might have arranged to be waiting for him – for he was almost sure that she had laid on this attack – in the complex of passages that led to the surface.

D0785634

ROBERT HOLDSTOCK

Eye Among the Blind

VGSF

VGSF is an imprint of Victor Gollancz Ltd
14 Henrietta Street, London WC2E 8QJ

First published in Great Britain 1976
by Faber and Faber Limited

First VGSF edition 1987

Copyright © Robert Holdstock, 1976

British Library Cataloguing in Publication Data
Holdstock, Robert
  Eye among the blind.
  I. Title
  823'.914[F]   PR6058.O442

ISBN 0-575-04010-6

Printed and bound in Great Britain
by Richard Clay (The Chaucer Press) Ltd, Bungay, Suffolk

*This book is sold subject to the condition that it shall not,
by way of trade or otherwise, be lent, resold, hired out, or
otherwise circulated without the publisher's prior consent
in any form of binding or cover other than that in which it
is published and without a similar condition including this
condition being imposed on the subsequent purchaser.*

for Sheila

Thou, whose exterior semblance doth belie
     Thy Soul's immensity;
Thou best Philosopher, who yet dost keep,
Thy heritage, thou Eye among the blind,
That, deaf and silent, read'st the eternal deep,
Haunted for ever by the eternal Mind, —

from 'Intimations of Immortality'
by William Wordsworth

prologue

He was brought among them and left for a while with his thoughts. He took the opportunity to make a recording of what had happened to him, an account of his journey which might one day be found by his own kind and used to enrich their understanding of this strange world.

He was in a valley of statues, a burial ground of the race, and he eased his way down the gentle slopes and felt the shapes of the creatures that had been carved in stone. His senses told him that he had been brought high, deep into the mountains, to a valley where vegetation was rich and animals solitary. His blind eyes looked out across the mountains and he felt the shapes of the wind, the towering bulk of the rock crags and sheer cliff faces.

They came back and clustered around him and he felt their sadness at his lack of sight, and by the time the cool of evening was bringing discomfort to his badly clad body, he was aware of what was going to happen to him.

In the darkness of the night there was the agony of waiting for the first true light of dawn . . . .

part one

chapter one

Moving faster than the dawn, the shuttle from the orbiting cruiser *Realta* might have been seen, by the sharpest of those eyes that watched from the landing station, as a flash of light, preceding, by just a few seconds, the first brilliance of Sigma-G53 as it began to rise above the eastern horizon. With the new day came the wind; an unobtrusive breeze at first, it rose, as the sun climbed higher, into a biting gale that flung the countryside into a frenzy of unwelcomed activity. It shook the tiny landing station with its human and native occupants, until both man and alien looked to each other for moral comfort and a reassurance that they would not at any moment be flung across the hills – with concrete base, wind-proofed towers and docked ships following in a turmoil of destructive energy.

As yet unaffected by the wind, the shuttle from the *Realta* continued its approach, unaware that it was not for the moment being monitored. With its three passengers it had dropped from orbit over the open sea and had approached the south-eastern shore of the larger of the two continents along a flight path with which Robert Zeitman was well familiar. It was this route, coming in from the south east and turning west across the land mass, that he had taken when he had first come to Ree'hdworld, an almost forgotten number of years in the past. Now he sat in the co-pilot's seat and watched the familiar ocean, the distant shoreline of Duchas, the swirling clouds that were evidence of a wind they hardly felt in the well protected shuttle. In a few minutes, Zeitman knew, they would pass across the city-installation of Terming itself; and then beyond, into the night, to where the reception party would be waiting for them. Perhaps Dan Erlam, with all his bluster and tactless humour, would be there himself, though Zeitman doubted it. It would be before dawn in Terming when they landed at the arrival port, which was much too early for the portly city father to have roused himself. Dawn, however, was not too early for Zeitman's wife, Kristina, and since he had overspaced a request that she meet him on his arrival he was confident that she would be there to greet him.

As the shuttle passed across the land-sea divide Zeitman was reminded of why this approach to Terming was the standard tourist in-flight. Although Ree'hdworld was similar in many respects to other Earth-type planets, there was nothing remotely Earthlike about the towering rock megaliths that reared up from the ocean, forty or fifty miles from the main shore, each reaching thin and seemingly fragile bridges of rock to the main land mass of Duchas. Within the vast area of fragmented shoreline below there lay concealed a whole world of animal life and hidden beauty; miles and miles of winding channels and rock ledges that had only ever been cursorily surveyed by the humans who lived across the hills. The sea and the wind, working with inexorable persistence, had failed – as Zeitman understood it – to make any major impression on the natural arches and pinnacles for many thousands of years.

The pilot of the shuttle, an ageing spaceman with a lifetime's fatigue etched into his face, seemed pleased that his three passengers were so awestruck.

'I've made this run a hundred times,' he said, glancing at Zeitman, 'and I still get that feeling. You know . . . ?'

'I know,' said Zeitman. A timeless feeling, a feeling of past and future, intermingled and indistinguishable. The ocean had beaten against those towers of granite before man had been conceived; the battle would go on after a great many things had died. And because the megaliths were a part of an alien world, and had seen an alien past, they inspired a thoughtful silence in those who regarded them.

The shuttle sped on across the mainland, taking them through gorges and canyons that seemed alive with movement. The movement was merely the wind that accompanied the terminator on its clockwork journey around the globe, and they were already heading towards the darkness of night and the relative calm before the early morning gale.

The coastal highlands dropped away after a few minutes and the eastern plain of Duchas stretched before the shuttle as it nosed lower. The concept of a plain, to Zeitman, was of a flat and barren land. Thus the eastern plain was merely a figurative description since there was nothing flat and nothing barren about the rolling hills and the untidy combination of forest, bush and jungle that covered them. Here, where the Ree'hd had spent their evolutionary history, the great dawn wind was split, divided into lesser gales, each of which followed a branch of the spreading rivers as they wound in through steep banks and deep channels in the land. The mass of purple-green vegetation that swept in belts across the plain moved and writhed with the dawn, seeming sentient in its own right, but hiding the only real sentience on Ree'hdworld from aerial view.

The pilot, used perhaps to answering a never-ending stream of tourist questions, seemed to Zeitman to be quite surprised at the persisting silence of his passengers. Zeitman saw him mentally summing each of them up. A nameless blind man, white hair curling over his shoulders, body clad in weather-beaten blue and brown rags. He sat in the back of the shuttle and played with the tarnished metal rings that covered his fingers, and smiled persistently as if nothing was wrong with his world; and he stared out of the window as if he could *see* the land below.

A girl, Susanna Neves – archetypal low-grav female – brunette, slim, smartly dressed and unhappy about something. She seemed very self-possessed so was probably rich, or younger than she looked, or both. And this Robert Zeitman. He looked important but carried no hand brief, bore no air of administrative authority or scientific abstractedness. He was dressed in the fashion of a European-Earthman, a one-piece suit, with a jacket, shapeless and gaudy, worn casually over the top. So the man had been on Earth; but he seemed, nevertheless, familiar with the world below.

'First time on Ree'hdworld?' the pilot asked at length. Zeitman had been waiting for the question and he smiled, shifted his gaze from the side to the forward port where he could see an approaching range of hills, and darkness.

'Second,' he said. 'I was here a long time ago.'

'Why'd you leave?' The man seemed oblivious to personal feelings. Zeitman glanced at him, and turned away.

'Private reasons.'

The pilot nodded slowly, as if everything had been made crystal-clear. After a moment: 'But you're back. For good?'

'I'm back. Hopefully for good, yes.'

'Are you all coming back from somewhere?'

The pilot's relentless interest was becoming an irritation. He had obviously spotted that they were not tourists; equally obviously he had seen the great clusters of ships in orbit around Ree'hdworld and had sensed that something was wrong. He was adding things up and concluding that his three passengers were something to do with the chaos outside the atmosphere.

The girl, Susanna, said, 'No. I'm new here. These two are the old timers.'

The blind man laughed at that. 'So old time that I can see changes even from this height.'

The pilot made a sound of amusement, not quite a laugh. 'I'd hardly have thought so,' he said loudly, then – immediately sorry – he expressed apology. 'Space drains a man's manners,' he added by way of explanation.

'No need to apologize,' said the blind man brightly. Zeitman looked back at him, met the white-eyed stare, the penetrating gaze that defied Zeitman's whole experience. It was unnerving to know – and to have had demonstrated – the blind man's uncanny ability to see despite his absolute blindness. He had never explained it, and since Zeitman had been working on him for nearly all of the three-month flight from Regan-M22, the last step of his journey home, he had concluded that whatever secrets the blind man bore in his heart would remain there.

The strength of the wind outside the shuttle was beginning to make itself felt. The pilot controlled the buffeting well, but was now distracted by his temporary interest in his three passengers. In particular the tall, quiet man who sat beside him.

'This is quite a world,' he said, as the first elements of darkness encompassed them. 'If you don't mind low grav. I already put in a request to be land-based here. A nice place to spend your dying days.'

'Don't you have a home base already?' asked Susanna. The pilot glanced at her in his rear observation mirror. 'My home base was on Sabbath. Three decades ago it was the second colonized world to get hit by the Fear. I was off-world at the time, but I lost a lot of good friends. The whole planet is deserted now, except for a few foolhardies who won't accept that Fear is an organic disease and think they can battle it with will power. They fail, of course; if they don't chop themselves to pieces they come running screaming back to saner stations.'

'Dominion has escaped so far,' said Susanna thoughtfully.

'Your home world? Yes, I thought it might have done. There's no reason why Dominion should ever be hit since it's a luxury world, and that – by definition – means Earthlike. There's no reason why the humans on Ree'hdworld shouldn't escape too. It's only holes like Sabbath that are falling prey to whatever is spreading the Fear.' He fell silent, almost sad. Zeitman thought he detected a sense of loss – even after thirty years.

Susanna said, 'I'm sorry that you lost your home. That must have been terrible.'

'Long time ago, now. Since then a hundred other worlds have gone the same way and I've been employed on more rescue missions than I can remember. Never does any good, mind you. Fear strikes, Fear kills. If you take a person with the Fear and whip them across the Galaxy to Earth they still die. All will to live goes – after the period of persecution, that is.'

The blind man had been listening quietly, intently. He seemed very puzzled, very distressed by what he was hearing. 'This is a disease you say?'

'Where have *you* been?' said the pilot with a smile. 'You've never heard of the Fear? The greatest decimator of human-kind since the Solar War?'

'I've heard of it,' said the blind man, not totally convincingly. 'I hadn't realized it occurred on Earth too . . .'

'I didn't say that. Mind you,' he turned towards Zeitman, 'They say – you know, the Universal They – that Earth *has* been hit by the Fear. You, er . . . you know anything about that?'

My God, thought Zeitman. Can no secret ever be contained? He said, 'I never take any notice of rumours. Hard fact is my discipline.'

The pilot did not seem convinced.

'You ought to know, I suppose. Myself, I'm inclined to doubt rumours too. But Earth is nearly as much of a hell hole as Sabbath was. And these days nothing would surprise me.'

The shuttle never reached total darkness. The land below became shadowy and achieved an atmosphere of mystery, but within a few moments the speeding vessel had risen over a low range of hills and the sprawling city of Terming was below them. It appeared, in the last of the night, as an area of grey and white, spread across the countryside of Duchas for as far as the eye could see in the dimness. In actual fact there was a very sharp and well defined border to the city, and the whole installation only covered a little over one hundred square miles.

The lights of the roadways and the centre were still alive. The centre, an area of ten square miles or so, blazed its greeting to the shuttle passing overhead, and the three passengers found they could discern individual buildings and vehicles quite clearly. As the city centre dropped behind they followed the twisting roadways that wound, snakes of glowing white light, towards the sudden darkness of the plains.

As abruptly as it had come upon them Terming was gone, and below were the dark shrouded ancestral grounds of the Ree'hd, the native race that lived across two thirds of the continent.

Zeitman relaxed back in his seat and anticipated the landing. He couldn't see behind, but imagined that the upper rim of the sun would be rising above the Terming horizon, and by the time the shuttle had landed (later than Zeitman had expected) the dawn would be breaking across those lands too, and Susanna, on her first trip to Ree'hdworld, would know the full fury of the *sam-hat-rhine*, the wind that came from the earth.

The pilot, now fairly busy with landing procedure, nevertheless seemed determined to avoid thoughtful silence. 'I don't know why the landing base has to be so far from the colony,' he said, shaking his head. 'Makes no sense.'

'Terming is not a colony,' said Zeitman patiently. He'd had this argument with Susanna, but in her case there was a good reason why he should make the effort to explain why the city was not a colony but an installation. He found no enthusiasm for pursuing the point with the pilot, beyond the correcting of his statement.

'Installation, then,' said the pilot, less amenably. 'An installation of two hundred thousand men, women and children sounds suspiciously like a colony to me, though.'

Terming, however, was not open to settlement and that was the whole point. The rationale behind a colony was that it was a base from which man the conqueror would spread his influence, eventually encompassing the planetary globe. Ree'hdworld was a world inhabited by an intelligent species, and a colony was not permitted. The Federation had permitted, however, the establishment on the planet of a single centre of learning, cultural exchange and industry, a city-installation financed by InterSystems Biochemicals who had discovered a considerable amount of the local flora to be of interest. The Ree'hd had given permission for that early base to be erected. The whole growing, processing and exporting business was undertaken within the confines of that hundred square miles of diplomatically owned land on Ree'hdworld. The borders were never extended, except to establish a landing station outside the city, and had not been added to, in fact, for three hundred years.

And the entire industrial process resulted only in organic waste which the environment devoured. Power was the least of Terming's problems. The dawn winds were harnessed every day.

Something detached itself from the surface of the world below, and rose rapidly to meet the shuttle. It was an invisible movement even to 'blind' eyes, but both Zeitman and the pilot knew that the probe was on its way. A few seconds later the tiny camera eye peered through the front port with unblinking concentration, then moved out of sight and attached itself to the hull of the ship, there to count sources of body heat. If there were more bodies than expected in the warmth of the shuttle, no landing was permitted.

A moment later: 'Hello shuttle, hello shuttle.'

'Shuttle *Realta* Nix Five. Ready to land,' the pilot signalled back.

'Go ahead *Realta* Nix Five.'

The signal was clear and free of static, and Zeitman searched the gloom for the lights of the landing base.

'Braces,' snapped the pilot. Zeitman pressed the switch on his couch and the whole couch changed shape to encompass him securely. The shuttle banked a little and the first sound of engine power crept into the otherwise still cabin. As the vehicle slowed into the hover mode Zeitman saw the landing base. It was a wide area of featureless concrete, with a small huddle of buildings and towers at one end. The towers reached very high into the Ree'hdworld atmosphere and near the top of one Zeitman could see a lighted window and three or four non-human faces staring out at the arriving vessel.

They sank towards a cradle that opened its arms like a giant anemone, enfolding them and securing them with much creaking and noisy clamping of supports. When the uncomfortable landing had been accomplished Zeitman found himself staring towards the highlands in the west where the trailing edge of Dollar Moon, the larger of Ree'hdworld's two satellites, could just be seen between the highest pinnacles of the mountains. To the east, over the hilly lands they had just traversed, the first edge of the sun was clearly defined, huge, red, sharp in the clear dawn air.

Everything fell silent except the world outside, and the sound of wind on the hull was a strange sound after so many months in vacuum.

Perhaps because they had arrived on Ree'hdworld so early in the installation's day, the air-lift to Terming was not waiting for them. Neither was Kristina. Hiding his disappointment, Zeitman loudly expressed his irritation that they would have to wait in this desolate landing station for an hour or so while Dan Erlam roused himself, fifty miles distant, and remembered his duties. But it gave both Zeitman and the blind man a chance to get the feel of the world they had both known before.

And it introduced Susanna to the sort of climate she could expect for the next few years.

They deposited their luggage with a tired female official who made them a stimulant drink and equipped them with the standard Ree'hdworld cataphrak, a body-hugging suit that would keep them warm or cool whatever the conditions they found themselves in. The blind man declined to dress in what he regarded as a restrictive article, but Zeitman was glad of the second skin, and he convinced Susanna to wear one too.

The wind blew strong and bitter for many minutes, but at length Zeitman detected its wane and he went outside into the morning air. Susanna followed him. They walked away through the grouped buildings, across the hard ground until they came to the natural soil of the planet. From there, buffeted by wind, Zeitman pointed out the sights: the Hellgate mountains to the north, that great expanse of valleys and pinnacles where the dubious remains of the Pianhmar had been found; the forests that skirted the mountains and stretched for thousands of miles across the southern extremity of Duchas and sent dense fingers of jungle across the plains and down to the seas themselves. In the jungles, lived the Rundii, the sub-intelligent second race of Ree'hdworld which had been responsible for a great deal of death among the early human population at the installation. Now humans and Rundii treated each other with respect and there was very little trouble. The Rundii herds stayed among the trees, and the humans stuck to the plains if they ever left the city.

It was as they walked towards the small tributary of a greater river, flowing some miles to the south, that Susanna saw her first real alien. It was a solitary Ree'hd wending its way painfully and slowly along the river bank towards its community.

Four years away had not lessened Zeitman's familiarity with the Ree'hd culture. He spotted the native immediately as a Wanderer.

Susanna had dropped into a crouch, a hundred yards distant, hidden behind a small rise of ground. She watched the creature with fascination bordering on horror. She had seen pictures, of course, but there was – and Zeitman realized and had experienced the fact – a certain shock in making the live acquaintance of a Ree'hd for the first time. It was a combination of the bizarre physical features of the creatures, and the fact that they were the only other intelligence in map-space, which was effectively the known Universe. To meet with a real alien was always a moment of great awe.

The Ree'hd, watching its lateral environment with infra-red-sensitive eyes, had spotted the two humans without any trouble. It turned its huge head and the colour-and-shape-sensitive forward eyes moved slightly as it accommodated for binocular vision. The eyes were small, but the mobile flesh they sat within covered half the creature's face. The great bulges on its temples became highly active, light flashing from the faceted surfaces of those night eyes.

It stopped and stared at Zeitman who raised an arm in greeting. The Ree'hd immediately approached, limping very badly. As it grew nearer Zeitman picked out the sexual characteristics: a particular pattern of scaly skin over the creature's belly. This was a carrier of young, a female.

Her left leg was grossly lacerated, and purple-red blood formed an amorphous pattern of clots and streaks from her crotch (which was featureless, no doubt to Susanna's surprise)

22

to her heavily muscled and widely splayed feet. As she approached so Susanna got an idea of the normal movement of a Ree'hd, an easy side-to-side swaying motion, the tree trunk legs moving almost without effort. The Ree'hd walked in a semi-crouch, body angled forward, long arms held out to the side; for hands they had disc-shaped plates with fifteen multi-jointed tendrils functioning for fine touch and smell sensitivity.

The Ree'hd female stopped a few yards away from the two humans and looked from one to the other of them. She touched her leg almost self-consciously. 'Looks worse than it is.'

The voice, speaking interLing with surprising fluency, took Susanna by complete surprise. She looked at Zeitman with a huge question in her eyes. Then she smiled, almost with embarrassment. 'I have a lot to learn,' she said.

To the Ree'hd Zeitman said, 'How long were you away?'

A great sigh escaped from the Ree'hd's wide fleshy mouth. Immediately a second mouth opened below the first. A strong belch of fetid breath assailed Susanna's sensitive nostrils and she winced, but was more surprised by the duality of mouth and lip.

The lower mouth closed and became almost invisible, the lips tucking inwards tidily and completely. 'A year,' said the Ree'hd. 'I wandered to the south, but there seemed no reason to continue.'

'What attacked you?'

'A *broo'kk*. As I traversed a small forest some miles from here. I should have known better.'

'What's a . . . broo-uck?' asked Susanna, addressing her question to Zeitman.

'*Broo'kk*,' Zeitman corrected. 'A foliage browser. A rare carnivore to encounter.'

'But an unpleasant one,' said the Ree'hd, favouring her companions with a human-like smile. It was an unnatural gesture for a Ree'hd, but it was an easy gesture to produce and was welcomed by the humans since it was an acknowledgement of friendship between the races.

The Ree'hd female moved away, returning to the stream she had been following back to its source.

Zeitman took Susanna's arm and walked her back towards the base. 'That was a Wanderer. She was lucky in a sense. Most Wanderers never return.'

'A Wanderer being . . . ?'

'A Ree'hd who has to leave the community to find an inner peace. I doubt that's anywhere near the truth, but the Ree'hd are difficult to understand in so many ways. If a kin dies unnaturally, or of disease, the closest kin wanders – that can be anything from a month to a year. Seventy percent of the time the Wanderer finds a sort of inner peace and commits suicide by drowning. Thirty percent of the time he returns and there is absolutely no change in his status in the community. The community reshuffles every year and the kin relationships change and our Wanderer participates just as actively.'

Wandering had been something that Zeitman had studied during his previous years on Ree'hdworld, and it was a phenomenon he had never satisfactorily understood. Nor had Kristina, who had worked with him.

He brooded about Kristina for a moment. He found it hard to hide his disappointment that she had not been at the landing station to greet him. But, in retrospect, he was not surprised that she had failed to show. It had only been during the last year of his time away from Ree'hdworld that his sporadic communications to her had taken on any sort of affection. Kristina was still his wife, although they were as good as separated. They had just never bothered to formalize the arrangement. For three years, on different worlds throughout the length, breadth and depth of map-space, Zeitman had pursued his whims, and had given no thought to his estranged wife. It was only after three years away that he had suddenly felt regret, and then a conviction that he had made a mistake, had acted atrociously, and should make every effort to clear the air and begin again. And even if it had occurred to him at first that such a beginning-again required two people's consent, and she might not be interested in such a rehabilitation, then by the time he had left Earth and made straight for Ree'hdworld Zeitman had been living his dream of reunion for so long that any other course of events was inconceivable and intolerable.

So her absence from the base was a blow, and the lack of any form of communication or explanation was an omen of foreboding, which was depressing him more with each passing minute.

As they came into the shadow of one of the control-towers, hidden from the orange-red sun that was now above the horizon and climbing steadily to zenith, Susanna stopped and looked back to where the solitary Ree'hd was a distant shape, still moving slowly northwards. She absorbed the view with obvious appreciation, her gaze lingering on the Hellgate mountains for some moments.

'They look forbidding.'

'The mountains? They are. They cover thousands of square miles and I don't suppose any human has ever penetrated more than the first two or three ranges. The wind, as you go deeper and higher, becomes too much for even our skimmers – and they're sturdy craft under most any situation.'

'But that's where that other race was supposed to have lived. Perhaps they were wind freaks.'

Zeitman laughed. 'Everyone on Ree'hdworld is a wind freak. The wind is our greatest resource. It's so predictable.'

As if to prove him wrong a sudden strong gust blew across them, propelling them at a run towards the warmth of the station. Susanna laughed loudly and reached out for Zeitman's hand as her hair obscured her vision and her feet began to find difficulty lodging. They collided with the door of the passenger lounge and – as if satisfied that blasphemy had been revenged – the wind dropped.

They waited for the airlift in silence. Susanna made her first effort to learn something about Ree'hdworld by studying the maps and guides that were hung, mostly for decoration though occasionally for information purposes, upon the otherwise bare walls of the lounge. Zeitman watched her, but his mind was on Kristina. How would she have changed, he wondered? She had been trim when he had known her before, but looking at the slenderness of the Dominion girl, the impression he had was that Kristina was fleshy. He lingered on memories of Kristina's physical form, and by doing so he managed to unremember the bitter arguments and stinging sarcasm that she had used as a weapon against him in the final months of the breakdown. More than anything, perhaps, it had been her hostility that had driven him from the world he had come to love.

So much for unremembering the bad times.

'What's the other continent like?'

It took several moments for Zeitman to realize that Susanna was talking to him. She smiled as he looked apologetic. 'Did I interrupt some tender memories?'

He shook his head. 'No. Not really. Wooburren? A desolate place. Deserted as far as intelligent life is concerned. I spent some time there with . . . people.'

'Wooburren . . . that doesn't sound like a native word.'

'It isn't. Nor is Duchas. The names go back to the early explorers, that's all I know. If you're interested, the Ree'hd call this continent *Sam'Hreeroill'ju'uk* . . . which, translated conceptually, means "the land with the life from the wind". The Ree'hd also have a thorough awareness of Wooburren, even though it's a legend to them and they think it's an island. They call the place – let me get this right – *Kranncaith'Samhaill*, "the island that floats in time and carries the spirit of the Earth Wind". As you'll find out, the natives believe in a metaphysical part of life that lives outside the community until there is a physical form for it to take on.'

'You mean, souls from God.'

Zeitman shook his head. 'The Ree'hd have no concept of God, only of wind power.'

Digesting that information, Susanna turned back to her scrutiny of the contour map of the world. Distracted from his reminiscences, Zeitman tried to engage the nameless blind man in conversation, but he seemed fairly melancholy. He

26

was sitting, tense and ill at ease, and his fingers twirled the rings on his left hand, sliding them up to the nail and back again. He stared into the middle of the waiting room and two thin trickles of moisture ran from each inner corner of his eyes – it was nothing but the dryness of the room, but it gave to the ragged individual an atmosphere of great distress.

Aware of Zeitman's silent scrutiny, the man smiled, his face creasing again into a thousand tiny folds. His skin was very tanned and when he laughed or frowned the already intricate folds of flesh formed into patterns of ridges as complex as fingerprints. He stopped his nervous game with his fingers and reached inside his brown leather jerkin to scratch the bare flesh beneath.

Zeitman opened the conversation. 'Strange coming back, isn't it?'

The blind man nodded slowly. 'Unnerving. Really unnerving. Everything is so different. The atmosphere, I mean. It's different.'

Zeitman could see, now, that it was not melancholia that was afflicting the blind man, but agitation; a distress that he was trying to cover but which was too strong for him. He went on as Zeitman, by his silence and his interest, invited a fuller understanding. 'I don't mean it smells different. And apart from this base, from here the world *looks* the same – and I mean that, as you know. But I have warning signals going on my head like crazy!' He slapped a hand to his thatch of white hair, shook his head. 'I don't understand it. The emotional atmosphere is different. There's tension, real tension. Perhaps you can feel it too. Great tension, Zeitman . . . as if . . . as if an emotional storm is about to break loose. I can't identify the source, but it's strong. Very strong.'

Zeitman couldn't feel what the blind man was obviously feeling. After a moment he changed the subject. 'When did you say you were here before?'

'Oh . . . years ago. A long time ago . . .'

Before Zeitman could pursue the point a small skimmer designed for six men plus equipment, fluttered on to the base outside the lounge and the pilot came in to fetch his passengers. He apologized for the delay but gave no reason, which meant that Erlam had been tardy in issuing instructions for the pick-up. Zeitman said nothing.

They battled through the brisk wind and secured themselves into the tiny vessel. When they were safely strapped down the skimmer took to the air like a leaf, almost somersaulting as it turned back to race, low, across the country towards the city.

Activity a few miles to the north prompted the blind man to ask the pilot to detour that way and, without commenting on the strangeness of the request, the man cut the skimmer across the wind and flew his passengers to what Zeitman had already noticed was a Ree'hd community. The community was in the process of dispersing after the mass crooning with which they, and other Ree'hd communities, greeted the dawn and the hostile wind from the earth. From their vantage point, high above the community and the river about which they had gathered, the entrances to the Ree'hd burrows were shadowy areas, difficult to discern as access points to the complex of underground chambers and corridors that would be spread beneath the ground for many hundreds of yards.

More interesting to Zeitman was the skimmer that stood some way from the river, being visibly assaulted by the wind. It did not have any characteristic marking that he recognized, and he saw no evidence of any humans among the crowded Ree'hd, but from this height the relatively small human frame would have been difficult to distinguish . . . .

Susanna screamed.

She was sitting behind Zeitman and next to the blind man and in the claustrophobic cabin her hysteria was shocking to experience. The pilot lost control of the skimmer for a moment and it slewed violently at the mercy of the wind, dipping and diving to within twenty feet of the ground before it straightened up and achieved a safe height again.

Looking round, Zeitman saw that the blind man was no longer in his seat, was not, in fact, in sight – and in the instant of acceptance of the fact came a crystallization of fear and feeling, a total acceptance on Zeitman's part of the sensation he had felt whenever talking to the blind man, that that strange individual belonged to no Universe with which Zeitman was familiar.

'For God's sake, what happened?' snapped the pilot irritably. He stretched round and looked at Susanna, and in the next instant he had seen the blind man's empty seat, and he was visibly confused. 'What happened?'

'He vanished,' said Susanna dully. She was shaking and was obviously reluctant to look at the blind man's empty seat. 'I wasn't watching him, but I saw him go from the corner of my eye. He just vanished in an instant . . .' now she looked at the empty seat, at the still fastened safety harness hanging limply and uselessly in the space where the blind man's body should have been.

Zeitman reached out and took Susanna's hand. She smiled and said, 'I'm all right. Really. It was just . . . well, a fright, that's all.'

She was still shaking, but there was nothing Zeitman could think of that was worth saying. He let go of her hand and lost himself in his thoughts. They completed the flight to Terming in total silence.

chapter two

It had rained during the short night, and Urak, with an uncharacteristic lack of foresight, had failed to secure the mud barrier at the mouth of the burrow. The substrate around the entrance had formed into a glistening paste and had run into the outer corridor system where Kristina, as she awoke from her usual heavy sleep, could see it drying in the fresh dawn breeze that ventilated the burrow network. Fortunately the rain had not been heavy, otherwise she might have found herself swimming in mud as many a thoughtless (or lazy) Ree'hd had done in the past.

Urak was not in the burrow. Kristina sat up and stretched, and in that simple movement was a luxury that she would never have considered when living her life as the human she still was. The chamber was in darkness, but by moving her head towards the burrow's entrance she could feel the filtered draught that kept the chamber fresh, and she could also see the shaft of light from the daylit world outside. Now that she looked more carefully the full extent of the damage was evident – the corridor outside was virtually unpassable.

She called for Urak, at the same time lighting the small power-lamp that the Ree'hd One permitted her to have. When she listened for an answering call all she could hear was the scream of the wind, distant and muffled. For a moment she panicked. Had she overlaid and missed the dawn singing? She grew calm after a few seconds when she realized that Urak, for all his consideration of her humanity, would not have permitted her to sleep on through the most momentous event of the day.

Muscles were aching in strange places, but mostly around her hips. Although her body was no longer complaining at this habit of rising with the sun, it was definitely complaining about the manner in which she had slept, squatting and upright, modelling herself on her Ree'hd 'lover', who was the most upright Ree'hd she knew. She began to exercise, calling for Urak again with human impatience.

In the middle of some vigorous toe-touching she heard several Ree'hd pass through the corridor outside, obviously irritated with the muddy slush they waded through. She paused in her toning-up movements and watched the shapes pass by the narrow burrow entrance; they were mostly immature Ree'hd, their spade-like forearms held rigidly before them. They would be set to the task of scooping the mud away before they began work shovelling out the extension to the burrow complex that was necessitated by the small increase in population this year.

The last Ree'hd to pass the entrance came in, and for a moment Kristina felt unease. The native was mud-spattered and wet, and Kristina did not recognize Urak for several seconds, during which her nakedness became acutely embarrassing. This was an irrational feeling, perhaps, since there was only the basic humanoid characteristic that was similar between human and Ree'hd; but with Kristina's growing affection for the ageing Ree'hd, Urak, had come the same self-consciousness of exposure that accompanies two humans at the start of an intimate relationship. It was a sensation she enjoyed, even if she did not fully understand it.

'Aren't you cold?' asked Urak, speaking his language slowly and carefully so that Kristina – not yet fully fluent with the dialect – would have no problem understanding. He began to groom himself, scraping the mud from his body with intricate strokes of his callous-covered forearm; his sensitive fingers attended, seemingly without conscious control, to cleaning more intimate and sensitive places.

'No. Surprisingly.' She began to dress. The small chamber, with its thick vegetation flooring, was fairly well insulated against cold, but was not a warm place. Kristina had grown used to the cool, but to face the biting dawn winds was a different matter. A cataphrak was the only protection against them.

'No *pins and needles* this morning?' asked Urak with his artificial smile. He used the English words (which had been retained in interLing), pronouncing them perfectly. Kristina shook her head and looked pleased. 'I'm getting to grips with my inferior circulation,' she said.

'Impossible,' said Urak. The Ree'hd found the concept of agony at returning circulation very amusing. His own race never relaxed, in one sense, since the circulation of blood at the body surfaces and extremes of a Ree'hd was highly efficient (surplus heat being lost by transformation into electrical energy that discharged through the earth). With any substantial lowering of a Ree'hd's body metabolism, or any compression of surfaces, the outer limit of the body became an isolated zone of activity whose behaviour was under conscious control.

'Is the sun up yet?'

'Just,' said Urak. 'There is a fairly heavy cloud covering moving along the horizon that will stop you seeing it, however.' Again the artificial smile, this time coupled with a boastful rolling of the lateral eyes, eyes which included complex devices for detecting polarized light as well as infra-red.

'Don't brag about your superior biology to me,' said Kristina, 'or I'll brag about some of mine to you.' She could hear the wind clearly now; a mournful humming that was, in fact, a full-blooded gale – polarized wind, blowing towards the distant mountains, sweeping as it did so across the thousand miles of forest that cut the plains of the Ree'hd from the mountains of another age. 'I don't want to miss the singing, Urak . . .'

'Don't worry,' said the Ree'hd. 'It won't start yet. There are too many repairs to burrow entrances. A few minutes . . .'

They looked at each other, human and alien, exchanging a gaze that each interpreted in his or her own way, but which both interpreted correctly: from Kristina, a look of absolute love; from the Ree'hd, warmth and affection, the alien version of emotions that ought to have led to the cementing of a relationship for life.

The barrier between them was too obvious to have even needed discussion. They touched, hand to sticky hand, finger on corrugated face, flexible digit on cool, hair-covered flesh, sending unbearably sensuous messages to the human brain, irritating the sensitive sucker discs of the alien as the invisible hair on Kristina's cheeks and chin played havoc with the nerve endings in Urak's fingers.

'Kristina,' said the Ree'hd, speaking interLing with what Kristina found to be a beautifully sexy accent, 'from what I learned whilst with you and Robert—'

Oh Urak! Why remind me!

'Kristina? You've gone cold . . .' A moment's query. 'Ah . . . I've mentioned the unmentionable.'

'You have indeed.'

'Is this a typical human reaction on being reminded of a fragment of the past? Hostility. Anger. Must I never mention Robert Zeitman again, even though he was a good friend to us both?'

'Never again.' He's coming, she thought. He's arriving today, back on Ree'hdworld, back on my home, and he thinks he'll be with me again . . . what a rotten, horrible turn of the celestial screw. Aloud she said, 'I've forgotten him, and I don't wish to be reminded.'

Urak made peace by touching her hands with his. 'I'm sorry . . . ,' in Ree'hd this time. The native could change language like he changed his chest tattoo. 'All I was going to say was that when I was with you . . . earlier, years back, when you were studying me for whatever reasons you studied me, I learned the difference between our races regarding sex.'

'Oh?' Kristina was intrigued to know what was coming next.

'I haven't mentioned it before,' in interLing now, using word contractions as if he had lived in human society all his life, 'but I've been worrying about it. Your race needs constant sexual communication, a physical need, a sensory need. I know this and see no reason—'

Kristina felt irritation rising within her, but she forced a smile and cut Urak short. 'No reason why I shouldn't go into "town" for an occasional thrill. You're very kind, Urak, but don't let human biology books be your only source of learning. Since a time in my past when my bonding to an unmentionable human became a nightmare I have lost all such desires. End of subject.'

Urak absorbed her statements with just the slightest tremblings of his song lips, an indication of relief. Relief? thought Kristina. Is he pleased I don't need sex? Would he have been jealous of that? Beautiful! A sexist Ree'hd, a very rare specimen.

The conversation ended there, abruptly, with an underlying tension that Kristina had been noticing for two days now. The tension was all on Urak's side, and Kristina was puzzled as to its cause. It had begun the morning they had first dis-

33

cussed the emotions they each felt, and tried to decide whether or not it was love. Urak's tension had arisen not from the mutual agreement that they *did* love each other, but from the reasoning, the discussion, that followed.

'The human body is not without its own beauty,' he had said.

'Thank you,' said Kristina. 'Mind you, there are more pronounced sexual differences than between the Ree'hd sexes, so I hope you find my body more attractive than a man's.'

Urak continued his pre-dawn grooming. His song mouth was stretched wide in his assumed expression of amusement.

'I regret, no. The female body of your race is clumsy. It's not made to merge with nature.'

'But this is an alien planet to us. You wouldn't expect—'

'But the human male body *is*. It's fast, lean – except for your friend Daniel – it's hard. Less susceptible. There is more beauty in the male body, despite its external weaknesses of neck and genitals.'

Kristina gave Urak an irritated look. 'We have a word for human males who think like you, but I'll spare you from it for the moment. My body is exceptional. Not exceptionally beautiful just exceptionally ordinary. But many female bodies *are* fast and lean and hard.'

'In which case they are less female.'

'No! Femaleness is a state of mind, not body.'

Urak struggled with the concept. 'Do you make love with your minds? I thought you had to have physical desire. Was I wrong?'

Kristina said that if there was no mind love there was only intercourse. 'Intercourse has two meanings to an Earthman, and both are necessary for love. Between bonded pairs, anyway.'

Urak finished his grooming and beckoned Kristina to him. She stood above his seated form and he reached out and felt her body in a most intimate way. His 'fingers' probed her sex and took the measure of her breasts. Kristina stood quite still, but gradually began to tremble. How did the Ree'hd see her, she wondered. To a human male she was a woman of medium

34

height and medium build, with black hair cut unattractively close to her scalp, and teeth stained yellow with her local vegetable diet. Her face was no longer smooth, but covered with the wrinkles of a skin that has been subjected to biting wind for day after day, month after month. She would hardly call herself a handsome woman.

Her moment of embarrassment faded quickly – what on earth (or Ree'hdworld) did it matter now?

'Physical attributes,' said Urak, 'are irrelevant to a Ree'hd . . . you know that of course. I can't conceive of a way of thinking that is dictated by superficial appearance. It seems shallow.'

Framing her words carefully, Kristina said, 'You must distinguish between love and desire. To most humans appearance is a secondary factor in establishing a relationship. Provided a good communicative contact is made first. Mind love above body love, like you said.'

Urak thought about that for a moment. He said, 'Perhaps between humans both physical and mental love *are* necessary, to the detriment of their understanding of each other.'

Kristina nodded, smiling. 'The body is only a limitation to physical love. True love is greater than the urge to couple, and there is no reason to confine one's search for love to one's own species. Our bodily differences are not limiting factors.'

It was then that Urak began to be ill at ease. Kristina had never seen such agitation in her friend (for months a friend, and now, for a day and longer, her lover). She reached out and touched him, touched his song lips and the sensitive skin beneath his lateral eyes.

The native stood up and remained motionless, surveying the girl. Beneath his flimsy wrap his sexual skin was dull green; there was no hint of arousal. But it was not in a sexual way that this strangely lovely alien aroused him.

It was in a way, he explained to Kristina, that frightened him. He was not ready to realize what was so obvious. He had a horrible feeling that once he sat, thought and documented what she was teaching him (*him*, the village One) his life search would be over.

He was afraid of achieving a goal. But he loved Kristina, and he could feel that love reciprocated.

From that time, two days back, to this they had limited discussion of the subject. Now Urak led the way from the small burrow and along the still muddy corridor to the egress on to the river slope.

The cold air was a shock to Kristina as she straightened up just outside the corridor exit. She shivered violently and stared up into the gradually clouding sky. The sun, still clearly seen from the community, was fully above the horizon. As she looked at the dull red disc she felt a touch on her arm, and heard the brief exhalation of a Ree'hd in great distress.

She knew who it was even before she looked, but after a moment she met the alien gaze of Reems'gaa, the small female Ree'hd who was (at this moment) a cause of great concern on Kristina's part.

Urak was still walking down the muddy slopes towards the river. He stopped briefly and looked back, gave no sign of any emotion, despite Kristina's obvious trouble, and went on down to the water's edge.

Reems'gaa, whose natural racial year-kinship to Urak, her rightful position, had been usurped by the human female, and was now lost and confused. She spent her days seated outside the burrow entrance, imploring Urak to take her into his burrow and not to leave her to die. Urak, since at this time he was the dominant of whatever year coupling he would assume, ignored her with all the callousness of a human adolescent. It hurt Reems'gaa to be treated so; it hurt Kristina to see Urak manifest such untypical contempt; and it hurt her to know that she was – to bring it right home – the other woman!

Reems'gaa made a strange low-pitched noise and closed her eyes. A gesture of pleading. She murmured words in Ree'hd, words that Kristina had difficulty in understanding and could not, for a second or two, figure out why.

Then she realized. Reems'gaa was speaking *with her food lips.*

'Oh God!' shouted Kristina feeling an overwhelming pity; there were tears in her eyes and she had to restrain herself from throwing her arms around the deserted Ree'hd and hugging her to her body. 'Oh Reems'gaa, don't ask me . . . don't make me lose him.'

All coherence gone, the Ree'hd female began to threaten, with sound, appearance and gesture. Her lateral eyes became swollen as body fluid pumped into the mid-facet vessels. Arms came up, palms spread, tendrils stiff and dry. Terrible, terrible anger!

Kristina ran after Urak, slipping on the muddy surface, straining a muscle in her leg, leaving her shame and her guilt behind as she tried to think of Urak and Urak alone.

As she sat down, three feet from the raging waters, feeling the icy splash of spray upon her face, she felt the eyes of several older Ree'hd upon her. Reems'gaa's plight, the unnatural turn of fate, was not a popular situation by any means.

The entire community was beginning to croon.

Kristina sat in the very middle of the gathered population, which had spread itself out along nearly four hundred yards of the river bank, and on both sides of the river. The Ree'hd sat, no more than three deep, all eyes closed, arms folded stiffly down their sides and bodies motionless. Only their song lips moved, almost imperceptible movements as they uttered the wavering notes of the dawn songs.

It was very cold and the wind was hard and unmerciful; it was building in strength still, though it would never reach the full strength it had once known when it had blown through this river valley. Kristina knew that it was a completely natural (and cyclical) decline. But most of the Ree'hd blamed the city of Terming. Six hundred years ago the newly arrived Earthmen had erected wind barriers to protect their growing installation – the Ree'hd had objected but because it was an irrational objection they had been ignored. There were, naturally, no Ree'hd alive who could remember the feelings that had flooded the continent in those days, but the memory lingered on, seeming to become a greater source of irritation the older a Ree'hd became.

The argument, six centuries back, had caused the division of the local Ree'hd community. Those that stayed moved into the overground buildings of Terming, abandoning their own burrows completely; those that refused to stay had moved along the river, away from the channelled gorges beyond the lowlands, and further into one of the evolutionary spheres of the *Rund-iamha-reach* (Rundii), 'the talking animals from the moving forests'.

Kristina squatted by Urak and listened to his voice join the swelling volume of voices welcoming the new day.

It would not have been proper for her to sing, though Urak had said that when she fully understood the significance of the singing, her high-pitched contribution to the sound field would be permissible. Now she contented herself by imagining herself singing, and her brain turned end over end (it seemed) with the ecstasy of the monotone harmony that the wind was picking up and carrying into the Rundii sphere.

The water rushed by and she found herself watching what some long-forgotten Earthman had termed 'silver-fish', the aquatic animals that filled the rivers during the winter and which, in the absence of any substantial land fauna, prevented the technologically incompetent Ree'hd from starving. During the spring and summer the 'fish' were never touched. There was food enough to be had by mindkilling the smaller burrow-dwelling animals, or running down the eight-appendaged game that symbiosed so cryptically with the moving forests.

The Ree'hd were fast runners. Their leg homologs were long and springy (becoming more so in the warmer seasons) and the tissue that mimicked muscle in function was what every skeletal muscle should be – powerful and capable of sustaining this power for days and days.

When a Ree'hd chased an animal it was no quick spurt and succeed or give up – he or she chased the animal for days, running virtually all the time, without water or food intake, without conscious functioning of any sort – a total closing down of systems apart from the fact of the hunt and the search for predatory animals.

It was frightening and yet . . . fascinating.

The thought of the fascinating fauna of Ree'hdworld led inevitably to thoughts of Robert Zeitman, her ex-husband. By now he would be somewhere in orbit, she imagined; perhaps scanning the planet's surface with a telescope . . . perhaps even watching her as she sat by the river and shivered.

When Zeitman had been here before he had been passionately interested in the biosphere of Ree'hdworld, convinced that there was something very out of balance in what he saw about him. He and Kristina had examined every animal they could catch, and it was during their various hunts that Kristina had first become aware of Urak (then a Ree'hd of low status) and he of she. Urak had been the Ree'hd that Zeitman had asked to examine, and the native with whom they had discussed the impossible actuality of a semi-humanoid race totally distinct from the human race of Earth.

It was still incredible to Kristina that for all Zeitman's being away for several years, it was only in the last few days that she and Urak had reached an emotional understanding that had resulted in him taking her as a 'lover'. It was time wasted, but Urak had merely been behaving properly. The interest had been there for a year, but Urak had taken his year-kin already and would not destroy that Ree'hd's soul by leaving her (it would have to be him leaving her since he was not the dominant of the pair relationship at that time). At the changing, four days back, Kristina had become Urak's year-kin instead of Reems'gaa – it was a choice that had been disapproved of by many of the local Ree'hd, but none had the right to argue with the burrow One.

That it was Reems'gaa whom she had displaced was an unfortunate coincidence. Six years previously Robert Zeitman, in one of his thoughtless moods, had made some ill-timed and inappropriate observations on Reems'gaa and caused her to lose her offspring and her chances of ever again giving birth. This had not affected her position in the community, but it was a severe personal blow to the Ree'hd female. Kristina, six years later, was compounding the wound.

She was drawn from her reminiscence by someone touching her arm. Urak was pointing to something in the sky, and looking up she saw a skimmer gliding high overhead.

A moment of anxiety and the slow calming of her racing heart. She knew Zeitman would be on that skimmer and that he was certainly very upset that she had not met him at the landing base. She knew, however, that if she had been there she would have been cold, incapable of warmth, and that would have made the meeting unbearable.

'Sorry Robert,' she thought after the vanishing vessel.

The singing went on, though the community was already beginning to disperse. The wind was less strong now, but just as cold, and Kristina drew her cloak more tightly around her shoulders. She looked at the ranks of natives, some swaying gently as their prayers and fears were offered to the remnants of the *sam-hat-rhine*.

With a start she saw an Earthman sitting on the opposite bank watching her. There were many Ree'hd on the other side of the river since the burrow community spanned below the river-bed through the solid rock. The Ree'hd were great tunnelers and in their 'adolescence', prior to the differentiation of their extremities into the sensitive appendages they would become, they had tough, shovel-like hands that facilitated the tunnelling through the hard-packed soil and soft bed-rock below this part of the continent.

The human who sat among the natives was staring at her, but there was something strange about the way he stared, something . . . blind. Perhaps her sixth sense, perhaps memories of seeing blind men before, but she knew without knowing that the man was blind, and as she thought that so she observed him lift a hand in salute.

She waved back. Could he see that? She pointed to the man and indicated that he should come across the river and sit with her.

The man across the water shook his head.

Kristina was uneasy. But her uneasiness was nothing compared to the agitation that Urak was showing. The dawn song was dying slowly and several Ree'hd were showing an interest in the blind man. He had not been to the community before and Kristina could not remember seeing him in Terming; and there was no sign of a skimmer or any means by which he had approached the community. 'Do you know him?' she asked Urak, imagining that the man meant something to the Ree'hd.

'No,' said Urak. 'Who is he?' Urak was tense and Kristina could not imagine why. She said, 'I don't know. I've never seen him before. Why does he upset you?'

'He fills me with unease,' said the Ree'hd, hunching forward and staring across the water. 'Something about him . . .'

'He can't go far,' said Kristina. 'Finish singing and we'll talk to him.'

But Urak could not finish his own song. He sat and watched the man with four unblinking eyes that had lost their sparkle as his tension grew. Around Kristina the Ree'hd song drifted away and more and more of the Ree'hd began to leave the steeply sloping bank of the river and return to their burrows.

The cloud-covering was now thick and oppressive, and the wind changed in character – no longer the magic sentience blowing in a single direction, but a playful sequence of gusts and eddies – the sort of wind pattern during which the bodies of dead infants were offered to the river.

This was early spring and the rushing waters of the river were the soul of a new season; their monotonous sounds were the prayers of the world as life cycles began to revolve.

Urak seemed to overcome his anxiety and he rose from the bank and turned to follow the stream of Ree'hd back to the burrows and the copious repairs that the rain had necessitated. 'Are you going to the city now?' he asked. There was a cheerfulness, a harmony in the air.

Kristina remained seated, watching the man opposite her. When Urak spoke she looked up. 'No . . . no, I'll stay here awhile.'

Urak's touch on her face was as gentle as it was reassuring. He said, in his own tongue, 'Don't postpone what might well be a pleasant meeting. Four years is a long time to be apart from someone. He may have changed.'

Kristina could not have agreed more. 'I know, Urak. That's

what I'm really afraid of. I've changed too . . . and not in the right way for harmony with Robert.' She shook her head. Urak walked away but, unaware of his departure, she talked on. 'It will be a frightening meeting. I can already see his eyes . . . full of despair, full of need. And what can I say? Just: "hello-goodbye . . . there's nothing left Robert. Nothing for us, so forget your romantic plans. Go about your business and leave me alone".'

The man on the opposite bank watched her. He seemed concerned. Kristina realized that Urak had left and that she sat alone by the river. She felt cold. Through a break in the cloud she saw a fragment of the dull red disc of the sun – she watched it and thought of Earth's tiny sun and how huge the sun of Ree'hdworld was by comparison. In the far distance she could see the energy accumulators above Terming and she could imagine the hideous bustle of human traffic, and the rape that they were perpetrating upon the Ree'hd culture, spreading out from the old burrows where they had set their first installation.

Kristina was ashamed to be pink, fat and bipedal. She wished she were a fish . . . a silver fish, darting upstream, as if inviting the watcher to catch it.

'Don't brood. There's no point.'

He was sitting by her and her mind could not accept the fact for a second. 'How . . . how did you get over here so fast?'

The blind man laughed. 'I move fast. Don't bother yourself with it. Concentrate on cheering up.'

Astonished by his matter-of-factness, Kristina stared at the blind man who turned his head to watch her with uncanny accuracy. He was very old, that was clear – and yet there was something very youthful about him. He wore clothes styled in antiquity, an outfit of leather, cracked and dulled with time. He wore no cataphrak and should have been freezing, but he seemed to find the climate quite amenable. Looking at his face, Kristina detected great warmth, and strong humour. Looking at his eyes she felt a chill, however; his eyes were white, completely white, with a few tiny blood vessels tracing a path around the very edge of each orbit.

As she moved her head so his head turned to follow; though his eyes never quite met hers, he almost certainly could see what she was doing. He seemed to enjoy her puzzlement and remained silent.

After a moment she said, 'I'm sorry if I'm staring, but I thought . . . I thought you were blind.' She was peering at him, searching, as if the answer to the paradox was written somewhere in the folds of flesh upon his face.

'My name is Kevin Maguire, by way of an introduction. And yes, I am blind. But I have extra senses and I can visualize you quite clearly.'

'You do? How? I don't know of any human that can do that. I'm Kristina Schriock, by the way.'

Maguire nodded. 'Yes I know – I just left your husband on a skimmer flying to Terming . . .' Kristina didn't even want to think about that. Did the man jump then? 'and you'd be right with what you say. There are no humans who can do what I do.' He grinned broadly. 'I'm unique. To change the subject, I'm surprised my name hasn't struck a bell somewhere in your head. Or has this world forgotten me already?'

Kristina thought hard for a moment, staring quizzically at the smiling man next to her. Kevin Maguire. She repeated the name to herself and tried to remember her first few years on Ree'hdworld. There was certainly something familiar about the name, but not about the man beside her. He looked almost too casual for a man from Terming. In any case, what would a blind man be doing in a limited installation? He could be of no possible use.

It came to her quite suddenly. 'Kevin Maguire – the man who left the Pianhmar search record.'

Maguire smiled. 'A search-and-found record. A record of feelings, of travel, of excitement, of sadness. I put everything into that little strip of tape.'

'The record gives no details of any actual contact. A few people think that the record is incomplete. Most think it's nothing but a record of failure.'

'Failure?' Maguire seemed shocked. 'Failure,' he repeated.

'I don't understand why anyone should . . .' he suddenly became angry. 'I gave Earth details of the first contact ever with a greater intelligence than ourselves – I gave the Ree'hd an account of the death of my friend, their brother, Hans-ree . . . I left it all at the base of the mountains before I went . . . what failure? Did they think I was lying?'

'Who was Hans-ree?'

'A good Ree'hd,' said Maguire. 'A very good Ree'hd. He was my guide to the mountains. In those days, you understand, I was truly blind. He took me as far as he dared, and when I begged him to take me further, up on to the first range, he agreed. It cost him his life and I buried him, and I even sang a song for him, and I only hope that that was enough – he was a good Ree'hd. Did the locals think I lied about that too?'

A sudden bitterness had entered his manner and Kristina wondered how she could make amends for a cruel twist of fate that had denied the generations on Ree'hdworld the knowledge of Maguire's activities. She decided honesty was the best policy. 'The tape was a mere fragment, rescued from the scattered fragments of a recorder. The fragment ended before any such contact details were given; there was nothing following a whispered message that you thought you were being watched by beings you thought might be the Pianhmar . . .'

Maguire had settled into silence. It seemed to Kristina that he was brooding over a loss that was no one's fault at all.

'Don't brood,' she said. 'There's no point.'

Maguire glanced at her and his blind eyes seemed to sparkle again. He laughed loudly and slapped his hand on her knee. It was then that Kristina remembered when Maguire's first contact was supposed to have been. Angry at having been deceived she snapped, 'You can't possibly be Kevin Maguire! He died seven hundred years ago. You bloody fraud!'

'Wait,' said Maguire, reaching out a hand to stop Kristina climbing to her feet and walking away. 'What do you mean – died?'

'How could he have lived? The lifespan of human beings on Ree'hdworld is cut to about a hundred and seventy years, so Maguire couldn't have lived past the twenty-fourth century.'

'But I tell you I *am* Maguire. I *am* the man who left that record. I'm the first man who ever contacted the Pianhmar, no matter what anyone says. I've been away and now I'm back.'

'You expect me to believe that? That you're . . . what, seven hundred years old?'

'I'm old,' said Maguire simply. 'Too old, perhaps.' He shrugged. 'In any case you're making a wrong assumption.'

'Tell me.'

'You're assuming that I'm human. That if my eyes are blind I cannot see, that if my age is greater than the sturdy oak then I should be six feet down.'

Kristina wondered – briefly – what the 'sturdy oak' was; then she shook the irrelevancy out of her head and said, 'Well you *are* human, I can see that.'

Maguire looked away. He pointed to the low hills between the community and the city of Terming. 'When I first listened to the world about the Ree'hd burrows, you know what I thought? And don't forget, I was really blind then. I thought: Earth.'

'I've been there on vacation and it looked very dirty to me.'

'Well . . . a lot can have happened in several centuries. But take it from me, Ree'hdworld is a very Earthlike planet in many respects. As Earth was when I was around, anyway. Looking back at those hills now,' he was pointing towards the Hellgate mountains, 'you know what I see? I see deep blue colours and shifting brown and green smeared vegetation. I see purplish tree forms wandering across the country, and outcrops of sodium-compound crystal formations. I see a world that I could easily believe was Earth. But it isn't. You and I and everyone on the planet can sense the alienness of the place. Take a non-colour picture and you'd not convince a child that you were on the single world of a class K2 sun almost diametrically across the galaxy from Earth. They'd say it *was* Earth. But sit, awhile, and feel the place and it becomes sinister. Ree'hdworld is so unlike Earth that it takes years to grow used to the place. You probably already know that.'

'Yes.' Kristina was feeling that alienness now. It was as she had felt it those first long months on the world, nearly half a lifetime ago and fresh from terraformed world of Kruzus B. It was nothing that could be expressed in words . . . it was, perhaps, a combination of feelings. A nature surrounding her in which she did not belong . . . the knowledge of the alien sun, the two moons that whipped the seas and vegetation in such frenzied bouts of activity. The fauna, fitting into all the expected niches, and yet not conforming to any evolutionary pattern that a human would be familiar with. Hostile animals that feared things outside their own experience . . . a planet where the air had never been conquered, but where the oceans supported a biomass so huge and varied that it had driven the catalog computer crazy.

She knew what the blind man meant. Ree'hdworld was alien on an emotional level, and she realized, as she experienced that alienness again, that she could probably never shake it off; unless . . . unless she could become a Ree'hd in spirit, if not in body.

As a human, after fifteen years, she had learned to adapt to the environment, and she felt Ree'hdworld nature just slightly closer.

Maguire said, 'In the same way, I may look human, but I am more than human, and less than human. I have lost my claim to humanity. But I've gained my sight.'

Kristina was unsure what to think. She hugged her knees and watched skipjacks jumping from the surface of the river in their efforts to catch drifting spores. Maguire appeared to be watching them too, and for a while there was no talk between them.

How could she accept that this stranger was the man who had gone down into history as the last man to try and contact the Pianhmar, a man who, by his own word, had been the first and last to actually contact them? He was six hundred years too late for his story to be accepted without incredulity. But life could be suspended, couldn't it? And if she assumed that the timing factor was explicable, then where was her objection? She believed in the Pianhmar as fact, not as myth. And, incomplete though Maguire's record had been, it had made definite reference to contact having been established.

She looked at him. 'If you are Maguire, and you contacted the Pianhmar,' Maguire nodded, as if he was anticipating the question to come, 'then where are they?'

'Why, gone,' he replied, as if nothing could be more obvious. 'They were almost gone when I contacted them. I found the remnants of their race, and they took me into their bosom.'

'You, but not anyone who tried before you . . .'

'I was blind, remember? No one who tried before me was blind, and the Pianhmar killed them. It was important to them, in the state they were in, that no sentience actually look upon them. But a blind man . . . that was different. And it finally came home to the bureaucrats in the tent-city – that's all Terming was in those days; it's bigger now, I notice – that the only way to make contact with the fabled race was to use a man who couldn't see.

'They brought me from Earth for that purpose. Did you know that? All the way from Earth.'

Kristina said flatly, 'No bodily remains, no tombs, no cities, no ruins, no traces . . . just myth. Hardly indicates the existence of a great race, a race who were supposed to have conquered the galaxy before man had even evolved on Earth.'

'They grew beyond such things. As you say, the Pianhmar had lived on Ree'hdworld for many millenia. In time, I don't know how long ago, they began the slow process of decay, of devolution. They cycled out. Time covered their tracks, and I caught them at the very last.'

'And there's not an atom of them left now?'

'On the contrary,' Maguire laughed. 'There are quite a few atoms left. And many traces. There are even a few Pianhmar, I should imagine, if you know where to look. I can't be sure.'

'Where have you been since? Where have you spent your extra six hundred years?'

Maguire considered the question for a long moment. 'With them. Moving with them, seeing and watching with them, experiencing with them.'

'On Ree'hdworld?'

'To begin with, yes. And later – everywhere. I've just come back. I've been away a long time.'

'But you already seem to know what's going on here.'

Maguire shook his head. 'That's not true; I'm not properly tuned into the place yet.' He smiled. 'You'll see what I mean.'

He climbed to his feet and Kristina stood up beside him and watched him as he looked all about him. A few adolescent Ree'hd stared at them from their burrows. Kristina saw a great troup of Ree'hd moving inland – to hunt, she presumed.

Maguire said, 'When did the Ree'hd establish this community? It's a little close to the burrowlands over there, isn't it?' He pointed towards Terming. It seemed to Kristina that he was becoming aware of a fact that he had not previously known.

She said, 'The terran city of Terming now stands over the old burrows. The Ree'hd moved here centuries ago, unless they wanted to integrate.'

Maguire was shocked. He stared towards where the city could just be seen as a glittering of high atmosphere antennae and the extremely flexible pylons that held the wind harnesses. 'You mean . . . you mean there are Ree'hd actually living in the city? What a stupid thing to do . . . what a stupid . . .'

Kristina stood beside him, confused. 'Stupid? Why?'

'No wonder they came back.' He began to stumble along the river bank, heading to the land where he had first lived. Kristina watched him go until he was just a brown figure moving across the nearest hill; then she walked back to her burrow to find Urak.

chapter three

The city of Terming, named for its first Governor, was a hundred and three square miles of angularity, built around a river, and covering with its skirts the ancient burrows of the Ree'hd who had once lived in this area. Nowhere in the city was there a building higher than seventy yards. Even with the baffles the city dwellers had erected, the dawn wind was too strong to make it comfortable to go higher.

Zeitman was accommodated in the military barracks, and he had no vantage viewpoint at all from his room. From the east window a sheer wall of green styrocon bricks was his to regard at leisure. From the north a long, unwinding road, filled with wind debris and wandering Ree'hd was his to contemplate. Seeing the city Ree'hd for the first time in four years, Zeitman felt a certain compassion. The Ree'hd all appeared drunk, but this was a symptom of their illness. Living under the wing of the human race the Ree'hd always became ill; their 'blood' thinned, they lost weight and co-ordination, and their thinking processes faded. They were good, at this stage, for many routine jobs and not surprisingly were mercilessly exploited. Since, however, their illness did not register as more than drunkenness and fatigue, and since the drug and social perks of living in Terming were attractive and seducing, the Ree'hd population in the city was enormous. And many of them had risen to positions of power and were able to exploit humans mercilessly in return.

Zeitman thought it was all quite disgusting but there was nothing he could do about it.

Towards midday he unpacked his kit slowly and thoughtfully, filled two of six wall repositories and found a complete wardrobe of travelling and military-style clothes waiting for him in the closet. The uniforms were the wide-trousered, long-jacketed regalia of a Major in the Liaison Corps, according to a note he found pinned to one of them. Zeitman smiled, partly at Erlam's humour (or *was* there such a thing as a Liaison Corps?) and partly at the necessary tradition of every member of the permanent personnel of Terming having an arbitrary military rank. He felt, however, a certain hypocritical pride. The last time he had been here he had been credited with a mere Captain's rank.

Promotion.

He stripped off his grey ship-suit and cataphrak and spent a few minutes squeezing the white-heads that invariably covered him after any length of time in space. Their cause was a bafflement to him, and he was fairly rare in showing the cosmetically unattractive feature.

He showered with the bitter water that Ree'hdworld offered and wondered what Susanna would make of *that*. The city did not bother to extract the excess of iron and potassium salts that were present in its water supply since every human on a colonial world had a biostasis unit built into his or her body, and these were efficient monitors of what came into the body, and equally efficient at getting rid of unwelcomed excesses – with exceptions such as alcohol and one or two other organic molecules, for which many citizens were highly grateful. Susanna, being a ninth-generation settler, probably had no such protection and would have the pleasure of unit installation to go through.

Having showered, he pulled on the most colourful of the uniforms and checked his appearance in the narcissistic mirror that glowed into being at the touch of a button.

Beyond the mirror? Zeitman would have bet a year's pay that robot eyes stared without interest at him. He didn't really mind. Apart from his white spots he was presentable, and not prone to private bad behaviour.

On the wall, just beside the mirror, a panel slid open with a noisy rasp and a message screen lit up. Zeitman read the words with interest and a certain excitement. Then he smiled and signalled the screen to fade. He didn't need a copy of what he had read.

So she was coming to see him. Did that mean (could it

possibly mean) that her failure to meet him had been a mistake on her part?

A woman's voice spoke from nowhere. 'Please connect your vone . . . please connect your vone . . .'

'I'm sorry? Oh . . . yes . . .' Zeitman found the vone and sealed the contact strip to the contact plate by his narrow bunk. Immediately the minute screen raced with static and then a man's face gazed out at him. Zeitman might have expected a beaming smile, but the man was solemn and it made him feel cold.

'Welcome back, Robert. We have lots to talk about, and we have to talk now. Did your wife meet you?'

Direct, impersonal, unconcerned about feelings – my God, thought Zeitman. He hasn't changed. Daniel Erlam, a City Father and the Director of the Department of Culture and Environment. An overblown, overweight man, pushing his century, but with the sexual drives of a forty-year-old man, the success rate of a college student, and the enviable position of being the only man Zeitman knew who commanded total fear and total respect from ninety-nine percent of the people with whom he came into contact.

Zeitman loved him.

'Hi, Dan. You look about three hundred pounds heavier than when I went away.'

Now Erlam smiled, slightly and without much feeling.

'I've put it on in the last few weeks, Robert. Worry, and you can guess over what, and while we're on the subject, it's classified, okay? There's only you, I and one or two selected top men in Terming who have any idea of the situation, so keep your mouth shut, right? And incidentally, what the hell happened to that blind man you illegally brought down with you?'

'It's a long story. I'll tell you later.'

'You sure will, Robert. You know better than to airlift unauthorized persons down to Ree'hdworld, and that man had no authority.'

'He worked on me when we were in orbit.'

51

'And he doesn't know?'

Zeitman felt disturbed at Erlam's abruptness. He had never been like this with him before. 'I don't believe he does, though the shuttle pilot had some sort of rumour that he spread on to us. So the information has leaked.'

'Leaking in orbit doesn't matter a bit . . . not to Ree'hd-world. It's the installation I'm worried about. So we have stopped all landings and will be shipping people offworld as fast as their stay here is finished. Have you made immediate plans?'

Zeitman decided not to mention the message from Kristina. 'Immediate like in the next hour?'

'Or two or three hours.'

Zeitman shook his head. The image of Erlam smiled sourly. 'When do you intend seeing Kristina again?'

'None of your business. How's your sex life?'

'Failing. I intercepted that message, Robert – you're meeting her at dusk at the burrows. I'd advise you to think twice. The burrows are closed at night for reasons that will become apparent. Listen, get on to Kristina . . . I can give you the skimmer contact she fired from. Tell her to meet you somewhere else.'

Zeitman declined, feeling annoyed at Erlam's confessed eavesdropping. 'The burrows have a special significance, Dan.'

'Tell me.'

'I can't. Not yet. Personal.'

Erlam swore under his breath. 'I'm surprised at the damn woman. She knows the trouble we've been having at the burrows. What does she think she's at?' He shook his head.

Zeitman smiled as he watched the expressions race across Erlam's full-moon face. 'You want me to come over right away?'

'That's what I intended,' said Erlam. 'But I think you'd better have a word with Harry Kawashima first – he's the man who took over when you left; he works in the same place. He'll fill you in on the Rundii trouble. Things are changing real fast around here, Robert. I'll see you later.' And he cut the circuit, leaving Zeitman shaken and puzzled. Erlam was rarely so abrupt . . . at least, he hadn't been when Zeitman had known him before.

He had hoped for transport to fetch him. Erlam had offered none. And so it was a question of footing it through the streets of Terming until a skipcab darted past.

Zeitman left the barracks and faced the Ree'hdworld atmosphere. He felt fresh and clean and fractionally more human than he had felt during the long journey in space.

The air was sharp. Trace elements in the atmosphere had different effects on different humans – Susanna, as they had walked in the open air for the first time, had stated positively that the air smelled sweet. To Zeitman . . . the tang of sulphur, the choke of chlorine, present just as a hint, no more. Not distracting, not uncomfortable. Neither element was present. It was psychological. It was the scent of home.

The barracks, Zeitman noticed as he made for the city centre, were larger and neater than they had been last time he had been here. They comprised, now, what appeared to be twenty parallel rows of bunk-houses, interspersed with smaller blocks of individual rooms such as that which Zeitman now inhabited. The admin. and mess blocks were further to the edge of the barrack block, and the flag of Ree'hdworld, an orange and red striped flag, with the code number of the world embossed in large, gothic silver letters, flew above this complex of buildings, fluttering below the larger, more pronounced standard of the Sector Federation. This was a plain white flag with the symbol of the Federation – a cluster of six stars arranged in a triangle – drawn in red in the upper left corner.

A skipcab cushioned up to him and an old and dishevelled Ree'hd stared out. His song lips stretched in a wholly unnatural smile. 'Need transport?' he asked in imperfect inter-Ling.

Zeitman was delighted to accept. 'I want to get to the Department of Behavioural Sciences; it's over on East side.'

'I know it,' said the Ree'hd, his smile never leaving his lips all the while he looked at Zeitman. 'Ten minutes round the edge, or half an hour through the centre which is a good ride.'

'Round the edge. I've seen all I want to see of tourists for a while.'

The skipcab darted off along the roadways; it was a small and uncomfortable vehicle, lent an almost tangible lethality by the atrocious handling of the Ree'hd driver. Zeitman felt tense and unhappy for the ten-minute journey, and was delighted to wave the cab away for the loss of a ten-credit bill (ten times the fare).

He checked at reception in the two-storey, white-bricked building that was his old place of work, but when he learned that Kawashima was up town at a sensudome he left to find the Japanese without visiting his old lab and the technicians and staff whom he had known before.

It was, he supposed, one more symptom of the insecurity he was feeling more and more these days. A feeling of sadness to think he had missed four years of scientific activity in the well furnished, comfortable laboratories. It would have depressed him to go deeper into the building.

His second cab ride was almost as bad as the first. The Ree'hd driver, a young, alert specimen, not yet irreversibly affected by the rigours and alienness of human living, was a better driver than the first cabby, but less responsible. He took Zeitman on a hair-raising ride through some of the dirtier of the East sector streets, and then into the brighter and busier centre.

Passing the skimmer-hire station Zeitman broke his journey to put in an application for one of the leaf-shaped vehicles that was as important a part of living on Ree'hdworld as was tolerance of wind. It would take two days for approval to come through (Erlam had slipped up again in not having approval through prior to Zeitman's arrival) and until then Zeitman would have to use a military issue skimmer, which was noisy and armed, something Zeitman did not approve of. Certainly he was armed personally (a B-type Kiljarold Vaze) but more as protection against other humans than as protection against the local Ree'hd population. The reverse was the philosophy behind the arming of the military skimmers.

By the time the skipcab was a mile from Kawashima's visiting place the traffic had been forced to a crawl by the pressure of tourists in the streets. It was all human traffic, of course; the only Ree'hd faces that Zeitman saw were those that peered out at him from acquisition booths or guide centres.

Everyone was well wrapped against the chill of the day, now half way through its twenty-eight hours, but the feeling Zeitman got was of excitement and pleasure. Terming was obviously as popular as ever.

The sensudome was one of only two that dished up a mixed diet of human and Ree'hd eroticism. As such it was something outside Zeitman's experience; in his previous years on Ree'hd-world he had spent a vast amount of time in the purely human establishments, from dining clubs that included striptease on the menu, to the drug and neuro-stim rooms where 'any and all delights' were available.

He had never felt any inclination to witness the necessary degrading of the city Ree'hd in those establishments that supposedly catered for both races.

It cost him a hundred credits to gain entrance to the complex of rooms and studios, but once inside he was his own boss; if it was available it was his, for an hour – or two hours if he paid an extra fifty credits.

He lingered for a while in the media entertainment section of the building, watching elaborate displays of human perversion, all quite aesthetic and arousing. He moved on and watched a mixed copulation display, a dynamic montage of male humans and female Ree'hd, a slowly performed sequence of actions that seemed almost comical to Zeitman . . . and yet the audience was large, and raptly attentive! It's the nude-on-horseback phenomenon, Zeitman thought to himself with a mental smile. But no grey dappled mare ever looked as uninterested as the participating Ree'hd. The male Ree'hd who were pseudo-raping busty, human females had their attention on anything and everything save the task at hand.

And the audience, Zeitman noticed, was almost totally human, about evenly mixed as regards sex. Such carnal displays were very far from the Ree'hd sense of the erotic – an interesting wind display might be a Ree'hd's idea of pleasure, but sexual motivation was lost before adulthood.

Zeitman followed a few human males into the brothel that spread out, a series of cubicles, around the strip studios. Some doors were open and males and females of both species watched him as he wandered by; only the humans made any effort to solicit.

He found Kawashima, then, and sat in the dimness waiting for the man's neuro-stim trip to end.

Kawashima was a small, fat Japanese – in fact a mixture of Japanese and North Continental Centauran, the eyes being testimony to the first; the wide, ugly hands evidence of the second.

He was seated cross-legged upon a mat, fully-clothed, eyes open but unseeing; a small circular metal disc was stuck to his forehead, feeding him the details of the experience he was undergoing. Every so often his eyes closed and he moaned, a sound of intense pleasure.

After a few minutes he seemed to relax and shiver. He came to full consciousness and reached up for the disc, and as he reached he saw Zeitman, hesitated in the action, then peeled the metal slither from his skin.

'Who the hell are you?'

'My name's Robert Zeitman. I used to—'

'Yeah, I know about you. Don't you know anything about privacy? I should beat into you for busting in on me.'

'I apologize, but I'm in a hurry.'

Kawashima climbed to his feet and sat down again on the small bed, picking up a towel and wiping moisture from his neck. Zeitman also stood up and moved round the room to stand in front of the scowling Japanese.

'Being in a hurry no excuse. I paid a damn lot of money for peace and . . . and what I got?' He spoke with an unmistakable accent, but it seemed to contain elements of both parental cultures: the nasal vowels of his North Continental Centauran dialect slightly overpowering the buccal predominance of the Japanese accentuation. Kawashima had almost certainly spent much time in each parental homeland.

'If you wanted peace you should have locked the door,' said Zeitman, unsympathetically. 'Which trip were you on? Human or Ree'hd?'

Kawashima was furious. 'Hey, you, Zeitman!' he shouted. 'What's your game? You bust in here, interrupt me, spoil the effect! And then you pry! Hurry or no, I think you'd better bust out until you can find some manners.'

Zeitman didn't move. 'Erlam said we should talk and I intend to talk. Cool down, mister. You've had your fun, now let's get back to work shall we?'

If Kawashima had been about to argue further, Zeitman's last statement stopped him dead. He stared at the other man for a moment, a mixture of emotions in his face; then he stood, flung the towel away and advanced on Zeitman. 'Work? Did you say work? Listen, *mister* – when you left four years ago or whenever you may not have left the planet for good, but you sure as hell left your job for good. And they appointed me in your place and I don't intend to let you snatch it away again, you got that clear?'

'Look, nobody said—'

'I said you got that clear, Zeitman? You deserted us, now you phase out.'

'I don't want your job, Kawashima! Will you shut up a moment?'

Kawashima smiled, a gesture of triumph, not mirth. 'You got that clear, that's good. Now. What the hell Erlam send you here for?' He picked up his towel and continued to absorb the sweat from his body.

'I'm going to be doing field work . . . I hope, simple liaison work with the Ree'hd—'

'In which case you'll be under my authority. I hope Erlam explained that to you.'

Zeitman affirmed, a little shocked, very annoyed, but he affirmed anyway and said nothing else about it. He went on, 'He says I should get an update from you. Major advances

57

only – he seemed to think there had been some.'

Kawashima made a sound that Zeitman interpreted as a sneer. 'Erlam is a pain, a real pain! Yes, there have been advances. Things are changing, Zeitman – rapidly and incomprehensibly things on Ree'hdworld are turning end over end. That's half the reason Erlam is a pain; that man, he likes everything *just* so. Nice orderly installation, nice orderly world, nice orderly biology; everything must fit a pattern. The man's on a bigger trip than I was just on.'

'To the point,' said Zeitman, irritated by this slandering of Dan Erlam. 'How are things changing?'

'I can only tell you what we've seen. Conclusions come later. First, the Ree'hd are behaving strangely. They are suddenly very angry and giving Erlam something to worry about. We've squatted on Ree'hdworld seven hundred years, Zeitman, and in all that time we've really been very good people – we've not interfered with the Ree'hd beyond inviting them into our installation. Everything – Ree'hdwise – is as it always was. But that is not enough for them. They want us offworld to the last man. Now that's *change* . . .'

Zeitman agreed. That was a change indeed. Four years ago he had visited the nearest three burrow communities to make his farewells and without exception the burrow Ones had urged him to return before too long. There had been nothing but friendship.

Kawashima, talking more relaxedly, went on, 'One of your jobs will be helping to figure out that change. As I say, it is Erlam's headache too because it is having an effect on the installation. He and his ugly henchmen are going crazy trying to keep their mega-vazes holstered.

'The second change, the one I think is the more significant, is the Rundii. In the last few months their behaviour has altered radically.'

'In what way?'

'I'd put it down to curiosity. They've started to take interest in things, in particular artificial things.'

The burrows, the city! It began to come clear to Zietman

where the source of Erlam's anxiety lay. He said as much to Kawashima.

'That's right. A thousand tourists a day go through the burrows. More, probably. But now the trips end sharp at dusk. I won't say the burrows swarm with Rundii, but they can be heard, prowling around; they even came up into the museum once! They've never been violent, of course, not deliberately violent, but they panic so damn easily. It has cost lives.'

Somehow it was impossible to imagine the Rundii as curious beings. They were Ree'hd-like animals, wandering in small packs, weaponless, clotheless, mindless, hunting by brute force, attacking when frightened (or as Kristina believed, when they met something outside their experience, a form of panic reaction) and generally staying in the deep jungles and forests of the continent. They showed no sentient behaviour whatsoever. And such developments did not occur in a heartbeat of time.

'Why should the Rundii cause Erlam to get so jumpy? A well thrown stone can still be dodged in daylight, and the burrows are well lit, aren't they? Just because they've found a possible new hunting ground doesn't mean a great change is taking place.'

Kawashima did not fully agree, but he said no more about the creatures. Instead he reached into his belt pouch and withdrew a small glass plate which he passed to Zeitman. It was a primitive form of photograph and when Zeitman held it to his eye and the content became internally illuminated, he thought that something was wrong with the focus. Then, after a moment, he realized that there was something wrong with the content.

It was a picture of the inside of a burrow, dim roof-lighting, crumbling walls. A white shape was seen half in profile, turning away from the observer – a Ree'hd shape, but transparent and unreal. Zeitman was looking at a ghost.

'And not Ree'hd, either,' said Kawashima when he spotted that Zeitman had realized what he was looking at. 'There's a spine ridge and a shape to the lateral eyes that can only mean one thing—'

'Pianhmar?' Zeitman shouted. 'Are you saying . . . ?' He looked again, more carefully, excitement rising within him. Yes, a spine ridge, visible through the insubstantial body of the creature. A spine ridge! The feature that distinguished the mythological Pianhmar from the two observable species on Ree'hdworld. 'A Pianhmar ghost. I can hardly believe it, I just can't. Who took this?'

Kawashima tapped his chest. 'It frightened the life out of me. And I'm not the only one to see them. Five reports in the last two months, four reports during the previous six.'

For a while Zeitman felt himself to be floating in a void, his mind unable to decide whether or not he was dreaming, while he waited for the impact of Kawashima's discovery to register fully. He thought of the Pianhmar, who were part of the legend of Ree'hdworld and in whom few humans believed (but he remembered that the Ree'hd themselves did not think of the Pianhmar as myths; they rarely thought of them at all, in fact). He thought of ghosts – ghosts, which were no forms of fantasy but very real echoes through time-space of particular human auras; ghosts which had been so well worked out and understood that they were no longer interesting. On Earth.

But Pianhmar ghosts!

chapter four

An hour later Zeitman arrived at Dan Erlam's office. He walked along a corridor that was filled with dictaprint chatter and busy body motion and passed through double doors that closed behind him and left him in a room where the only sound was the almost inaudible (but annoyingly intrusive) whirr of heating systems in the ceiling and wall. A large, green room, walls sloping inwards giving a sensation of greater depth, with a glass-topped desk sprawling across nearly one third of the floor space – and sprawled across the desk, head down, arms outstretched, neck connected to the mobile masseuse that Erlam had had specially imported – Erlam himself. He waved a hand as Zeitman came into the office and reached out to switch off the robot rollers. The skeleton-thin machine reeled up and slid away into a corner and Erlam straightened in his seat, feeling the back of his neck and smiling with pleasure.

'So you're back. I should have expected it, I suppose. Everything else has been going wrong these past months.'

'Nice to see you too, Dan,' said Zeitman, smiling broadly and sitting down across the vast desk from Erlam. 'Rheumatics?'

Erlam scowled. Rheumatics! Zeitman could almost hear him saying. There's no such thing as rheumatics, only disused muscles and under-oiled joints. 'Been doing a lot of reading lately, and this gravity on heads as large as mine . . . well, you know how it is.'

'I understand fully,' said Zeitman, inspecting the decor of the office. Erlam followed his meandering gaze, smiling. 'Impressive?'

'Hideous. You have the tastes of an adolescent.'

'Young at heart, Robert. The only way to be on an age-breaker like Ree'hdworld. Young at heart. You yourself are looking gaunt, underfed.'

'I've done a fair amount of travelling,' replied Zeitman, as he finished his scrutiny of the murals from Morgansworld. They were crude in execution, not to mention content, but their interesting feature was that they moved – ten-second cycles of frantic, sweaty activity. 'What do they call them? I've seen them but never heard them referred to.'

'The holodynes? Holodynes. The three-dimensional effect isn't wildly exciting unless you're up close. Forget them. We have things to discuss.'

Zeitman sat and took a good look at Erlam. The man was grossly fat and his bulging forehead seemed to bulge even more as his hairline receded beyond the horizon. Zeitman was glad he didn't look moist. Rather, Erlam – for all his excesses – seemed cool and at ease. His thin lips were perpetually stretched in a natural smile, though today, for some reason, Zeitman could not feel the warmth he usually felt from the Director.

'You get to see Kawashima?'

Zeitman nodded, slowly. 'An aggressive man, to say the least.'

'He's like that with everybody. Mind you, most people around here are going through it too: snappy, jumpy, easily irritated. Something to do with the moon, I expect.' He stared straight at Zeitman as if willing him to disagree, to tell him something far worse. But Zeitman just shrugged and smiled, and the moment passed.

They drank *baraas*, and chased it with genuine Irish, and talked about Zeitman's time away from Ree'hdworld; they found their feet with each other again, became the old friends they were, relaxed with each other. But there was an underlying tension in Erlam that Zeitman felt was directed at him; Erlam was unhappy about something, and not the greater worry shared by them both.

Zeitman told of his wasted months, brooding over the world he had left, wishing he had never gone away. Then the gradual realization that Kristina had meant more to him than he thought. There had been pleasure all along the line, of course. New challenges and old problems that he could have set his mind to. But he had participated in these things very little. He travelled a huge circle, went to Earth, and came back – ultimately – to Ree'hdworld.

'Why?' said Erlam. 'Why back here? There's no *pleasure* here – not on the same scale as some of the colonial worlds.'

'Did I give the impression I wanted pleasure? No . . .' he fell silent for a moment. 'You know why, Dan. You know why I'm back.'

Erlam watched him, then nodded. 'Kristina.' He suddenly

became angry. 'For Christ's sake, Robert – you've got a damnable cheek! You treat the woman like . . . like an inferior being for years; you walk off and leave her, and then expect to come creeping back! It's not fair of you, damn you. Not fair.'

Surprised at the outburst Zeitman was at a loss for words, for a second or two. 'Dan, it wasn't just me, you know. There was fault on both sides . . .' What on earth was the matter with Erlam? Why so touchy about the point? 'Anyway, Kristina is only a very small part of it. Very small.'

And the rest was Ree'hdworld and Zeitman himself. Ree'hdworld because of the fascination the place held for him (as indeed it held for Erlam), a fascination based on his own understanding – and that understanding was shared by very few others. There was the biology of the world – previously his full time study – a biology that he could not accept as being everything it seemed. There was the Pianhmar legend, and who could resist that? Every world that Zeitman had ever visited claimed to have *some* mysterious past intelligence, but only on Ree'hdworld did he get the feeling that the legend was substantially more than myth. And with Pianhmar ghosts moving through the burrows near the city, how much longer could widespread scepticism last?

And Zeitman himself. It was no surprise to him to find he looked gaunt and underfed. He must have looked a wreck, contrasted with how he had looked four years ago during the phase of his life when he felt confident and secure among his colleagues. All that was gone. In only one thing did he find security – Ree'hdworld! A world substantially free of humans, where he could lose himself, if he wanted, in an alien nature and alien environment, and not be forced to play tough games with aggressive Japanese biologists, and behave in a way that was contrary to his inclination.

He was running back to the warmth of familiarity, and in so running he hoped to find again his old confidence, his youthful carelessness. He hoped to shake off that terrible thing that he knew had afflicted him, the almost unmentionable disease that was spreading through map-space and decimating colony after colony, and which had taken a hold of him and was wearing him down.

He said, simply, 'I like it here.'

Erlam burst out laughing. 'I know how you feel, Robert. The place sort of gets under your skin. How about the job? Like it?'

'Liaison Corps? Since when did we have a Liaison Corps attached to the military?'

Erlam grinned. 'We never did. You are it. Your old job had been reassigned, but the city fathers all agreed with me that you were worth getting back. And the old fool in charge of the military happens to be . . . well, we drink a lot together. Listen, don't bloody complain! You're lucky to be allowed back at all.'

'Fine . . . fine . . . I'm not complaining. I accept – gratefully.'

Erlam was flushed and getting happier. He reached across the desk for Zeitman's glass. Zeitman reached out and stopped him from refilling him with Irish whiskey. He was already feeling light-headed and the strange colour combinations of the murals in the office were merging and mingling to form an almost white sensation in his head. Years since I threw a drunk, he thought angrily. Why now? Why on my first day down when there's so much to learn?

He tried to shake the dizziness off and the room swam back into focus.

'Strong stuff,' said Erlam, waving the flask of *baraas*. 'From Dominion. Susanna Neves brought it in and we confiscated it, naturally. It was my turn for a favour. Breathe deep. The active ingredient disperses quickly, but more so if your blood is well oxygenated. Alcohol should be so delicate, huh?'

'Liaison Corps,' repeated Zeitman. 'You want me to run a team of people . . . doing *what* to human-Ree'hd contact? Stopping it? Monitoring it?'

'Whatever you like, Robert. Do as you please. The whole thing is just for officialdom's sake, but it gives you the legal opportunity to get back among the Ree'hd. Your actual assignments will come from . . .' Erlam looked suddenly guilty.

'That bloody Japanese, I know!' shouted Zeitman. 'If he thinks he's going to tell me what I should and shouldn't do, a moron who's only been here a fifth the time I have . . .'

'I'm sorry Robert, I really am. I can only bend the establishment so far. You know very well the position you had, which Kawashima now has, was the boss-position. I can't change that.'

Zeitman swallowed his pride. 'But you can tell him to lay off. That Robert Zeitman goes where he wants, does what he wants. Right?'

Erlam acquiesced. 'Robert . . . it is already done. My, you're a touchy fellow at times.'

Zeitman felt better already, but it wouldn't last.

'Incidentally,' Erlam continued, 'Susanna Neves might be useful as an assistant, and there are a few diplomatic corps people in Terming with too much time on their hands if you ever want a team of more than one.'

'I thought Susanna was here as a secretary to some diplomatic topman . . . so she told me.'

'It's true – I got here off the hook just two hours ago. She'd have hated him. It's a sad story about Susanna – parents kicked her here to help her find some responsibility. If she travelled with you I expect she already found some . . .'

He couldn't possibly know, thought Zeitman, but he was impressed at Erlam's guesswork.

Erlam went on, 'In the meantime, the world of contact is yours. As Kawashima told you, I expect, the Ree'hd of several communities are giving us trouble. My worry is that the city-living Ree'hd will start acting up.'

'There's something very patronizing about your tone, Dan, and it damn well shouldn't be there. Anyway, I can't see that you have anything to worry about. There's essentially no social structure in Terming – among the Ree'hd that is. They drift about between their own sector and the centre – they'll do anything to help, and make every cent they can. You don't get rebellion without organization and the only thing our home-grown Ree'hd seem anxious to do is to follow the human way of life. They don't give a Rundii's spit about money, but they seem to think it's the thing to do, to make a profit.'

Erlam laughed. 'You're right. And make profits they do. Every so often one of the topmen Ree'hd throws a party – one of those Ree'hd who are a little *more* organized than you seem to think – to which I get invited and I don't come out of it for a week. If you'd spent more time in the city during the last twenty years you could have shared that perk. They're great lads, Robert, those few. Things have changed in the last few years.'

'Not to mention the last few hundred.'

Erlam shrugged, looked a little fatalistic. 'Can't help the past, Robert. Can't help the way things were left to us.'

Seven hundred years ago, thought Zeitman through a fast clearing head, there were just the Ree'hd, their burrows, and a few humans in tents, living in harmony, living as Ree'hd. The Ree'hd, in those days, had all been as the hill-dwelling Ree'hd of this century, gentle and quiet beings. Apparently empty vessels on a strangely still world.

Humans.

Wherever they went they took change, and change had come to Ree'hdworld within three centuries. At first it had been the installations – scattered beacons, way stations, geophysical units and training stations. A few hundred humans taking scant interest in the Ree'hd (though more in the occasionally violent Rundii) going through the motions of their human functions, exploring, probing, documenting. There had been a few, even then, who had found the myth of the Pianhmar a challenge, and in his reading and listening to records from the past, Zeitman had found much to suggest that there had been scientists and observers who had also felt uneasy about the world, about the way things were.

Zeitman had his analog back through time to the moment of discovery of the only other intelligence besides man in mapspace.

Things were different now.

The town had appeared first, an expanse of tents gradually replaced by less wind-susceptible buildings. Five hundred years after man's arrival on the world the first tourists showed their faces, in an installation that was by then a city.

By the time Zeitman had arrived on Ree'hdworld there were over twenty thousand humans in the installation, and the two cultures, human and native, were very mixed within the artificial boundaries of Terming. And it had worked well, until now. Suddenly, within a few months, the Ree'hd communities scattered about the continent had begun to object to the human presence on Ree'hdworld. Some of them, Erlam pointed out, had probably been nursing a grudge against the invaders for centuries – he meant, of course, those who had moved from the burrows upon which a part of Terming lay.

Zeitman wondered if he would go on to rationalize that ancient trespass with a cursory 'had to have something to show the tourists'. But Erlam went on, 'It began some months after you left. For a while there were little armies of outside Ree'hd moving continually through the city streets, trying to convince the Ree'hd living here to move away. A few of them did, but most of them would have nothing to do with it. When they saw that their policy of persuasion was failing, then the acts of open aggression started.'

'Killing?'

Erlam grimaced. His gaze was openly surprised. 'This isn't Earth, Robert. The worst aggression a Ree'hd will demonstrate is destruction of personal property.'

Zeitman could guess. Air-cars, installations . . .

'That sort of thing. We've lost all our geophysical installations, but managed to rebuild the two beacons that they burned down. The most annoying thing they've done is to burn clothing. They capture tourists, strip them and send them back to the city in the raw. Bloody unsociable behaviour these chilly spring days, but imagine the winter! We lost two tourists from exposure and are having an almighty struggle to keep the whole business quiet.'

'Indirect murder. Do the Ree'hd know?'

'No. Why bother? They have no conception of how inefficient the undressed human body is. That's something you can do: drop the hint that human temperature tolerance is restricted to *warm*.'

'I'll do my best. Have they said they want us off-world?'

It was not a pleasant thought, and was not the case. If the Ree'hd *did* request the evacuation of Ree'hdworld, then, by their own laws, the Federation would have no choice but to evacuate. While Zeitman would have loved to have seen Terming gone, if Terming went, so would he. He couldn't have it both ways.

Erlam said, 'All they've asked is for us to stop interfering with their evolution. I presume they mean their cultural development.'

'Well, we're not. Those communities are left very well alone.'

'Apart from the busloads of intrepid explorers . . . but that's not what they're worried about. It seems their anxiety is restricted to the Ree'hd in the city. Our population of terraformed natives is increasing and they want us to give them back. How do we tell them there's more than a thousand Ree'hd visiting other map-space worlds at this moment?'

'Let's hope they're not susceptible to . . .'

That stopped them both, and for a long while they sat and gazed at the table that separated them. There seemed to be a great sadness in Erlam's expression, and Zeitman could well understand it – he himself had managed to overcome his own emotional reaction to the fate of Earth, the effective loss of the homeworld, but it still gave him sleepless nights and frightening waking-dreams – it was as if some essential sentience in the Earth was screaming across space to each and every one of her offspring, sharing her death-dream with them all, for Zeitman had not met a single man or woman, born (like him) on the homeworld, who did not feel that something was wrong.

Erlam's was a secondary emotion since he had never been on or seen Earth, merely heard . . .

'You've seen it, Robert. You've seen the evidence?'

'Yes. There's no hope.'

'But how? Why? I'd always thought that the Fear was something restricted to hostile worlds, planets where man really had to fight to survive. Why Earth?'

It was true. Whatever caused the disease known colloquially as the Fear – the irrational development of auto-destructive psychoses – it had always had its effect on worlds of darkness, of mud, of rain and storms, of dust, of hostile atmosphere.

Erlam had never seen Earth and he entertained the romance of green hills and idyllic existence. He had a dream of the homeworld and it was his right to die with that dream. But the dream was a myth. The Earth, the world of man, was the most hostile world that Zeitman had ever visited. He had stood in an atmosphere so thick with man-made dust that he could see no horizon, and he had wondered what had taken the Fear so long to strike this, its most logical victim.

He had seen cities laid waste, the ensuing destruction of whole landscapes. It would take a thousand years to accomplish, but the death of Earth was, without doubt, in process of accomplishment.

'What ideas? What reason?' said Erlam. 'Surely someone has an inkling of what man has caught.'

'The most widely held idea – no evidence for it, but then there's no evidence for anything – is a virus-symbiote, something we all have that has not troubled us for thousands of years, but which in certain environmental situations gets activated with the consequences we have seen. A modification of the theory is that it is the psychological climate that's important.'

Erlam poured himself another drink and after a moment pushed the flask across to Zeitman, who decided he would indulge this time and filled his own glass.

'When you called me at the barracks you said it was classified information. Half the galaxy knows about it by now, so how are you working that?'

'Simple – we're not telling anybody.'

'Yes but why? Why not let them know?'

Erlam was suddenly irritable. 'Oh come on Robert,' he snapped. 'Use some imagination. The moment a world hears about Earth, what do you think it does? Sends a bunch of flowers and a "get well" card? It panics! Hostile worlds are one thing, but when Earth goes – that's something else. I mean, if Earth goes, everything will go eventually – the thing to do, so the worlds unaffected until now reason, is to get to a place as far away as possible from the colonized worlds cluster, and find the most Earthlike world – a longer chance of survival means more time for a cure to be found. There are about ten worlds that qualify as such temporary havens – and one of them is Ree'hdworld.'

'You mean there's an exodus on its way here?'

'That's exactly what I mean. And I don't mind admitting that it scares the hell out of me – within a day the leaders will be arriving, demanding landing rights—'

'Oh my God.'

'Oh your God nothing – they're not coming down, and if they try we'll shoot them down.'

'But hasn't the Federation warned them to leave Ree'hdworld alone?'

'The Federation, as far as I can see, is too busy planning to cope with millions of panic-stricken humans. They do not apparently care about our intelligent natives any more. Fortunately I do, and so do the other city fathers, and we'll allow no single ship to land – not even a Federation ship.' He rose and walked to the window, pointed down into the street below. 'There's a tourist population of several thousand on the world, scattered across the globe, but mostly in the city, and they all have their ships with them, and they're all ignorant of what has happened – and over the next few weeks they'll be leaving and good riddance. We want them to go. If we tell them about Earth they will want to stay for sure and there's just no way short of murder that we'll be able to stop them. We're not telling the legitimate inhabitants of Terming, either. My big worry, you see, is panic. Panic might cause one or two things to happen. There could be those individuals who would attempt to sabotage our efforts at keeping the planet free of extra refugees – reasons might range from feelings of good samaritanship to wanting to get their families together from all over. Panic might also cause mass migration from the city into the surrounding countryside and I want that as little as you do. It means we get a colonized planet and soon we breed like flies and goodbye Ree'hd, not to mention Rundii, and the fauna you find so fascinating. If we keep everyone together in the city, the worst that can happen is that we extend our borders by a few miles, but the very nature of our physical environment cuts down birthrate. We'd be no trouble to the natives at all.'

Zeitman said, after thought, that he agreed with Erlam's reasons, but didn't find his policy practicable. Surely there were radios among the tourist population?

'No there aren't. A restricted artifact – you should know that – but to be honest, yes, it's just a short-term plan. Eventually of course everyone has to be told, but hopefully by then they can be told in such a way that panic can be avoided.'

Erlam sat back down behind his desk and emptied the flask of *baraas* into his glass. He looked at it sadly and then threw the empty container into a disposal chute out of Zeitman's sight. 'A good drink,' he murmured, then drained the glass and settled back, contemplating Zeitman for a long time. At last he said, 'One other thing. This . . . blind man that you were supposed to be bringing down with you. The *Realta* sent down his picture. It's very interesting. What did you know about him, Robert?'

'Virtually nothing, Dan. We got friendly on the *Realta*, shortly after it stopped at Eternity. He wasn't really blind, you know. He had some sort of extra-sensory perception.'

'Not to mention travel abilities of an unusual nature.'

'Yes indeed. I can't explain that – he just vanished in mid flight.'

'I find that disagreeably metaphysical,' said Erlam, scowling slightly. 'But never mind. Look at this.' He skated a photoblok across the desk and Zeitman reached out to look at it. 'He's younger, but yes. That's the man.'

Erlam shook his head. 'That is a man called Kevin Maguire.'

'Maguire? I've heard of him . . .'

'The Pianhmar record, in the museum. Remember?'

Zeitman remembered. 'Of course. Kevin Maguire.' He looked at the photoblok again. Then it struck him. 'Look, wait a minute – let's not confuse ourselves too much . . .'

'Why? Because Maguire lived seven hundred years ago?'

'That's good enough.'

'Explain the likeness.'

'I suppose he could have had descendants.'

Erlam was unimpressed. 'All the records I checked – which were all the records we have – said that Maguire went off into the mountains with a native guide called . . . Hans-ree, yes Hans-ree. The guide was found dead six weeks later, and the only sign of Maguire that was ever found was a shattered recorder, discovered by a wandering Ree'hd nearly a hundred years later. I don't believe Maguire ever left the planet. I believe his destiny was to die in the Hellgate mountains. What I want to know is, how did he cheat that destiny? Because that's Maguire, all right, and he's seven hundred years out of time.'

Later Erlam said, 'I'm glad to see you back, in one way; in another, I'm not. I wish you'd stayed the hell off Ree'hdworld.'

'I don't understand, Dan.'

'I resent you. It's not a feeling that can be talked out of my system, either. I feel resentment, and that feeling will grow. It's something that has to be faced.'

It was Kristina, of course. Zeitman realized that without even thinking – by intuition, perhaps, something he had long ago felt draining away from him. He stared at Erlam and felt a mixture of emotions. He felt sympathy for his friend. He felt anger at the extra level of complication. He felt annoyance that Erlam should interfere. 'I'm sorry you feel that way, Dan. I really am. I'll try not to cause too much trouble between us.'

He felt cold, felt the warmth slip away, evaporating with the alien drug in his blood stream.

Erlam stared down at his hands, clasped before him on the desk. He seemed to be regretting what he had said, but after a moment he looked up sharply. 'You're a scientist, Robert, and – let's indulge in a little false flattery – a very good one. So go out and be a scientist . . .'

'It's difficult to involve oneself with the mysteries of an ecology when all you can think of is a woman, and how to repair four years of battling.' He smiled, but the smile was not reciprocated.

'You're a fool, Robert. You always were. You're a self-pitying, self-centred fool, and it will break you. For the last time—'

Zeitman couldn't believe what he was hearing. 'Dan! What the hell's happened to you? This doesn't sound like—'

'For the last time, Robert! Pull yourself together. You've been sitting here for the last hour oozing redundancy. I can't use a man who can't see beyond his own skull. I want you like you were, Robert, and that means putting your emotions down . . .'

'Easy for you, Dan; not so bloody easy for most of us!'

Silence. Regret. Erlam stared sullenly across his desk.

'All right, Major Zeitman. All right.'

'Look, I'm sorry Dan . . .'

'I said it's all right. We're both jumpy, so let's forget it. Keep in touch—I'll want to know how you're getting on.'

'Sure.'

Zeitman rose and left the office.

chapter five

Sunset, with Kristina watching. The river was quiet now, the air still. Her senses were sharp and she could smell the vegetation smell of Ree'hdworld, the effusion of waste products from the mat covering and from the micro-fauna that lived in the well drained earth.

The sky was orange and the clouds ran across from south east to north west in parallel rows, and they were highlighted by the last light from the setting star.

Urak sat beside her, asking her not to go.

'I must, Urak. I must. You said yourself that I shouldn't put the unpleasant task off for too long.'

'It's not the meeting, Kristina,' said Urak. His anxiety was very great, a yellow flush spreading across his chest and down his arms. 'It's not the meeting, it's the old burrows. Why go back there? They're empty of true meaning, and H'sark has told us that he saw Rundii there when he last visited them.'

Kristina shook her head. 'I must go. The burrows have a special meaning for both Robert and myself. I can't explain, Urak. It's too . . . human.' She was aware of the Rundii sightings, and she knew of the ghosts as well (which Urak did not). She had never seen a ghost, but knew that they were not ghosts in the terran sense, echoes or projections. She was intrigued, certainly, but for the moment there was only Zeitman, and what she must reveal to him, and how he would respond to her, and what it would do to her.

She kissed the Ree'hd and was pleased to notice the natural brown colouration return to his skin. Urak, of all the Ree'hd, should know that she could look after herself. She walked with him to her skimmer which stood, slightly askew, right upon the water's edge.

The sun dropped out of sight and there was total stillness. From the Rundii sphere came the sounds of beasts and moving earth, carrying through this calmest of moments for many miles. Ree'hd, gathering along the water's edge, sang their still-songs, praying for the lost. Always, at this time, it was the lost Ree'hd of all ages who were foremost in the Ree'hd minds. Urak walked away from Kristina and squatted among his kin, facing the Rundii sphere and the unknown lands to the north. Tonight he was close to Hans-ree, the Ree'hd from the time of Maguire. Tomorrow, perhaps, he might tell Kristina what he learned.

Finding no immediate interest in such things, Kristina concentrated her thoughts on her 'ex'-husband. The skimmer lifted and glided away into the gloom. She wondered if Urak was watching her departure. As the skimmer passed across the distant hills he might see the silver surface flashing as it caught the last rays of the sun, still visible from this higher elevation.

In all probability Urak was unaware of these things.

Zeitman arrived at the burrows an hour after dusk. By now the life of the city was beginning to peak. From the depressed, almost aimless wandering of the day, the population outside the centre began to move with vigour. Work was finished, trade and exchange centres were closed, schools – segregated and mixed alike – were putting up wind shutters, and streams of young Ree'hd and humans paced in three-abreast columns through the streets towards the public transport station.

Zeitman found the bustle very pleasant, for a change. He immersed himself in the flow of visitors that moved through the main streets of the southern part of the city, and finally came to the gates of the museum. They were electrically charged, electronically controlled, absolutely impenetrable barriers, still manned by three uniformed servicemen. Zeitman showed his identity card and waited for the usual call to higher authority, but to his surprise, this time his arrival had been anticipated. He passed the gates and walked into the squat dome that covered the museum.

The interior was still fully lit and there were servicemen moving through the exhibits and checking each display for damage. Zeitman stood in the doorway for a moment and looked around at the vast array of statues, photographs, obscure objects and preserved animals. There seemed to be no order in the arrangement – a cluster of things of interest and education, designed for the impatient visitor, not the enthusiastic student. There was a second museum devoted to biology and behaviour some miles away, and a third devoted to the geology and human involvement on Ree'hdworld very close by. But neither of those museums allowed access to the burrows, and were the least popular two houses of history.

Zeitman walked round the exhibits until he came to the wax models of the three intelligent and pseudo-intelligent species that inhabited the planet, the Ree'hd, the *Rundiamha-reach*, and man himself. In a case, next to three naked males that stared blindly out at the visitor, was a model of a Pianhmar. It was labelled as such, with great emphasis being laid upon its existence being only in legend. Zeitman smiled to himself, and wondered how many times a Pianhmar would have to show itself before the label on the display would be changed. And quite suddenly the hair on Zeitman's neck prickled and he found himself looking into the glass eyes of the model and feeling a strange tension, a feeling of wonderment and fear that a past might have been coming closer again, making itself felt in a universe that scorned it . . .

'Major Zeitman?'

Zeitman jumped as the voice spoke from just behind him. He turned to see a serviceman staring at him. 'Major Zeitman?'

'Yes. Sorry, I was engrossed in this beast.'

The serviceman nodded, looked the wax Pianhmar up and down. 'I guess we'll have to change the display soon,' he said, then looked at Zeitman. 'You have heard about the, er . . .'

'Ghosts? Yes, I've heard. I was just thinking that the spine ridge on the model is too small. Imagine being able to say a thing like that with authority! The spine ridge is too small . . . the eyes too Ree'hdlike.'

'The model was made from Ree'hd description as handed down in their legends. Details were bound to be wrong.'

They stared at the three species for a moment, comparing and contrasting, and it was so clear that the three local breeds were from a common stock, somewhere in the distant past.

'Any time you want to go down, Major . . .'

'I'd like to see the Maguire display first.'

'Sure; it's across the far side.' The serviceman led Zeitman across the museum and stopped him in front of a small cabinet. Zeitman stared at the incredibly fragmentary display of one man's life – wallet contents, a photoblok showing a young Maguire on Earth (a photo that Zeitman must have looked at many times in his own youth, but had failed to remember). Prize item was the recorder that Maguire had taken with him on his journey into the hills, seven centuries previously. The machine was broken and incomplete. At the touch of a button a copy of the fragmentary recording that he had made could be heard. Zeitman was tempted to take time out to listen, but memory returned to him and he could hear, as he had heard years ago, the soft voice, speaking so urgently, so finally.

The serviceman said, 'A blind man. You'd think it a crazy thing to do, wouldn't you? Send a blind man into those mountains. But there was a legend that the Pianhmar would only contact a man without sight – a superstition on their part – they feared being seen.' He laughed. 'Like the Ree'hd hate being photographed. Primitive, isn't it?'

Zeitman declined to comment. He knew the legend about the eyeless being the only ones who could contact the Pianhmar and live, a legend that had been dashed when Maguire had failed to return, like so many sighted humans before him. Now the serviceman had struck an interesting chord, since Maguire *had* returned, and under unusual circumstances to say the least! If the Pianhmar did still exist in the mountains, Maguire might be needed again.

The barrier to the burrows was unlocked and Zeitman was at liberty to enter. The serviceman said, 'I'm going to remain here all night, Major. When you come up it will be necessary for me to let you out. Precautionary, you understand.'

'The Rundii, right. I understand.'

'A small group of them came into the museum one night – after that we got a lot more security-conscious. It could have been nasty – you know how they react when they're panicked.'

'How about the entrances out on the savannah. They blocked off?'

'No, and it's very easy to get access to the burrows. There must be hundreds of entrances and miles of tunnelling. Most of the passages we take people around are blocked off, but you can take this key which will get you through them. I guess you know what you're doing.'

Zeitman hoped the serviceman was right. Kristina would know the way in from the plain, south of the city, and where they would meet would be a place no tourist was ever taken to, or serviceman ever inspected; a place that, to Zeitman's uncertain knowledge, did not appear on any chart of the labyrinths.

He passed through the barrier and walked down the tunnel into the cool air of the Ree'hd burrows.

At first, of course, the burrows were well lit. Unobtrusive strip lighting illuminated every crack in the hard paste walls of the tunnels and Zeitman walked along them without hesitation. At each branch, each tunnel that led down or off, he took an alternative with hardly a thought. He knew where he was, and where he was going, and he was only vaguely aware of the uncomfortable pressure of his vaze, tucked in his belt.

Thousands of feet pacing these tunnels every day, thousands of hands touching the walls, thousands of voices chattering in the restless air, had led long ago to the secretion concrete of the walls cracking and flaking. The Ree'hd, in the centuries before man had arrived on their world, had burrowed this tunnel-city with the shovel-like forearms of the adolescent males in the community . . . and they had compacted the walls and made them safe, with clay and sand, and a female body secretion that hardened to a very tough, transparent film. This, in nature, was used to coat the female's body during the long, metabolically static time of parturition. The film was protection against the cold (the act of birth was performed upon the open plain, alone) and dehydration.

The use of the secretion in the walls was one of the few innovations that the Ree'hd culture demonstrated, and it had become fundamental to their way of life.

The walls of the tourist burrows were now replaced with man-made products, indistinguishable in sight and touch from the original, but far stronger and far safer. Since the atmosphere in the authentic burrows was different from that here, Zeitman had no misconceptions as to the cultural worthlessness of the tours that filled this place by day.

There were, certainly, many artifacts, standing now as they had stood for centuries. Zeitman recognized various 'prayer' forms, for want of a better expression – hand-carved blocks of stone and what he chose to call 'dried wood' cemented into the walls and floors of the burrows at the time of building, and carefully replaced at the time of rebuilding. There were other objects that had been left in the burrows when the Ree'hd population had moved site and retunnelled, away from the human city. To protect the memories that would linger in the old site, grotesque statues, squat idols, distorted caricatures of the Ree'hd, were left in many places. Some were as large as two feet high. The heads were bowed, the arms wrapped round the body, and always one lateral eye was open and one closed. The eyes (went the story for the tourists) were the eyes of stillborn Ree'hd infants, preserved and used in the sculpting.

Zeitman walked through living chambers that were now souvenir shops. The Ree'hd had lived in communal groups, up to thirty or forty in each chamber, and within that thirty or forty were formed the complex year-kin relationships. But intercourse between chambers was common, and at sunset and sun-up, all Ree'hd were as one family, moving to the river to 'pray'.

Tired of walking fast and breathing badly, Zeitman squatted in one of the more natural-looking chambers. It was a cave some fifty feet in diameter, the floor being piled with a terran mock-up of the vegetable matting that the Ree'hd used. In the centre of the floor the matting was several feet thick. It was firm but spongy. Ramps had been placed across it because, strong though the pseudo-matting was, it would not support the shuffling crowds that passed across it. All around, the walls were carved with the strange figures that were Ree'hd symbols. Each carving was a complex of names and lines and told the story of the year-kin relationships, the dying and the birth within that burrow. There were accounts of the losings and the wanderings that had once fascinated Zeitman, but he had seen those records so many times before that they occupied his interest only briefly. He had read and reread the translations from so many burrows, and when it came down to it, the repetitive nature of the content was very boring.

In the absolute stillness Zeitman's breathing was loud and

he held his breath for a moment and listened. No ghosts or invading Rundii. But he had a long way to go.

He pressed on, deeper into the burrow complex, and after some minutes he arrived at the edge of the tour section. He unlocked the screen and went on through. For a few yards the burrows continued to be lit, but as soon as he was out of sight of the screen, the lighting ceased. He switched on his belt light and felt the change immediately. Here the walls were the original burrow walls, and in many places their condition was obviously deteriorating. There was a peculiar odour associated with this type of burrow, caused by the breakdown of the female secretion on the walls. It was not decay, not staleness, rather a slightly alcoholic smell, a heady odour that could make minds spin.

Now navigation became more difficult. Zeitman held a string of seventy-three numbers in his head, all of them remembered mnemonically. They were his guide and without them he was lost.

Increasingly he had to drop down the vertical shafts to reach deeper layers. In many places the burrows were bare, no artifacts, no floor traces, in places the carvings cut from the walls for study in laboratories in Terming. But as he walked deeper, so a more natural order descended upon things. Here were statuettes and wall-embedded blocks, literally as they had been for over a thousand years. Here a section of the wall had crumbled and the corridor was heavily blocked by rubble. Occasionally a cross-breeze drew his attention into the gloom of a side passage and he logged the position against his mnemonic scales, for that passage led to the plain above. It was a way out.

And in.

He was being followed; of that he was sure. He had known of the follower almost as soon as he had left the tour section. A footfall, a caught breath in the sudden silence. At first he had thought that it might have been Kristina following at a distance, but after a while he came to realize that it was no human who trailed him so steadily.

He walked faster, passing through empty-floored chambers, the mattress long since rotted and vapourized. He saw, on the floors, embedded in the substance of the cavern lining, the bones of Ree'hd, many years old. Below each vegetation floor was the burial ground for those of the community who had died in the burrows themselves. It was like this across the entire continent – whenever he had sat and talked with a Ree'hd in his natural environment, he literally squatted upon the remains of the dead.

He checked off number sixty, visualized the route ahead and realized he did not have far to go. He could not recollect having drawn his vaze from its pouch, but he held it now in readiness for anything. When he stopped and held his breath he could hear the approach behind him.

The Rundii surprised him from a totally unexpected position – from the front. It was gruesome to look at, being lit by the yellow glow from his belt. Its four eyes were turned towards him, fully dark-adapted, swollen and black.

Before Zeitman could lift his vaze it had spread-eagled him on the burrow floor and hit both his shoulders, numbing his arms and making him feel sick. He stared up at its oversized head, straining against the thick tissue that disguised any neck it might have had. It was naked and its sexual orifice was a dry slit running down its belly, pulled tight by contractile tissue and giving no clue as to the sex of his attacker.

It shrieked in its meaningless tongue, and the sounds remained with Zeitman for a long time.

It spat then with its song lips while its food lips, the sensory flesh around its ingestion sac, fluttered and moistened. The spit was a wholly human gesture, but it was an increasingly popular gesture among the Ree'hd for it had come to mean what it meant to a human. Where, then, had a Rundii learned the significance of spitting?

There was no glint of metal, no flash of knife, no lifting of hammer-sized fist to pound Zeitman's face to a pulp.

One moment he was trapped beneath three hundred pounds of odoriferous Rundii, the next he was sprawled on the burrow, staring at the ceiling, and still feeling with his nerve endings the weight of the beast upon him.

He eased himself up and picked up his vaze. I'm getting slow, he thought, and brushed himself down. The Rundii were not automatic killers, and for that he was thankful, but its behaviour had been . . . wrong. Why would it attack having followed him so deliberately? If he had surprised it, it might have been expected to have reacted even more viciously . . . but such calculated behaviour! And the strange sounds it had shouted at him – not human echo, not Ree'hd echo, but something new. He wrote the sounds down phonetically and stared at them. Meaningless. Not even a basis in the guttural, simple sounds that the Rundii made between themselves and which, Zeitman was sure, were a developing language – a simple word-object association, nowhere near conceptual communication.

There was a sound ahead in the passage and he ran to it, this time prepared for shock.

Kristina stood there, and she smiled. 'I thought you might have been hurt,' she said. 'I heard the scream from the deep-place.'

'Hello, Kristina.'

'Hello, Robert. You look . . . thin.'

'Gaunt? Haunted? I am. You look . . . plump.'

'Enough compliments,' she said. There was a terrible expression in her eyes. Zeitman, still shaken and physically upset, found he could not interpret it. They walked to their special place.

They alone knew of the chamber. It appeared on no map of the burrows, and in all the years they had used it as their hiding place, as their *special* place, they had never been disturbed, nor even heard a human or a Ree'hd approach them.

They found out later, from talking to Ree'hd living in a nearby community, that this had probably been the deepest part of the burrows, and the most revered. It was not a religious centre, not a place to pray, not even a place to leave remains, though the remains of several Ree'hd had been uncovered when the vegetation mattress had decayed and vanished. It was anomalously warm, whereas in most chambers it was chill. Here, they knew, had gathered the spirits of the unborn, floating in the still air and waiting to possess the Ree'hd as they came into the world – a gathering place of souls, and they had made love here a thousand times, and not a breath of wind, or a moaning ghost had objected.

That had been long ago and they would never make love here again, but to both Zeitman and Kristina the chamber called, welcomed . . . here, and perhaps only here, they could talk together and reach some level of understanding.

They stood in the warm place and Zeitman's belt-light showed them the chamber unchanged from when they had been here before. Bones arranged symbolically formed a belt around the lower part of the cavern. The scrawled figures and texts were faded and could only be seen close up, and for a moment they both walked across the artificial flooring they themselves had installed when they had discovered this place, reading the inscriptions and remembering the fun they had had trying to decipher what they meant. A slight draught was blowing from the tunnels, aerating the chamber and bringing with it the scent of vegetation from the flatlands above.

'How have you been, Kristina?' Zeitman turned round and sat down cross-legged upon the mats. Kristina sat in front of him and her fingers played nervously with the pressure pads on her boots.

'Happy,' she said after a moment. 'I think I can sum up the past four years in that single word.'

'Happy,' repeated Zeitman. 'Content?'

She nodded. When she said no more Zeitman pressed. 'Lovers?'

'Are you really interested?'

'A little. Tell me to mind my own business if you like.'

She looked at him, thinking hard. He could read her well, now. She was weighing him up, wondering whether it was worth keeping things from him, wondering whether he was worthless enough to be told all about her emotional life of the past few years.

'Lovers? Yes . . . several. All very early on. They're all off-planet now, and none of them lived in my heart much beyond two or three days.'

'How long did I?'

'A little longer. Don't become tedious, Robert. It's difficult enough for me to be here with you without you building up to an adolescent tantrum.'

Zeitman felt struck between the eyes, but forced a smile. And he conceded that she was right, albeit a silent concession.

In the harsh illumination from his belt light she seemed hollow-eyed and fierce. He toned down the emission and a softer light filled the chamber, and she became suddenly a different person to behold – rounder, gentler.

'I had a hell of a four years,' said Zeitman. 'I presume you thought of me some of the time? You must have wondered . . . .'

'I received your madly passionate communications from Orgone and Necroman 3. You sounded like you were having fun. From the tone of the letters I assumed they were sent to hurt me, rather than inform me.'

'I can't remember. I was pretty bitter in the first few months, and I did have some fun, yes. But it didn't last. Orgone has a strange effect on male humans – it makes them very juvenile. Some form of micro-flora that upsets the hormones; so they say, anyway.'

'In other words,' said Kristina with a humourless smile, 'I'd better make allowances.'

'I don't think the effect has lasted. If I look younger it's because I've lost weight. If I seem emotionally less mature it's because I aged prematurely in my last few years on Ree'hd-world – and I've corrected the fault.'

'Are you attempting to insult me?'

'No, not at all,' said Zeitman quickly. 'We were different people then, Kristina, and in four years we've changed. Right now I only know one thing for sure . . .'

Kristina dropped her gaze from his. 'Don't tell me.'

'I want you back, Kristina. Now. As we were, together, researching, exploring . . .'

'Stop it, you fool. Stop it!'

Her shout died away. Zeitman sat and stared and she couldn't meet his eyes.

'Fool,' he stated without emotion. 'I don't understand that.'

'You don't understand a thing, Robert. You never did. That's ninety percent of why you're such a dislikable person.' She was flushed and trembling, an expression of anger, perhaps, or bitterness. Zeitman sensed that she was preparing to leave. 'You never understood me,' she said, 'which in itself was acceptable – just. But Robert, you just did not listen when I told you things. You always had to believe that our life here was fruitful and uncomplicated, and you became so indifferent . . . Inside I was dying faster than I thought was possible.'

'Oh come on, Kristina . . .'

'Shut up and listen. I'm not staying here, Robert, and I'm certainly not getting together with you again. You have nothing but the original Robert Zeitman below that juvenile flesh and bone exterior . . . There's no book that lists the lessons learned from this, or that, or him or her . . . There's no file headed "how I get up Kristina's nose, and ways and means and self-denials necessary to negate this contrast of personalities". You never grew up, Robert. Orgone didn't touch you – it had nothing to touch. You have grown up a little now, but at the time you lived your little dream relationship and *killed* me, and I will not run the risk of being hurt again. Not that you could hurt me any more. I have no inclination to know you, to talk to you, to lay with you or do anything with you. I want you to forget me, and when you've forgotten me and what I mean to you, then maybe we can set up together in a purely scientific way, studying the Ree'hd as we used to. Understand?'

Zeitman understood and it hurt him very much. She was trying to send him away with a half-promise that she, and he, knew would never be fulfilled.

He let his head hang limp and for a long time there was just the sound of Kristina's breathing. What went through Zeitman's mind was a confused and illogical sequence of fears and feelings, and when he looked up he said the worst thing he could have said, and this was so predictable to Kristina that she laughed.

'Why must it always come down to suspicion? Hell, Robert. You're a cliché unto yourself.'

'I asked you a question.'

'I already told you I had lovers.'

'That's past. I mean *now*.'

'Very well, Yes, Robert. There is someone else in my life right now. He is my lover and I love him.'

'Dan bloody Erlam . . . it has to be him!'

Kristina laughed, the bitter laugh that was all Zeitman could remember of her expressions of amusement. 'Dan is a very fine man, and he makes his feelings for me well known. But he knows the score and he accepts it, even if he does rally his forces every so often and come courting. No Robert,' she seemed to be almost goading him, baiting him. 'My lover is someone much more interesting than any human . . .'

Zeitman shook his head, an expression of utter disbelief in his eyes. 'Not . . . not Urak . . . surely not a bloody Ree'hd!'

'Right on, Robert Zeitman. My lay has four eyes and an erotic zone beneath his para-arms. What do you think of that?'

Zeitman's response was a cry of anguish. He struck Kristina and, climbing to his feet, reached a vantage point from which he could strike her again.

'Leave me alone, you bastard,' she screamed, rolling away from his first vicious kick.

'A bloody Ree'hd . . . I heard you were living with him, but I never realized . . . You bloody stupid bitch! How could you, Kristina. How could you!'

She climbed to her feet and held the side of her face where blood seeped from a two-inch graze. 'Easy . . . easy. Come and watch us sometime. It'll make your hair curl.'

'You bitch . . . I – oh my God!'

'Hit me again and I'll kill you!'

He pulled the blow as he saw the pin gun in her hand. She walked sideways round the chamber and came to the entrance.

He was conscious of tears streaming down his face, but he stood still, watching her, fists clenched by his sides.

She said, 'You may well have destroyed everything I ever wanted, Robert – a chance to become a part of an alien world . . . a chance to become an alien myself. I was nearly there, Robert, and you may have destroyed that. If you have, I hope you rot in hell. If not, then I don't intend to let you have a second chance.'

'A Ree'hd, Kristina! They're not human. Kristina, you can't love a damn animal.'

Her smile was almost triumphant. 'I loved you, didn't I? And that's enough said. Leave me alone. Just leave me alone!'

'NO!' He shouted, anger making an irrational animal of him. As he reached for her she shot and he felt the sting of a needle and the sickening sensation of paralysis.

chapter six

From the position he had adopted upon falling, Zeitman could see his wrist chronometer. He watched, paralysed, as the seconds passed. Each second seemed to take an hour to tick into non-existence, and in the time taken for the seconds hand to register a full minute Zeitman had several times lived and relived and regretted the incidents of a few minutes before. His mind lingered on Kristina's words, rephrased them, re-expressed them: had he really seemed as an animal to her? Or was that just spite, bitterness on her part, causing her to invent past hatred she had never felt? Was she really without *any* feeling for him? Could she love a Ree'hd . . . could she really become a Ree'hd? And if she could, was it possible that he, Zeitman, could follow her . . . into the culture of the

Ree'hd, into the world, into a peaceful, non-competitive existence?

Two minutes.

He felt the sensation of anesthesia wearing off. First his fingers and toes, then, quickly (five, six seconds) his arms, legs. He staggered, stumbled, stood up straight and leaned against the wall of the burrow, staring at his knees, at the ceiling, at his knees again, as he tried to shake full consciousness back into his head.

Two minutes thirty seconds. He listened carefully, applying his whole awareness to the task of searching for Kristina's departure.

There was no sound at all.

Three minutes and he felt in full enough control of his muscles to give chase to the woman. He crossed to the narrow entrance of the chamber and leaned against the wall again, peering into the corridor outside, the light from his belt giving him a view for twenty feet in either direction.

He didn't notice the Rundii at first. It was standing more or less where the corridor twisted out of sight and the light was weak. When he saw the shape standing there watching him, he froze.

It was the same creature that had so recently attacked him, of that he was almost sure. There was a difference in the native's attitude, however. It seemed hesitant, unsure.

Zeitman realized, as he acted, that the time between becoming aware of the Rundii, and drawing his vaze to shoot it down as it leapt at him, was less than a heart's beat. He shot, and the Rundii screeched loud and long as it lay on the floor, and pumped its body fluid on to the hard rock.

When it screeched it identified itself not as a Rundii, but as a Ree'hd. Zeitman, confused, approached cautiously and stared down at the dying creature. Sure enough, there was something very artificial about the characteristic yellow sexual skin of the Rundii below each arm. Yellow paint, already smudged and smeared.

Checking the wound Zeitman realized that it was not, for a Ree'hd, as serious as it would have been for a human; in all probability the native would survive. Zeitman left him lying there, and began his pursuit of Kristina, knowing neither where she had gone, nor what else she might have arranged to be waiting for him – for he was almost sure that she had laid on this attack – in the complex of passages that led to the surface.

He climbed, and ran, covering several miles of winding, crumbling burrows. Every minute he stopped and listened. He heard nothing.

At last he came to the first exit corridor to the surface of the planet: a steep, ridged slope, with a circular entrance, three feet across and just accessible to a fit human being. Through the hole in the roof he could see clouds, lit by the weak reflected light of Other Moon.

He was well outside the city, probably more than two miles under the natural plain across the river from Terming. He climbed to the surface and took great care as he made his exit from the burrows. There was nothing waiting to attack him, or to greet him, or watch him, and he felt mildly grateful. There was, less fortunately, no sign of Kristina.

The plain was a black, featureless area. In the very distance he could see, against the horizon, the beginnings of a small 'forest' (an accumulation of the moving tree forms that roamed during winter, and rooted during spring) restricted in dimension by the shallowing of the top soil as the bed-rock waved close to the surface in this particular area. He imagined he saw the flickering light of a fire, but there was nothing, or no-one, that would want – or have been mad enough to light – such a fire in this area.

Behind him, as he crouched facing the darkness of the plain, Terming was a wall of bright light, promising security. Between Zeitman and that security there flowed the wide, uninviting river, and to cross it would mean re-entering the burrows and negotiating their complexity with only a vague idea of the route he should take, now he had been rash enough to leave his mentally encoded route some distance behind.

Unsure of what he should do next, he spent some moments in indecision. Should he make an approach to the woods? Or go back below the surface and find another of the back exits from the complex and hope for better luck? Or should he give up altogether and return to the barracks?

His mind was made up a moment later when Kristina screamed from a distance of at least half a mile. For a moment Zeitman's heart stopped, then he was off and running, forgetting the the scattered ground holes that could have claimed a limb if not his life.

In the darkness he became aware of an area of light, the light from Kristina's belt. He could see, as he approached, the stooped shape of a Ree'hd bending over the prone form of a human . . . Kristina!

With a cry (designed to inspire fright – as if the Ree'hd would respond to such a thing!) he closed the distance with speed and determination. At the last moment before he would have fired his vaze, the Ree'hd turned and stared at him.

He recognized her immediately. A middle-years Ree'hd called Reems'gaa, now demonstrating great distress, great anger, great frustration – such a mixture of emotion that Zeitman knew one thing only – she was about to kill.

A Ree'hd never killed another Ree'hd except in times of great (truly great!) stress, or if that Ree'hd were mad. On Ree'hdworld humans were regarded if not as Ree'hd, then certainly as equivalent beings, and were never attacked with murder in mind, although he had once seen such a thing happen by accident. Humans *were* affected by the Ree'hd mind-killing ability, and this, it seemed to Zeitman, was what Reems'gaa was doing to Kristina. Kristina was quite obviously unconscious, and the Ree'hd had been slowly killing her by closing down the human's body systems. It took time, obviously – or was there such a conflict of ideals within the Ree'hd that she was unable to bring her powers to full fury?

When Ree'hd and human met each other's gaze there was a moment's tenseness, an instant recognition, and on Zeitman's part a deeply situated fear that gripped him from the inside and said, 'kill her, she's going to kill you!' The Ree'hd obviously remembered Zeitman. Strangely, when Zeitman had encountered her before he had been alone, and not with Kristina – so why was she attacking Kristina?

Had she been harbouring a hatred for him all these years? It had been . . . six years, a whole six years since they had met last! It came back to Zeitman as if it had happened just the day before – a clarity of image, frightening in its intensity. It was day, the time of day (apart from dusk) when the wind was at its least intolerable, perhaps midday, a little after – the cloud covering, as deep and dark as any winter cloud-covering ever was, prevented accurate time telling, and Zeit-man, in those days, did not wear a chronometer . . .

He had come out of his burrow (not really his, merely hired for the period of study with the Niimyr Ree'hd, his main source of study these days since the wind had become so strong as to make distant travelling dangerous and uncom-fortable). A female Ree'hd was moving slowly away from the area, almost staggering as she walked up the slopes behind the main burrows, legs splayed a little more than was usual.

The Ree'hd was in the later moments of gestation, and the phenomenon of parturition among the Ree'hd was something Zeitman had never witnessed (although it had been witnessed on many occasions in the past). There were many reasons for this omission – the main one being that it was virtually impossible to tell that a Ree'hd female was with offspring until the last seven local days of gestation. At this time the developing foetus grew almost visibly fast, and the female took her leave, without consulting even burrow-kin, and de-livered the young in an open place, where the full force of the wind could carry its soul from the place where souls waited!

With scientific callousness, and childish excitement, he set out after the Ree'hd.

Reems'gaa walked for an hour, oblivious of her shadow; she finally came to a stop in the middle of an exposed rock face on the side of a hill, and turned to face the biting wind. Zeitman dropped to a crouch, fifty yards away, using the naturally rising and falling terrain as cover. He began to speak into his belt recorder, reporting every motion, every gesture, every sound that Reems'gaa made as she began to produce her offspring.

Squatting on the rock she began to croon softly, and as the tenor of her voice grew in volume, so a sparkling liquid oozed from the sexual crevasse at the base of her torso. The liquid, thick and translucent, began to blow into a huge bubble that completely covered the lower part of her body, and formed a tent against the wind. In seconds the shining dome had lost its lustre as the material hardened.

A moment later the birth began, Reems'gaa's belly opening wide between mid-torso and crotch, and the arms of a tiny Ree'hd pushing through and grasping thin air inside the cocoon. At the same time Reems'gaa began to scream.

It was a perfectly human scream of terror, a sound so filled with meaning and emotion for a human that Zeitman reacted almost by reflex.

He ran towards her. To help.

He had run perhaps ten paces when he realized his mistake and stopped. In the same instant Reems'gaa's scream ceased, and she turned her huge eyes upon him, and there was just the whine of the wind, the distant roar of a water cascade, and a sense of stillness . . .

The unborn Ree'hd fell from Reems'gaa's belly, its head crushed to a red and black pulp by the plate-like bones of the womb cavity that had pressed irresistably together at the moment of the mother's shock. The tiny form lay in the protection of the cocoon, limbs twitching slightly, spreading the freely flowing blood about the bare rock.

Reems'gaa began to keen, her arms extending, fingers tense and splayed in a gesture of distress. Her forward eyes never left Zeitman. The human was shattered; he looked at the dead Ree'hd child, and at Reems'gaa and he saw a symbol of what he hated most – human interference. He ran down the hillside, and fled the burrows for a while, and as over the days he pieced together what he had really done, so his crime, and his anxiety, became greater – not just a single abortion, but the loss of fertility of a female Ree'hd. When he had surprised and frightened Reems'gaa she had reflexly aborted the lining of cells within her cavernous womb that were the part-formed bodies of all her offspring of the next fifty Ree'hd years. The Ree'hd way of birth was insemination when just sexually mature, by all those male Ree'hd in the community who would, through life, become year-kin; thereafter offspring were produced where and when required, selecting for characteristics, according to the feeling of the community, from the range of types the mother carried.

Zeitman had destroyed her as a natural Ree'hd, and she had obviously never forgotten or forgiven. He came back to the present, losing the image of the younger, panic stricken Reems'gaa, and facing her furious form as she stood before him, and prepared to attack.

'Reems'gaa! Wait ... please!'

In the half-light from his belt his perspectives were confused; he had thought the Ree'hd was still motionless, but she was approaching, fast, heavy. In an instant Zeitman felt the wind driven from his body, found himself driven to the ground beneath the weight of the native. Reems'gaa stared down at him, her eyes hugely dilated, her squat form pinioning him securely and irresistably.

Zeitman struggled with his vaze, but a strange paralysis affected him. He found he was unwilling to defend himself. The energy seemed to drain from his arms and legs, from his whole body ...

There was a whispering sensation in his head; not words, not even coherent sound. A noise like the distant hiss of static on a primitive radio receiver, and it spread to fill his conscious mind. His heart stopped.

His last thought was, interesting, this is how it affects a human being. Fascinating. Fascinating. Fascinating ...

Something hit him in the face.

Cold wind chilled his flesh, and a human voice was shouting 'Robert Robert Robert ...'

There was a smell of decay. A pain on his left cheek, then

on his right. Something was pulling his shoulders.

His first visual awareness was of the gaping food mouth of a Ree'hd, from which the revolting smell was issuing; his second was of being pinioned beneath the bulk of a dead Ree'hd.

He used all his strength to shift the inert form, and eased himself into a sitting position. Kristina was crouched by him, her face pale, her eyes wet.

'I had to do it. Oh God, I had to . . . but . . .' she began to cry.

Reems'gaa was dead, the burn hole in her back being ample evidence to the fatality of Kristina's rescue operation. 'I didn't want to kill her . . . I never stopped to think, I just . . . reacted.'

There was a certain irony in the situation – Kristina had just killed to save his life, whereas a few minutes before she had left him to die at the hands of her hired assassin. Could it have been that she had no stomach to witness his death? Or might there be some deeper, more selfish reason for her sudden preservation instinct?

Kristina was still shivering and staring at the dead Ree'hd. Zeitman tried to comfort her. He could imagine how she might be feeling – she had reacted as a human being when she saw one of her own race being slowly killed; and this was contrary to the way she thought of herself, as only half human. She had killed her racial half-sister.

'Urak had turned her away. She is – was – Urak's natural year-kin, but he refused to acknowledge her at the changing ceremony.'

'And took you instead,' said Zeitman, immediately understanding the deeper source of Kristina's distress. She was feeling guilty.

'I didn't realize how destructive such a thing could be, but poor Reems'gaa – she was totally lost, totally dependent upon Urak who wouldn't pay any attention to her at all. As Burrow One for this year he had a responsibility only to his nearest kin.'

'Did no other Ree'hd help her?'

'There was a lot of reaction against me, mostly from the males, mostly from the younger males. Reems'gaa wasn't starving, but I don't think she was being helped by any other burrow. She spent nights inside the outer corridors of the city, and her days by the river bank, watching whatever Urak did. Finally she turned her attention to me, just this morning begging me to leave and let her live normally.'

'And you didn't.'

Kristina turned on Zeitman, snapped, 'I have my own life, Robert! What was I supposed to do? Sacrifice my own happiness to give one female her own? It was her or me, and I regret that that was the way of things . . .'

She fell silent, perhaps aware of the very humanness of the things she said, perhaps ashamed, perhaps thinking that it was Zeitman who had brought this reversal upon her. They stood in the darkness, a small circle of light, two humans regarding the sprawled body of a murdered Ree'hd. After a while Kristina grew very tense and switched off her belt light; the action drew Zeitman's attention to her and she said, 'Turn off your belt.'

Zeitman obeyed. He had noticed her gaze, directed into the distance, towards the beginnings of the forested lowlands behind Terming. Directing his attention in the same direction he felt a sudden chill, a quickening of his heart.

Four shapes stood there, in the absolute darkness, discernible only by the slight glow of the sexual skin areas on their torsos. They made no sound. They watched.

'Rundii,' whispered Kristina. It was an unnecessary observation since Zeitman had noted their nature immediately, but when she said the word he felt that chill again. In the darkened plain an accurately thrown rock was far more lethal than a blindly discharged vaze.

Human and Rundii stood motionless and silent, watching each other. This was only the second time that Zeitman had come close to one of the forest-living primitives, but the first time he had been secure in hiding, unobserved, unbothered.

This time he had been caught unawares, and the Rundii were unpredictable creatures, increasingly unpredictable as their violent outbursts declined, not quite to negligibility, but sufficiently to inspire a false sense of security in new human arrivals on Ree'hdworld.

'Let them move first,' Zeitman whispered. It had occurred to him that if four faced from the front, there could be a larger band approaching from behind, possibly just curious. And if curiosity in the dead native was all that motivated them, he saw no sense in giving them reason to attack.

The shapes faded away with a gentle padding sound until there was no sensory indication of them at all. Zeitman whirled round, fast, vaze in hand, searching the darkness for any other Rundii prowlers. He noticed, as he did so, that Kristina was doing the same.

'Let's follow them,' she said, and it was as if there were no distance in time between them. They were Rob and Kristina Zeitman, and you wouldn't find a better biological team this side of Earth.

They followed, stealthily, carefully, picking up the trail in a very short time, and depending on keeping the quiet walking of the Rundii just in earshot. With their unrefined infrared senses the Rundii might not notice their pursuers, unlike a Ree'hd who would not have failed to notice them.

Dollar Moon began to rise, away to the west, above the mountains. Kristina registered some alarm, but Zeitman urged her to be silent and pulled her to the ground. Ahead of them the Rundii had stopped, and were staring at the leading edge of the moon's disc as it appeared, outlining the peaks of the Hellgate mountains.

For some minutes the four creatures stood and stared at the moon; then, as more than half the disc came into view, they turned back to their original route and vanished into shadows.

Zeitman remained where he was, watching the moon, then staring after the Rundii and thinking hard. He had never ever heard of the Rundii being fascinated by the lunar rising. No account of them, however detailed, had ever referred to such curiosity. Was that an omission of observation? Were these Rundii unusual? He discussed the phenomenon with Kristina.

'To my knowledge,' she said, 'The Rundii are primitive, closer to the common ancestors of Ree'hd and Rundii than are the Ree'hd. We have never found artifacts, though they use stones and will use knives that they steal; they have no organized community life outside the natural racial patterns. They have no self-awareness . . .' she stopped; her eyes bright in the new light on the plain, were wide. 'What are we witnessing, Robert? Two scientific minds, frustrated by inactivity, reading significance into nothing at all? Or a change?'

'I have no idea,' was all Zeitman said, thinking of what he had learned from Kawashima, but impatient to follow the Rundii group. 'We're losing them.'

They followed on. By the time they were passing through the sparse bush and twisted tree-forms that marked the first ten miles or so of the impermanent forest, Dollar Moon was riding high, speeding through the heavens towards its setting point out across the ocean.

They came to the Rundii community suddenly and without warning. Community. Zeitman could use no other word.

They were grouped in a clearing, squatting in a wide semi-circle about the body of one of their kin. The corpse lay prone, and facing the sky, its limbs broken and bent across its body in a fashion that neither Zeitman nor Kristina had ever seen. The Rundii gathering just sat, and stared at the body. They seemed to be contemplating what they observed. They seemed to be thinking about death.

After a while Kristina slipped away from Zeitman. He followed her, not wanting to remain so close to the animals on his own, and found her seated in the full light of Dollar Moon, back against a tree-form, arms around her legs, her frail body shivering in the cold night. Zeitman sat beside her, debating whether to put his arm around her shoulder and warm her, or leave well alone. While he was still thinking about such trivial matters, Kristina said, 'Did you feel it?'

'The confusion?'

She nodded. 'Terrible confusion. They have faced death

for generations, but now they fear it. They're aware, Robert. They're fully aware. In less than a heartbeat they've crossed the barrier. They're really alive now.'

'That's an enormous assumption . . .'

'But you said you felt it! That was no animal empathy. That was the confusion of an intelligent, emotional being, facing life objectively for the first time in its life.'

Zeitman agreed. 'I *did* feel it, and if they had been old apes of Earth sitting there, I'd agree. But they are Rundii, and this is not Earth. There have been guns jumped for centuries – the so called speech of the Rundii for one thing . . .'

'I know. Just defensive repetition of sound. I know. But this is different. We're sensitives, you and I. Don't you have faith in that ability any more?'

What could he say? All his life his capacity for empathy and sensitivity had been his major laboratory instrument, allowing him into the minds of animals and men. Six years ago he had failed to understand human beings, the ability had gone and it had helped destroy him and Kristina. How could he fully trust what his senses told him about an alien? His feelings might be as distorted now as they became those several years ago.

'We could . . . we could work together on this Kristina . . . as we were . . .'

'No way,' she said coldly.

'Not as man and wife, just as a biological team—'

Kristina struggled to her feet, saying, 'I told you Robert. I don't want to know.'

'Kristina – just for a while. Don't you sense the change that's going on? I honestly don't know if I *can* trust my sixth sense any more, but if I can, then it tells me that something big is happening, and we could explore it together.'

Kristina stopped. She didn't look at Zeitman who stood behind her, but she softened. 'There is something happening, I agree. I've been feeling it for a long time. I've felt it in the Ree'hd, though Urak seems oblivious of anything happening to him. I've felt it in the ecology, in the air. I've even felt it in the humans I know, especially Dan Erlam.' She turned

98

and faced Zeitman, and there was something confused about her expression. 'It's a change I don't think any human could cope with, and it is probably the reason I'm so desperate to become a Ree'hd.'

The thought of it! To become totally intimate with an alien culture – to *become* an alien! To die an alien. For a moment he forgot that he was Robert Zeitman, that he wanted a relationship with a human female that he had had once before. For that same moment he thought how absolutely *right* it was to shake off the human guise and to become immersed in Ree'hdworld. It was what he had always wanted, but perhaps never realized. And Kristina was suggesting that she knew how to do it; and if she knew . . .

He said as much to Kristina, but she remained apparently unimpressed. He said, 'Kristina – help me to find the way into Ree'hdworld. I can't do it alone . . .'

She was quiet for a moment, thinking. 'I could help you, I suppose . . .'

'Christ, Kristina – we could be really great together—'

'Togetherness I *don't* want. Don't get carried away, Robert. I'll help you now, this instant, for a few weeks if you need it . . . but that's all.'

'That's all I ask, Kristina, a few weeks, the security of your presence. Hell, I don't know why I'm saying this, but I mean it. I'm lost without you, Kristina – I'm in a vacuum . . . I'll be unable to do anything meaningful unless I have your strength.'

'I've told you I'll help.'

'Not right away, though. Not just yet. We must find out what is happening here . . .'

Kristina's laugh was almost insulting. 'You'll never make it, Robert. You have no sense of urgency, and if any human feature is required to lose humanness it's a sense of urgency. Forget I ever offered. I want no further part of you.'

She was gone, consumed by darkness and her hatred for Zeitman, a silent animal, making her escape through the night.

Behind Zeitman came the sound of animal voices, crooning, singing, perhaps, the first death song.

part two

chapter seven

In a dream of Earth Zeitman became encased in fire, and ran screaming and blistering through rows of gutted buildings. He cried out in his sleep and Susanna reached across and shook him awake.

Shocked by the abruptness with which his nightmare fled, Zeitman sat bolt upright and stared into the darkness of the chamber. He could hear the shuffling approach of a Ree'hd and Susanna's voice was an urgent droning that slowly began to assume coherence.

It had been a nightmare and nothing more, and after a moment he relaxed. When Grai, the burrow One, peered into the chamber and expressed concern for her guests' well-being Zeitman apologized for the disturbance. When Grai hesitated before withdrawing, Susanna switched on their small lamp and the Ree'hd took a long and hard look at her guests from the thousand-mile-distant city, and satisfied herself that all was in order. She backed out of the chamber quietly and Zeitman heard a low exchange outside between several Ree'hd.

Susanna felt his brow. 'You're soaking.'

Zeitman wiped his face on the thin sheet that covered them. 'I'm fine – I'm just very tense, that's all.'

'What about? Here, lie back.'

Zeitman shook her off and climbed to his feet. He dried the sweat from his body and dressed slowly and with shaking hands. He had difficulty with the magnetic fasteners of his 'phrak and finally left it open. 'I need a walk.'

'I'll come with you,' said Susanna, throwing the sheet off and reaching for her clothes.

'Alone.' He smiled at her, but he could see that she was upset. 'I haven't been relaxing at all well . . .'

'Is what happened on Earth still on your mind?'

'Of course it's still on my mind! '

She fell back on the mattress and said no more. Zeitman

almost apologized for shouting but decided against it. He walked from the burrow and out into the end of the night.

Earth. He looked for Sol and saw where it lay in the heavens. As a star it was nowhere near sufficiently bright for its light to be seen from Ree'hdworld, and anyway lay far round the rim of the galaxy so that a veil of light frustrated his search. But it seemed to Zeitman as he gazed into the night sky that where Sol lay there was a black hole in the star spread, and he tried to reach through this to Earth. He stared at that gap and imagined the solar system with its myriad comets, its gas giants – and the radio-wave-filled aether, the noisy babble of thousands of solar stations greeting the approaching voyager. He had been back to Earth several times in his life and one of the great excitements of return was the thought of that rich human greeting as the ship coasted through solar space, seeking its specific beacon.

His last trip home was likely, he reflected now, to have been literally his last. He had wasted his time there, spending the few days he was on-world exploring his childhood haunts, looking up his colleagues from training days, and paying a short and agonisingly nostalgic visit to his parents – both now looking frighteningly old and haunted. Neither of them had ever forgiven him for leaving Earth so permanently. With a solar system to play with why, they asked, did he have to go so far away? It made him tired to hear the argument again, so long after he had thought it was resolved; but of course, it was merely a symptom of what was happening to Earth.

In his last days there he had been told of the spread of Fear across the globe, had seen it for himself, and had been terrified. By now, even as he sat on alien cliffs, his parents and earth-bound friends had succumbed, and would in all likelihood be dead.

He would never go there again, the distance being prohibitive if nothing else. Strangely, Zeitman never felt he was far from Earth. It was impossible to conceive of the immensity of space, especially since a trip from star to star was made for the most part locked in one's cabin, thinking (without comprehension) of the distance being covered. Zeitman could never cope with watching endless star-fields passing, and worst of all was looking back into the blaze of lights behind and thinking 'what if we were lost, what if we couldn't find home again . . .?'

All quite normal fears for quite normal men, and Zeitman was normal in every way. He had even found a more normal feeling for Earth – instead of his indifference of a few days earlier. Now, as he went through a phase of depression, he began to realize that if Earth *was* gone, then man had lost more than he could, in all likelihood, cope with. A complete volte-face had set Zeitman to brooding about the mother-world in every spare moment.

In the Ree'hdworld night he watched Dollar Moon sinking below the southern horizon, its brilliance setting the sea on fire. There were many Ree'hd squatting on the cliff-tops also watching the descent. Very few were paying attention to the red glow of Other as it cast a diffuse light across the land to the north.

Zeitman watched Other and thought he could see the winking lights of the check-stations and signal-installations, but only those with perfect eyesight could see such phenomena, and he was probably imagining what he saw.

What he saw without doubt were the lights in the heavens . . . so many of them! They passed overhead in regular streams, some flashing, some steady beacons. Ships, hundreds of ships with no possibility of landing since the installation was not prepared to assist, but was only too prepared to use missiles to discourage any landing.

The necessity of missiles on Ree'hdworld was something that Zeitman was just prepared to acknowledge, but he hated their presence. What, he wondered, would an innocent Rundii circle think if their night sky suddenly erupted into a double explosion, filling the night with magnesium-flare brilliance and a thunder the like of which they might never hear again? Would they read some religious significance into it? (Might it spark the development of a religious awareness? That was an intolerable thought!). Or would they think of it as a natural phenomenon and forget about it?

Quite apart from their obvious danger, thought Zeitman, the missile-installations are potentially the most destructive to the native cultures of all man's introductions to the planet.

With the approach of dawn the on-shore wind grew in strength and Zeitman pressed against a rock pillar so that he ran no risk of being blown over. The sea was growing wild and he could hear the sound of its relentless beat against the cliffs and the rock platform that formed a natural promenade at the water's edge. At this point, on the coastline, the cliffs were sheer and simple. A few miles to the east were the beginnings of the fragmented coastline that Zeitman had observed on his arrival, and he could see the black archways of rock reaching out into the ocean, and the sea dashing itself against these invaders from the land, swirling through the caverns and channels in its attempt to destroy.

At this time the Ree'hd of this smaller community, nearly a thousand miles from Terming, came out of the ground and spent a few minutes breathing the *Sa'am-cri-orog*, the past and future spirits of the sea wind. Almost immediately, however, they turned from this precarious dawn position on the top of the cliffs and began to move inland, to where the beginnings of a river cut in between high, sheer cliffs. Some Ree'hd were so bold as to sail inland, manipulating their coarse fibre boats with a great deal of facility. The in-blowing wind assisted their efforts.

Always wind, thought Zeitman, as he followed at a distance. Susanna had remained behind to record any activity in the burrows at this time of day.

Zeitman walked the hard way, along the edge of the channel, looking down through nearly three hundred feet of cold air to the turbulent waters below. He could see rocks and ledges below the water's surface, and he could see them carved and pitted with life-holes, each representing a Ree'hd who had died in the community, his spirit committed to the *Sa'am-cri-orog* and to the inner land spheres.

The burrow One, who was Zeitman's host, saw him staring into the canyon and approached him, walking against the raging wind with seemingly little trouble. Zeitman held on for his life to one of the rock pillars that had been driven into the ground, a long line of life supports – the Ree'hd population advanced inland from post to post and it was rare for one of the community to be swept away by the wind.

Grai made no effort, Zeitman was thankful, to adopt human mannerisms; the attitude at which she held her arms told Zeitman of the Ree'hd's pleasure. It was always a pleasure to have a sensitive human to stay under one's burrow roof. There was a difference, of course, between humans like Zeitman, who were scientifically interested in the natives, and the tourists who came to stare and were more frightened than intrigued by the strange creatures they pretended they were *not* holospanning. (Zeitman was guilty of such breaches of trust himself, and had an extensive collection of pictures of Ree'hd. The Ree'hd did not care to have their pictures taken and Zeitman was always disappointed that their apparently primitive culture should manifest itself so blatantly.)

'Are humans not afraid of these distances?'

Zeitman shook his head. 'You mean the height? Most of us would be petrified. That's a very long drop.'

Grai followed his gaze downwards. Zeitman, feeling instability affecting his legs, turned to regard the Ree'hd. Grai was a small female, and quite old. She had been burrow One several times, and her offspring numbered over twenty. It was rare for a Ree'hd to grow so old (Grai was close to one hundred Earth years old) since in all that time the loss of a brother- or sister-year-kin was inevitable. In fact, twice Grai had lost such kin and had wandered for several seasons in the inner lands; but both times she had returned. From his understanding of the burrow records, and from listening to accounts of kin movements, Zeitman knew from long experience that to return *twice* was very unusual.

Grai had said simply that she had felt it was right to return, right that she should remain alive. She had wandered and become a part of nature, but there had been only negative responses to all her thoughts. Not understanding further, she had returned. The next time she might well discover what she had been denied on two occasions.

'A long drop,' echoed the Ree'hd, raising her voice above the wind. 'I have dropped it twice. The water is deep in the middle of the channel and when the wind dies it is possible to guide your fall clear of the rocks.'

'That's interesting. There is a burrow community living near the human city that has no such water-embracing habit.'

'Do they live by the cliffs?'

'No, but they live along the shores of a very wide river, and they share the dawn and dusk meditation with this community. But they never touch water except to catch fish or die.'

Grai made a strange noise with her song lips. Amusement? 'If there are no cliffs they cannot jump. Are you wondering what special significance there is in such an activity?'

Zeitman nodded, thoughtfully. Below him the sea heaved and crashed against the rocks, and the wind brought a fine icy spray up through the enormous chasm to where the two figures stood in such precarious defiance of the forces of nature. The embracing of water could be a part of the Ree'hd desire to embrace all of nature. But there had to be an easier way of doing it than jumping three hundred feet. He said as much to Grai.

'Easier, yes. But not as much fun.' She 'laughed' again, and walked along the cliff-top with Zeitman watching in annoyance. So why shouldn't the Ree'hd have fun as well?

He caught up with the burrow One and apologized for his naivety. They walked in silence, braced against the driving force of the wind, and eventually the cliff-top dropped nearer to the river, and they came to the place of communication where there were several hundred Ree'hd already squatting along the water's edge, among the tree-forms and sheltered among the rocks.

Zeitman and Grai walked down-wind, picking their way carefully, in the half-light, between the motionless shapes of the Ree'hd. They stopped at a place where the full volume of the dawn song reached them, and Zeitman fell soul-silent as the shifting monotone penetrated his awareness and he became a part of the dawn. Grai sang beside him and gradually the sun peered above the horizon, and as full light was shed upon the community the song died away.

'What did you think about?' asked Zeitman, breaking with manners. Grai was not angry. She picked up a small stone, a glittering red crystal shard, and turned it over and over in her sensitive fingers.

'Today my thoughts were of humans, and that overground burrow system you have, and of my third son's kin, Woork-Ree, who has decided to live with the humans.'

'And he needs your prayers because of that?'

Grai stared at Zeitman with an unblinking lateral eye. She was detecting Zeitman as an infra-red emission and she must have seen the flush upon his cheeks, and possibly she realized that Zeitman was uneasy in his probing into the private thoughts of the burrow One.

Grai said, 'There was another Earthman who was interested in our thoughts, and in our relationships with the wind. A few years ago. He had a female with him, as you have.'

Zeitman remembered his previous visit here. The burrow One at that time had stated quite clearly that there were things no Ree'hd would ever let a stranger know, but that Zeitman was welcome to study them if he was prepared to accept that limitation. It had quite unnerved Zeitman at the time, since he felt he was becoming close to the Ree'hd psychology.

He said, 'That was me too. I looked different then, and the woman was my . . . breeding-kin?' He couldn't bring himself to say 'wife'.

'I didn't remember you. I was wandering for most of your previous stay. I came back as the humans – yourself and your kin – were leaving. Is it correct to say 'breeding-kin'? Do you have young by her?'

'No.'

Difficult. He explained that they were married in the sense that they had bound to stay together for five years. For what purpose? Love, companionship. No, not at the expense of love and companionship with others . . .

Zeitman had a feeling inside that Grai was quite aware of the situation regarding human relationships, but it was hard to tell. This community was sparsely visited, even by students. Tourists viewed from a distance; there might be mutual exchange, especially of food, and then the air-bus whisked the visitors away, leaving very little mark upon the community. In all the years of human visitation the Ree'hd here had never learned interLing. Zeitman, however, had rediscovered his earlier fluency in the Ree'hd language and now struggled only with the deeper throat presentation of emotional concepts. To Zeitman it seemed that the group were almost shy to express their inner feelings. The sound volume dropped and the words were forced out between narrowed 'lips'. It was a variant he could not cope with himself.

If Grai was more aware than she was pretending, she never let on to Zeitman. It was not *that* alien a concept to the Ree'hd that there should be a long-term bonding between two individuals for the purpose of physical love, and occasionally for procreation. Among the Ree'hd physical love was an unimportant and occasional indulgence, and did not involve intercourse in the human sense. All but the burrow One were a part of a complex grouping of kin-pairs within which pleasure and emotional communication were shared freely. The burrow One was restricted to a single kin (of the opposite sex) but for the year was the focus of the dusk meditation and the kin was important only as a replacement should the burrow One die.

Gradually Zeitman came back to his original question. 'Does your son's kin need your thoughts?'

'I hope not. But the balance is upset, Zeitman.' Her pronunciation of his name was so strange that for a moment he wondered what it was she had said.

'Which balance is that?'

Grai did not answer immediately. When she did, it was the answer he had been given so many times before. 'The development balance. The balance of nature.'

'Upset by human interference? We try and steer well clear of the Ree'hd communities in all our various enterprises. And we've not despoiled more than a tiny corner of the ecosphere. Is it fair to say we've upset the whole balance?'

110

'Is it fair to allow the imposition of your way of life upon ours?'

'I think you mean the Ree'hd in the city . . . well, as you say, we *allow* it, but we don't force it.'

Grai turned her forward eyes upon him, seemed to find a cause for anger in his words. 'Then you should disallow it, Zeitman. I have a small conception of your world, Earth,' she said the name in interLing, this time a more successful use of the human name. 'Am I right in believing that it is a world where nature is in very small pieces?'

Zeitman thought of the national park he had visited in Kenya-green, when he had been a child (the park was gone now). So many miles of continually recycling, sun-baked but rich, green bush, so vast an area that at the time he had felt terrified and would not leave the security of the coach. He had been thirteen years old and he could remember the thought that went through his head, screaming at him. If I step out there an animal could *get* me. There's no protection, no force-field, no fence, no inbuilt command to turn and run as they got to within ten feet of a human. Naked animals!

Thirteen and afraid of what little nature Earth could offer. By his mid-thirties he had landed on worlds where there was no artificiality at all and, after the predictable panic and depression at knowing there was not a metropolis over the next hill, he had come to love open spaces.

Again an easy adaptation. Now he could revisit Earth (until recently, at least) and lose himself in the shadows of buildings higher than the clouds, and feel no sense of loss, because he could step off-world to the exact opposite. He had access to everything he could want. There was only the voyage between them that was fearsome.

'I suppose it was.'

'Was? Past tense?'

'Past tense.' He decided to say no more about the fate of Earth; instead he went on, 'There's very little left to study. Well, that's not strictly true. Everything that ever lived on Earth is somewhere in one of the Federations, still being

111

studied or preserved. All the questions are being answered about Earth's natural history, but Earth itself grew a little too small for everyone who wanted to stay there. So they took the natural history somewhere safe.'

'So: at least there is something left.' Grai seemed very depressed. 'And that which is left, can it function on its own? In parts?'

Did she mean monoculture? 'I think so,' he said. 'We used to grow just one species of a plant in an area, or keep animals of the same kind in confined spaces. For consumption. If a weed grew up to threaten the monoculture we could eliminate it with no difficulty.'

Grai seemed very perturbed. She picked up another crystal shard and flung it into the river; a flattened stone, it skipped across the water's breaking surface for a few feet. 'Then the balance of nature was not very delicate.'

'Oh it was.' Wasn't it? He should know the answers to these things. Perhaps the delicacy of the balance was not as pronounced as had once been thought, but throughout his history man had been aware that to take too many liberties with his environment had meant to destroy. There had been, Zeitman remembered, a time of ecological conservation, of resources consciousness, but whatever the men of old Earth had done the natural flora and fauna had survived because it lasted, until it was deliberately destroyed, for thousands of years. He said, 'It was delicate in that to eliminate one particular parasite, for example, might allow another parasite to grow up simply because it had once been the victim of the eliminated species and now was free to breed. So it was possible to . . . rearrange things.'

'But a new balance was found very shortly?'

'Yes, I suppose it was.'

Most of the Ree'hd had returned to their burrows on the cliff-tops. It was developing into an overcast day, very cold, very damp, and the flora of the river-bank, the great sprawling brown and blue tree-forms, were unnaturally quiet and closed up.

'On this world,' said Grai, very slowly, 'Everything counts.

112

Everything is important. And not only that, but the individual is important – though perhaps not at the mat level,' she dug her scratch-pads, the horny extremities midway down her arms, into the tight vegetation mat they sat upon. Pulling up a piece she shook the yellow top-soil from it and held it up. It was tinged blue, as was everything on Ree'hdworld, and Zeitman, without effort, remembered why – copper ions, important in the surface temperature energy generation process that the flora used to complement its inefficient photocoupling processes. Blue, yes, but when the light was right the land could seem as naturally green as any pasture on Dominion.

'I don't suppose I have insulted the balance of nature by doing that,' Grai said. 'But Ree'hd, and Rundii are not species of the ground. There are so many Ree'hd in your city that we cannot but feel uneasy. The individual is important. So, in a way, the human city is causing distress to the ecology.'

Grai threw the piece of sod into the river and rose to return to the burrows. Zeitman declined to return with her. Instead he walked away from the river, deeper into the land around this particular Ree'hd sphere.

In the several days since he had met Kristina he had seen and travelled much. Susanna, his constant companion, was nothing more than a distraction. She shared his days, and for the last two nights had shared those too. They found each other mutually exciting, and sexually fulfilling, and had developed their relationship to nicely distanced intimacy. During the days, however, Susanna let her youth become obtrusive, sulking continually when Zeitman was rude to her (which was often); when she wasn't sulking she talked of the most trivial things, talking Dominion out of her system, perhaps talking her previous domestic repression out of the same system. She showed no inclination at all to accept and sympathize with Zeitman's new-found feelings for Earth.

What was increasingly bothering Zeitman was a sensation of pointlessness.

Why bother to continue on Ree'hdworld, or on any world, in an investigatory capacity? Liaison officer, yes, with its defined functions, but these meant nothing simply because Zeitman was a scientist, and an observer, and was inclined to do nothing but observe and interpret. Kristina was very similar; as an object-empath she may well have been psychic to a considerable degree, but her preferred pursuits were as academic as Zeitman's. Zeitman and Kristina had been a good team, and in Zeitman's mind they would always be so; they were on Ree'hdworld not to throw fits at each other, not to fall in love with the natives, not to get unnecessarily irritated with little Dominion females, but to understand the planet, and its people, and its history, and why it was suffering so much from what was possibly the gentlest, most unobtrusive presence the Federation had ever demonstrated.

But why try and understand now? Who would they report back to with Earth virtually gone? What was the point? Wouldn't it be better to take Susanna, and maybe another couple, and stake out a nice piece of land, somewhere miles from the nearest Ree'hd sphere (perhaps on Wooburren) and just survive?

But there was a scientist in Zeitman and the scientist was emotionless, without personality. It was dominant and it was interested in Ree'hdworld; it was interested in mind-killing, and the sudden evolutionary development of that most useful of powers. It was interested in why only non-Ree'hd animals could be killed in this way. It was interested in the 'silver fish' and their totally atypical winter behaviour, shirking the deep waters of the oceans where many closely related species vanished to. Zeitman, the scientist, had the obvious answer to it all, but Zeitman the man would not accept what his common sense told him!

The scientist inside him would keep him functioning in the way he wanted, even though his humanity was dying. All around him he could witness panic, suicide, the drive to destruction of humans suddenly realizing that they were not, as they had thought, immune from the spreading disease they so feared and had named Fear – he could witness all this and still concern himself with questions about the wind and the animals, and the minds of the Ree'hd, and why they seemed so unconcerned about the Pianhmar, neither denying their existence, nor asserting it, and pretending (it seemed to Zeitman) that such things were unimportant.

Zeitman felt a tremendous calm. As he walked, thinking over his presence on Ree'hdworld and his dead relationship with Kristina, so he unwound, and the tension that had built up during the night fully dissipated. It was very cold and wherever he walked he could see the tree-forms in frantic motion. They were gathering into temporary forests in places, where perhaps, they might harness any rain or wind to the best advantage.

A stinging rain fell for a few minutes, driving across the country and down. Zeitman made no effort to shelter, but he turned his respiration over to the small face-mask he carried on his belt. For a moment the more terrestrial oxygen-nitrogen balance, adjusted by the mask, was uncomfortable. He breathed deeply a few times and continued to walk.

With the passing of the rain the land became alive with the sleek blue-skinned animals that filled one of the herbivorous niches on this world. They drank water from the saturated turf, and played in the dampness with a great deal of exuberance. From a distance they seemed almost otter-like, though they were difficult to observe properly, they blended so cryptically with the background. From a closer vantage point their six-legged forms were disquieting. All fauna on Ree'hdworld were six-legged, even if only during embryonic development. The Ree'hd and Rundii were no exceptions, but the middle pair of limbs (in the Ree'hd at least) appeared to have been modified into the plate-like endo-skeleton around the mid-quarters of both sexes (in the females becoming associated with the womb). In the absence of a fossil record the theory was not universally accepted.

For a while Zeitman crouched on his haunches watching the frivolity of the life around him, and conscious that that life was watching him back. He was about to continue his walk when a distant droning caught his attention and he stood, adjusting the binocular lenses of his mask's eyepieces until he could detect the cause of the noise, about a mile away, skimming low over the steep hills.

It was a Terming air-bus, packed with leering tourists, and making its way to the ocean-edge commune that Zeitman was currently visiting.

Furious, he shot a burst of his vaze at the air-bus and felt no satisfaction as the charge blasted out a great chunk of rock, sending a deep booming explosion echoing through the humid atmosphere.

Erlam had promised that he would reroute any tourist venture away from Zeitman's planned visit route. Erlam had let him down.

Zeitman began the long trek back to the burrows. It rained again for a few minutes, and this time he found his saturated situation a very great irritation.

When he arrived at the burrows, he found several Ree'hd lined up along the cliff-edge, staring down to where a shelf of rock formed a natural promenade, wide enough for an air-bus to land upon. Zeitman, without acknowledging Grai or Susanna, found the wide-cut pathway to the sea. He stumbled twice and sent cascades of loose rock and earth, fallen from above, pouring into the air and on to the ground below. His approach was so noisy and his shouts so venomous that eventually the milling crowd of bio-stat-suited visitors turned to see him. Some waved, some brought out their holospans and blatantly photographed him, and took the opportunity to turn their sights on the Ree'hd as well.

A large gathering of Ree'hd adolescents was the main source of attraction for the humans. These young natives were on the rock-shelf to swim and fish, and Zeitman could see several dark shapes a few hundred yards offshore, and every so often a Ree'hd head poked above the water's surface and regarded the scene on the promenade. A few older Ree'hd were crouched in the shadow of the cliffs, watching impassively as they were subjected to the scrutiny of a hundred human nonentities. There was little attempt made to communicate; obviously so, since tourists never bothered to learn the language of the natives, and the natives here were content not to learn interLing. The exchange of food items (permissible trade) occurred as usual, the adolescent Ree'hd supervising the trade, and this was in progress as Zeitman arrived angrily at the air-bus.

The Ree'hd adults all raised an arm in salute, and Zeitman waved back. He could see from the pursing of their food lips that they were fed up, and probably thinking it was up to him to get rid of these irritations.

Zeitman swung himself into the air-bus where the driver sat, bored and half-asleep. 'Get these bastards out of here!'

The driver came fully awake and stared up at Zeitman. 'Who the hell are you? This is a scheduled stop.'

'It's just been unscheduled, driver. Now get these . . . get them back in the bus and lift off. You had your orders from Dan Erlam . . .'

The driver seemed quite upset now. He cast anxious glances at the crowd of humans who, sensing that something unexpected was happening (were they all as bored as the driver?), began to approach the air-bus.

'Patrician Erlam? He said nothing to me . . .'

Damn you, Erlam, thought Zeitman. Aloud he said, 'There is a scientific study being undertaken in this group and I don't want any dumb visitors spoiling the atmosphere of the place. Now get the hell out of here.'

'Look, I can't just pull these people back in the bus and fly off . . .'

'Why not?'

'Well, for one, I'm tired. It's a long haul to the next stop and I've been flying this thing for the last three hours without break.'

'I'll shed a tear for you just as soon as you've gone. Now I'm telling you again, get these creatures on the bus and lift off! Those aliens there are waiting for one word from me and they'll pitch every last one of you into the sea . . . and, mister, I'm not joking!'

The driver hesitated for a moment, then rose from his seat and went outside. Zeitman followed, glancing up the cliff to where the whole cliff-top was alive with Ree'hd faces peering down. Were they enjoying the spectacle, wondered Zeitman? Could they hear his raised voice?

'Back on the bus,' said the driver, and the tourists, objecting loudly, began to file back into the enormous vehicle.

They were mostly middle-aged, and in their eyes Zeitman could see all the intelligence of people visiting a zoo. They were all angry, not surprisingly, and several demanded who the hell was Zeitman to stop their paid-for, promised tour?

Oh God, thought Zeitman. To be able to tell them that their precious Earth is probably a pile of radioactive ash by now . . . that their relatives and friends are at each other's throats and jumping from high places . . . just to see their faces, to hear their own fears coming out . . . just to see their destruction! But he said nothing except that he was acting on the city father's instructions to keep tourists away from this burrow community.

The air-bus lifted and swung out to sea, skating across the high waves, and then finding height and vanishing across the broken shoreline a few miles away.

'Very nicely done,' said a familiar voice behind him, and Zeitman turned in surprise.

chapter eight

'Where have you been?' asked Zeitman.

'I've been here,' said Maguire. 'All the time.' He stood staring out to sea, his face far dirtier than Zeitman had ever seen it, his hair unwashed and hanging lank across his forehead. He was still dressed in the casual clothes that Zeitman had last seen him wearing. Now they were torn and filthy. Maguire was scratched, and dried blood added the final touch of raggedness to his disorderly appearance.

'I've been going dizzy with the things you've been up to . .'

'Such as?'

Zeitman said, 'Such as living to the age of seven hundred years. Such as the feat of parascience you performed, that I suppose you're going to explain as just that. Such as leaving the planet without anyone knowing. How did you manage that?'

Maguire chuckled, and turned his head to look at Zeitman with the same blind expression he always wore. 'Try metaphysics.'

'Would I be close?'

'Ah, Zeitman. So many questions, so much intensity. Relax. I'll tell you something – remember how depressed I was when we came down? How I said there was a terrible atmosphere about the place? Perhaps you still don't feel it, but it's there, and it worried me for a long time. Within two hours of landing I was sick to my stomach with what I was "seeing" on this planet. It's taken me four days to come to my senses. Right now I feel like strangling every human in Terming—'

'Me too.'

'But no; I'm accepting what I see and feel, and now I want some help to put things right. But that's okay. The Ree'hd, and the Rundii . . . even the Pianhmar . . . they've waited seven hundred years, they'll wait a while longer now that they realize what truly rotten beings we humans are.'

Zeitman shook his head. 'You're losing me, Maguire.'

Maguire reached out for Zeitman's shoulder, turned as he turned, and together they began to walk up the cliff-path. 'I can't say a lot, Zeitman. I'm not sure myself, yet, about everything. You'll find out in your own time, and that way you'll come to love this place like I do. Like Kristina does. You'll want to stay. And don't worry.'

'About what?'

'About anything. Anything that's worrying you. Stop it. Things will work out.'

Did he mean Kristina? He had obviously seen her in the last few days. Had he talked to her and found out that she was beginning to miss him at last? Or did he mean Earth? Or the tourist blight? Or . . .

All Maguire said was 'leave it alone. Just don't worry'.

What about the vanishing trick?

'Couch it in any semantic disguise you like. I used my mind, and my body is attached to my mind. Okay? Where one goes, the other is sure to follow.'

'Teleportation,' said Zeitman flatly.

'What's so ghastly about that?'

What indeed? If the so-called para-normal phenomena were as rare now as they had been a thousand years ago, and as little understood, there was no denying their actuality. There had always been the Malsenn effects, and the Roanscott effects, and the Geller effects, and they were all still classified as para-normal, when they were, in fact, quite normal, just very rare – and occasionally liable to cause some observer shock!

They reached the top of the cliff and Zeitman was breathless. Maguire seemed quite at ease. The wind, at this exposed locale, was strong and Zeitman found himself gripping Maguire as much for his own support as for the blind man's.

Susanna and the burrow One were waiting for them. The girl seemed wary of Maguire but said, as he reached out and touched her face by way of greeting, 'Hello, mister mystery.'

'Hello Susanna. How do you like Ree'hdworld?'

'Cold,' she said. 'And sickly smelling.'

Maguire laughed and looked at Grai. He became solemn as he exchanged a silent gaze with the Ree'hd. Grai said nothing but the lustre of her eyes faded for a moment, an indication that she had responded to something in Maguire's manner.

Grai said suddenly, 'Some of the young have caught a good harvest of *tucc'f* – come and eat some with us.'

They followed her towards the wide burrow entrance (this community had a single entrance to the complex). Maguire took Zeitman's arm again, this time more for personal contact than support. As they walked Maguire whispered to Zeitman, 'You two getting it together?' It was a loud whisper and his head inclined almost imperceptibly towards Susanna.

'Between times,' said Zeitman flatly, slightly perturbed by Maguire's tactlessness. Susanna had heard and looked embarrassed. 'I didn't do too well with Kristina, as you probably know.'

Maguire looked sad. 'The Ree'hd, Urak, yes. I didn't find out about him for a while. I talked with Kristina the day we arrived, but that was at the time I was building to my first big heartbreak and I wasn't too sensitive to her, though I could tell she was anxious, even upset. But I was impressed by her, really impressed – a sensitive and frightening woman.'

'Frightening?'

Maguire nodded. 'I find the sort of personal courage that she possesses very frightening. Don't you? How many other people do you know who will risk their very humanity to explore a facet of an alien way of life?'

'She told you that?'

'Not exactly *told* . . .'

Zeitman was about to say it was more than a temporary exploration that Kristina had planned, and that he didn't think it frightening, when Susanna took Maguire's other arm and said, 'You mentioned heartbreak – a girl of your own?'

'No – no girl,' laughed Maguire. 'There have been a few, mind you. But no, this time my heartbreak was from memories of a people a little more innocent than I find them now.'

They were in the burrows then, and they found their way to Grai's small chamber. Zeitman turned on his belt-light so that he and Susanna would not have to sit in near-darkness. Grai did not object to the light in her chamber, and nor did her kin, Sakk'ree, who sat beside her. Maguire, as he sat down in the circle, said, 'I always enjoy a small feast with some good friends.'

Feast? thought Zeitman grimly. He had managed to avoid sharing the Ree'hd food the day before, but now he would have no choice. The 'fish', *tucc'f*, was far more analogous to terran fish than the staple winter diet of the near-city Ree'hd, but it was more eel-like, and very nasty tasting. Zeitman, as he picked at the raw flesh, imagined he could feel his biostasis unit working hard to convert any reasonable semblances of human amino acids to their human form. In this way, he guessed, the *tucc'f* was supplying him with three such digestion products, and from his subcutaneous store he was making up for the others.

More worrying than taste or lack of nutrient value were the possible parasitic life-forms that might be chewing their way through his gut wall. They wouldn't last long, certainly, but they could be damaging while they did. When he commented (on being asked why he ate so slowly) that – even after so many years on Ree'hdworld – he was still used to cooked food, and when he elaborated as to the possibility of infection from semi-raw food, the Ree'hd One gave a demonstration of thought-killing that Zeitman had not seen before, and which reminded him that para-normal powers were somewhat less rare on Ree'hdworld than on Earth. The One killed a living, squirming eel-form, slit it along its midline and opened the ingestion sac. Parasitic jelly forms wriggled and flattened in the sudden light, but died instantly when willed to do so. 'Why cook?' said the One, 'If infection is all that worries you?'

'But what about the bugs you can't see?' asked Susanna. The Ree'hd looked at her, raised her arms in query. 'Which are they?'

'Bacteria, viruses, single-celled animals . . . you have similar forms here . . .'

'That's not strictly true,' said Zeitman. 'There are no virus analogs, and bacterioforms have never specialized beyond saprophagous and symbiotic modes of behaviour.'

'No bad bacteria?'

'Not to the Ree'hd, at least. To us, certainly. Why do you think you had your Overload?' Susanna touched her arm delicately. It was several days since she had been immunized but the enormous reaction she had produced to the tiny scratch was still sore and red. Zeitman said, 'That was anti-a-thousand-and-one things.'

'Including anti-me,' said Susanna.

Maguire grinned, and said loudly, 'When I was here before,

properly here, that is, I knew a Ree'hd called Hans-ree who could mind-kill across miles. He was the only Ree'hd I ever met who wondered about mind-killing, and also the only one who ever tried it on another Ree'hd.'

Zeitman shivered as he remembered that awful sensation of slipping into submission and feeling his heart stopping. What sensation, he wondered, would a Ree'hd feel? 'What happened?'

'Nothing. The Ree'hd was old, had decided to die but couldn't find the strength. Hans-ree helped him, tried mind-killing him and failed. To his knowledge no Ree'hd had ever tried that before. How about you, Grai?'

Grai, and indeed, Sakk'ree, had been becoming increasingly uncomfortable. Zeitman gained the impression that mind-killing was a very personal subject, but that was illogical since it was merely a tool of food supply. Perhaps, then, Grai felt the talk of murder to be personal. She said merely, 'It isn't something I ever think about; I can't understand the use of mind-killing for taking Ree'hd life when there are so many easier ways for a Ree'hd to die.'

'Enough said,' said Maguire. He waited for Zeitman to finish translating for Susanna, then asked, 'Have you got an evolutionary reason for the development of that ability? Can you rationalize such a weapon?'

Zeitman said that he couldn't. He was puzzled by such power existing in a culture otherwise devoid of mind-power. There was no apparent mind-linkage between Ree'hd, no ability to teleport . . .

Or . . . was that true? He settled into silence, rejecting the remainder of his food and hoping that he would not be considered rude. Grai and Sakk'ree talked about the burrows and the fishing life, and the plague of the human tourists; Susanna talked about her homeworld, and how like Ree'hdworld it was in many ways; and Maguire sat silently and smiled, and his blind eyes seemed turned on Zeitman all the time.

Zeitman remembered a few years back being amused at a low-intelligence Ree'hd called Wor-F'kar who said he had talked with one of his kin-ancestors of two hundred years before. The praying by talking to one's dead kin was well established as a semi-religious manifestation on Ree'hdworld (as on Earth – was this an example of a Universal axiom?) and Zeitman had laughed at Wor because Wor, in Zeitman's presence, had sent Zeitman greetings from the one he prayed to. Had Wor-F'kar, in his innocence, broken some code of non-revelation practised by the Ree'hd? A few days after the encounter Wor-F'kar had left the community and had not returned.

If the Ree'hd never exhibited their mind talents, excepting mind-killing, how would an alien know what they were capable of? For seven hundred years the contact between cultures had been a fact, and in seven hundred years an indifference had grown up between those two cultures, and it was only the tourists (for their reasons) and a few other humans, Zeitman and Kristina included, who took an active interest in the Ree'hd.

Scientific study on Ree'hdworld, it had to be admitted, was minimal and poorly supported. And yet, to Zeitman, it was all there was of importance. Being minimally and poorly supported, however, had resulted in knowledge of the Ree'hd, and their cohort-brethren, being severely limited, a limitation not helped by what Zeitman was convinced was the Ree'hd being very unforthcoming about themselves.

In all probability the existence of Terming was an expression of the human ego, a stronghold on a world where they knew, deep inside, they should not have set foot.

The day moved on and Zeitman, Susanna and Maguire found their way down the cliffs to the rocky ledges at the exit of the river. Maguire seemed remarkably at ease, and it was unnerving to see him moving with such facility down rocky precipices which Zeitman and Susanna traversed more with adrenalin and breaking nails than skill. When challenged with his versatility, Maguire laughed. 'Who needs eyes to feel? I can feel every crack, every nook, every loose stone. I feel them with my toes, which you also have and could use to the same extent, were you not so dependent on your vision. Climbing is easy. Look, Zeitman, stop trying to invent abnormalities in me.'

On the ledges, ankles awash with the stingingly cold water, they poked fingers into the life-holes, tried to imagine a younger Grai leaping from the cliffs high overhead and plummeting into the deep waters mid-channel.

'How about the Pianhmar?' asked Zeitman after a while. It had been on his mind for hours. Maguire was the only man who claimed to have seen them, and it was apparent that he had survived. And knowing that, Zeitman felt almost afraid of asking. It was the same feeling he had felt on meeting Kristina a few days earlier. An unbearable anticipation preventing him from reacting normally. Now he had brought the subject up and Maguire had not responded badly. He laughed, splashed through the water up on to a drier part of the ledge, and stared blindly at the younger man.

'Pianhmar . . . what a beautiful name, isn't it?'

'The people of the past,' said Susanna. 'I like our translation better.'

'Why, yes. I agree. Human translation of Ree'hd has something very magical about it. Charismatic is the word, I think. I always think of the Ree'hd as "the people who gain spiritual strength from the air". It's a bit of a mouthful, I suppose, but no more than some of the old non-interLing tongues of Earth'.

He's dodging the issue, thought Zeitman, but as if he had heard, Maguire went on, 'The Pianhmar. Have you ever seen them – Zeitman? Susanna?'

'There are no such things,' said Susanna, glancing at Zeitman. 'Figments of mythology. Legends. And not very interesting legends at that. There are no representations of them in the Ree'hd culture.'

'Legends.' Maguire worked that one over in his mind for a while. The tides, complicated movements and dangerous when not predicted, were rising. They might rise slowly for an hour and then rapidly for five minutes, trapping the group on their exposed ledge among the memories of the fishing commune. Maguire led the way to higher ground. Zeitman stayed at the water's edge for a while, trying to decide just why Maguire should be so unforthcoming about the Pianhmar. Could it be that he had never actually seen them? That he had found they *were* a myth? Then how to account for his obvious teleporting ability? And could anything that was so taken for granted among the Ree'hd, and so basically a part of their culture, be, in fact, mythological? Certainly it was not impossible for a myth to become a way of life, but only on the *edges* of culture. Saint Nick, Dragons, Bogie men and Giants in the Earth, all different types of legend, all just peripheral: the cultures that held them in fear or reverence were not dependent upon them. God, of course, was a different matter. All gods, by their nature, were integral with the culture that worshipped them. But the Pianhmar were not gods, nor revered as such. Not revered at all. They were just . . . assumed.

Zeitman rose and followed the other two up on to a higher ledge and along that ledge to reach an overhang where he found Maguire holding Susanna's hand very tightly, and worrying her very much.

'Nice-feeling girl,' said Maguire, grinning broadly. 'Do I look old and unattractive to you, Zeitman?' Yes, thought Zeitman. Maguire looked far older than a few days previously when they had been together on the *Realta*. His hair was white, dirty, his face was covered in the stubble of days. His eyes, white and unseeing, were rimmed with folds of flesh, the make-up of stress and strain. Only his grin remained young. Wild and hungry, to put it romantically.

'We don't change, do we?' said Maguire. 'Men, I mean. It's seven hundred years since I danced a bedside bolero . . . that was on my way to Ree'hdworld the first time I came here. It was a long journey in those days, very long, and the major shipping lines had just started running ship-mates, girls and boys both, available to passengers for free. That was some journey. You know, I forgot all manner of things in those few weeks . . . I forgot Iylian – my wife – I forgot being blind, I forgot depression. You know what? I could have stayed on that ship, indulging myself, and just forgetting that the Universe existed. But the A and E man, the Associations and Escape man on board, said I was being irresponsible, and they

126

booted me off when I got here anyway. That was a long time ago, and I'm damn glad I landed here. I found Iylian again, and I found sight, for what it was worth. The Pianhmar were a real turning point for me. In the first instance for something very small: for all my life I'd been hoping for a glimpse of colour . . . colour, Zeitman. Think about it. Colour . . . reds, blues, whatever. When I was with the Pianhmar they let me see colour and I didn't like it. Green, blue or red, a mountain is still a mountain, and that's what I could see anyway.'

He stopped and let go of Susanna's hand, smiling as he did so, and rubbing his eyes as if he had just risen from sleep. When he looked back at Zeitman his eyes were the same pearl-white orbs, blind, yet full of expression. 'I don't have to see colour any more, not if I don't want to.'

'How do you see me, Maguire? What sort of images?'

'I'm just aware of you, what you're doing, the expression on your face. There's no colour in it, but there's much more. Wind currents round your face, static electricity in your hair, your eyebrows, moving systems deeper within you, giving a shape to your body. There's an alarm clock thundering away down there somewhere. I have a sort of X-ray view of you . . . both of you.'

'Peeper,' said Susanna. Maguire nodded. 'In a way I am.'

Zeitman: 'Tell us about Iylian.'

'Iylian. My beautiful wife. I was so anxious to find sight that I left her for space and she grew old very quickly. Every time I returned to her I could feel the age in her body, while I remained young – I was travelling in space, and ageing only weeks to her years. The trouble was, I always forgot her when I was chasing a dream – a drug to restore sight or a so-called magic valley on a world where men never managed to establish a colony. I found nothing to give me vision, and eventually I returned in time to see her die, and suddenly I felt terribly alone, even though I had many friends on many worlds. I hadn't finished burying her before I was called for a mission on a world I'd only ever heard about in cheap newsfacs – Ree'hdworld. There was a race of beings, they told me, who – if they existed at all – would not allow the contact of a man with sight, and all their attempts at contact had led to the explorer being found dead some months after his attempt. They needed a blind man, a man who could see everything except light, and they had heard of me. I agreed to go. I thought I would make contact and leave and continue my search for sight, but I found sight with the Pianhmar. Strange how things work out.'

'Where did you find them?' asked Zeitman. He was aware that he had to keep Maguire talking. The tides had risen very high, and the on-shore wind carried salt spray up and over the huddled group of humans.

'Where did I find them? I couldn't really tell you. By a river, beneath a night sky I couldn't perceive, high in the mountains where the air was bitter. There was ice on that river, and the turf was crisp and one night, as I lay in my body sack, thinking about Iylian, and missing her, I became aware of six shapes standing in a circle around me. Maguire, they said in my mind. Maguire, what have you come for? And I told them and they accepted me, and took me even higher into the mountains. They were very old, very deep into their devolution. I suppose if I'd come two hundred years later they'd have been gone completely . . . or almost. They had lived on the world for thousands, perhaps millions, of years. They had accomplished what they were to accomplish, achieved the totality of their lives, and they were evolving out, returning to the biosphere. Slowly, gradually, individual by individual. Devolving.'

'What did they seem like?' asked Susanna. 'Were they like the mock-up in Terming?'

'Never seen the statues?'

Zeitman said, 'We've looked for the burial statues, of course, but we've never found one. The Ree'hd themselves model a burrow statue, a guardian spirit, I suppose, on the attitude of the Pianhmar statues as you described them. But we've never found anything that is convincingly pre-Ree'hd.'

Maguire turned to Susanna and reached out to find her hand again. She allowed him to take it, but cast a despairing glance at Zeitman who forced himself not to react. 'And you,

Susanna . . . I suspect you still remain unconvinced about the Pianhmar.'

Susanna said she was. Zeitman had heard her argument a hundred times before, from many different sources – so many times that he became irritated with it and with her, and even with whoever else might be voicing that same argument. Yes, he thought to himself, there are no cultural artifacts to be found, nothing, at least, that could be proven not to be early Ree'hd. The Ree'hd lived along the rivers and by the sea, and their spheres left the huge inland tracts free of influence. There, in the jungle, in the highlands, were the Rundii, semi-sentient (but was that strictly true now?), primitive of language, custom and practice. Like the Ree'hd yet unlike them – part of the same stock, certainly. To many people it seemed obvious that the Rundii were at the end of their civilized period, having never achieved a civilization greater than barbarism. Zeitman had many times heard the statement, delivered dogmatically and with authority from someone who could know nothing of what he talked about, that the Rundii were the Pianhmar in a stage of cultural ignorance. It was nonsense. It had to be. The fossil evidence was poor, some might say inconclusive since Ree'hdworlder bones did not undergo the necessary changes for an extensive survival in the earth, and the remains dated back only a few thousand years. Nevertheless, better men than Zeitman had shown how what little there was *could* be interpreted as three subspecies existing concurrently, and probably radiating from the same stock. Zeitman also knew that the remains interpreted as Pianhmar remains were arguably nothing of the kind. There were, however, no Rundii remains in the mountainous areas that were known with certainty to have been the fabled haunt of the Pianhmar, whereas in the mountain areas within the Rundii spheres, the remains of their development were plain to see.

Susanna believed in the legend theory, that the Pianhmar were invented to act the role of gods. Why, she argued, should a god need to be something greater than the race that had invented it? That was a specifically human version, the superbeing with absolute control, to whom all would return at the end of life. To the Ree'hd a god seemed to be something that reflected the greatness of the past, a lie to impress, a form of self-delusion or perhaps a means of impressing foreigners. Never mind what we are, look where we've been. So: the Pianhmar – reflections of the Ree'hd as a great race, long gone, still revered. Zeitman had tried to point out that the Pianhmar were not revered, but that particular criticism was not particularly relevant.

Susanna stood unshakingly by her feelings, while Zeitman tried harder to understand how a race such as the Pianhmar could vanish so completely.

Maguire had listened to Susanna's argument and seemed impressed. When she had mentioned the lack of traces he had shaken his head. Now he said, 'What is it they say? You can't see the stars for the Universe.' He turned to Zeitman. 'How apt, don't you think?'

Zeitman felt a strange chill. In Maguire's eyes was an expression Zeitman could not have conceived of. Blank white, they nevertheless radiated encouragement. Zeitman said, 'I'm right then?'

Maguire shrugged. 'Of course.'

'What's that all about?' Susanna was annoyed at missing the implications.

Zeitman held a finger to his lips. After all, his ideas were wild at this stage, and there was much he didn't understand. But he knew, with absolute certainty, that the Pianhmar had existed. There was no single element of doubt left within him.

'Are you saying that there *are* Pianhmar remains?' Susanna was insistent. Before Maguire could reply, or not reply . . . before he could make any motion, Zeitman said, 'I have to admit that it's strange the Pianhmar left nothing in the way of pots and pans.'

'You're thinking human again. I agree that this is a very Earth-like world, and the Ree'hd are fairly predictable, as are many of the non-intelligent cultures – well, I shouldn't say non-intelligent – semi-intelligent, I think that covers it.

It's a meaningless expression anyway. You might predict pots and pans but it all depends on how temporary things could be made to be. And anyway, the Pianhmar were a space-travelling race.'

Zeitman reacted with remarkable calm. He queried Maguire's statement and Maguire answered irritably, 'Why should I be kidding? Look, either believe me or don't believe me, but don't just select what you want to believe. The Pianhmar travelled space a lot; they've left their marks on many worlds. Think about it. Check your history books, your stories of the early probe groups, the robot monitors that virtually catalogued every blade of para-grass on a world and micro-stored it in the libraries of the Solar System. Look and see how many artifacts of inexplicable origins have been picked up. It's thousands. It's so many that no one gives a damn any more. It's so many that when the sole intelligence was found in our Galaxy it got an estimated hour and a half of media coverage on Earth at first. That's going way back, of course. In the thousand years since, I suppose there have been many mentions, and your tourist trade tells you that a lot of people are interested still; but when Ree'hdworld was put on the map it was a "surprise surprise" reaction. "That elusive ol' intelligence has cropped up at last, and guess what, viewers, it's all primitive and muddy." Terrible lack of appreciation.'

'So we *do* have Pianhmar remains, but from other worlds.'

'Sure we do. Thousands of them – shapes carved in stone, guardians, little statues, scattered across a newly visited world, the normal debris of living, metal containers, crystal shards, all manner of remains. The Ree'hdworlders could have been used to explain every artifact ever found in the Galaxy, but when Earth saw how lowly they were, that air of mystery came back. Human beings *need* a sense of mystery, so the Ree'hd were not considered as being the originators of those traces. Anyway, they'd have been close but not close enough. It wasn't the Ree'hd, it was their predecessors.'

'Prove they are what you say they are,' said Susanna, obviously not impressed by Maguire's story.

'I can't.'

'And there won't be any to be found now, I suppose. On Ree'hdworld I mean.'

'The Pianhmar destroyed all their remains, I believe. Yes. You're right. There are none to be found here. But your colleague, Kawashima, is finding something right now, something very interesting.'

'How do you know?'

'I found him unearthing what you'd call a burial statue. Would that be artifact enough for you, Susanna? A real, whole, life-sized burial statue, intact and unsullied by the passage of time? And there are others to find, one or two others; but frankly I don't see the point. When you've seen one burial statue you've seen them all.' He laughed. 'Are you breathless, Zeitman?'

Zeitman nodded slowly, comprehension filtering through the confusion in his head. 'You told him where to look, of course . . .'

'What if I did? Would you like to see it? It's the genuine product, probably nine hundred years old. Take my advice, Zeitman – fly up there as soon as you can. You won't regret the experience.'

'You'll tell me where to go?'

'I'll come with you,' said Maguire. 'I'll travel conventionally for once.'

They waded through the ice-cold water that now covered the lower ledges, and scrambled back up the pathway towards the burrows. Susanna gained on the two men until she was a long way ahead. Maguire stopped, suddenly, stared at her for a moment, then looked at Zeitman. 'This world is in danger, Zeitman. It's in danger because humans cannot think like non-humans . . . like Susanna with her artifacts. You're coming to an understanding of this world and very soon you'll be ready to become a part of it, like I am. And when you're at that stage you'll understand why we have to get Terming and all that goes with it, *off* this world, and fast! Believe me, Zeitman, this is one hell of a world to be a part of, and for a few humans it promises a veritable haven.'

Susanna shouted to them, and they continued to climb. Zeitman found himself thinking of Kristina, and how near she was to him, and yet how far; and how, when he needed her strength more than anything else in the world, it was more inaccessible to him than it had ever been.

chapter nine

Kristina, flying low over the broken hills behind the burrows, spotted Dan Erlam's approach from the east. His skimmer, with its characteristic black and yellow striping, was instantly recognizable and she sent a hailing pulse towards him to attract his attention. She touched down a hundred yards from her burrow entrance and watched as Erlam performed an elegant left-hand spiral and nosed his skimmer to the dry earth, close enough to her own vehicle for the downthrust of his jets to send her short hair bristling. Erlam dropped through the undercarriage of his skimmer and opened the neck of his cloak. He came up to Kristina who greeted him with a short kiss and a big smile. She looked him up and down with pointed disapproval. 'You won't be able to walk soon.'

'I'll roll,' he replied, and she laughed.

'And to what do I owe this pleasure?'

'My displeasure,' said Erlam in deep, paternalistic overtones. 'I'd have been out sooner, but I have a city to keep in order, and entropy insists on increasing.' He took her by the arm and they walked up the sloping river-bank towards the burrow entrance.

'Nice place you have here,' he said as usual, chuckling at his own joke. They were inside and seated on the odoriferous flooring and Erlam was making a great show of his discomfort at the alienness of the living conditions.

'I've decorated the walls,' said Kristina pointedly. 'Bet you didn't even notice.'

Erlam scanned the scratched walls of the burrow and saw the pin-woman figure amongst a yard of Ree'hd inscriptions. In the flickering light of the lamp the figure seemed to dance and writhe.

'Your sign?'

Kristina affirmed. 'My sign, Dan. I am now a Ree'hd. You may cease to impart to me terrestrial courtesies. I no longer desire them. Just don't ask me to sing first thing in the morning.'

'No, Kristina, I shan't ask you to sing.'

Kristina's smile faded as she stared at the solemn features of the city father. 'So serious Dan. Why?'

Erlam stared at her and felt an unaccustomed heat in his face. How difficult it was with Kristina, now that she was so convinced of her increasing alienness. She was not attractive, not by Erlam's standards, but then Erlam was not so much interested in looks as in finding someone to share his excessive personality. Kristina, he had always felt, was his ideal. He had once lost her to Zeitman without her even realizing he was in the running for her affections. When Zeitman had left Ree'hdworld Erlam had compensated for his sorrow at the loss of a friend with the thought that now Kristina was again available.

And, after a string of brief affairs, she had finally walked straight past him and into the arms of a Ree'hd!

What must she think of me, he thought? Rotund and red. I can feel the moisture on my face, and there's nothing I can do about it. She must look at me and see a functionary, and in second place, a colleague, and nowhere in her eyes does she see a potential lover.

'What is it, Dan? Why are you staring at me?'

Her voice was cool and calm and it penetrated Erlam's momentary haze of self-pity. He came back to the issue at hand and shook his head.

'I can accord you Ree'hd status in everything except murder, Kristina.'

Kristina's face turned pale. In the dim light it seemed to Erlam that her eyes suddenly became darker, her expression just that fraction more defensive. 'I haven't murdered anyone, Dan.'

Suddenly angry, Erlam snapped, 'Come on, Kristina, this is Dan Erlam, remember? Not some white-faced junior from the Agency. That was a stupid trick, sending a Ree'hd to kill Zeitman and trying to blame it on the Rundii. If the Ree'hd had succeeded, you would now be in serious trouble. Whether or not you regard yourself as a Ree'hd, you go and commit murder and you'll end up in our own courts and be tried as a human.'

He stopped talking abruptly and stared at the woman. The burrow suddenly seemed empty, empty of all warmth, and Erlam found himself looking around, trying to see why things were so still. When he lowered his eyes to Kristina's they were cold. Kristina was solemn and sitting perfectly still.

'I'm sorry, Dan.'

'Okay. You see my point . . .'

'Dan . . .' she struggled with the words. 'Dan, I'm a Ree'hd now. I'm a Ree'hd in all that matters—'

'I accept that—'

'No, Dan. Listen to me. Let me say it so that you understand. If I were still human, if I had even felt human when Robert arrived, I would have tried to kill him on my own. But killing by unnatural means is something I've conditioned myself to think of as alien. The Ree'hd I asked to help me was from the city. It was only when I heard him really going through with the attack that it came home to me just how *dead* those Ree'hd are. And there are hundreds of them, Dan. They're dead in every way that makes a Ree'hd, and I'm alive in every way that makes a Ree'hd. I feel so angry with the city, with my own physical kind. I feel so angry that I even feel angry with you, but it's difficult because I know you too well to categorize you as just another human. You're an individual and a friend. But my greatest friend is my year-kin, Urak, and my greatest love is Ree'hdworld, and my greatest fear is that we'll never finish the development of our lives because of the interference of Earthmen and those dead Ree'hd who walk the streets of Terming.'

'I'll say this for you, you sound like a bloody native.'

'My God, Dan, you sound nearly as bitter as Robert – why so upset?'

'It's disorderly, Kristina, that's why so upset! Imagine if every other human in Terming decided to become a Ree'hd and demand Ree'hd privileges – imagine the chaos! It's irresponsible, Kristina!'

'Irresponsible! And isn't it irresponsible to imprison hundreds of Ree'hd in your filthy, human city? Oh Dan, get your values right!'

Erlam found the smell in the burrow overpowering. After a moment's cold silence he rose and went outside and watched the heavy skies. Being the season of change, rain – forceful and penetrating rain – would soon sweep the continent from east to west. Not gentle rain such as fell for a few minutes a day all year round, but a drenching, dark, fearful rain that drove down to the earth for hour after hour.

It was the time of year that Erlam hated most, a time when Terming seemed to drown beneath the natural forces of Ree'hdworld, and every dawn the streets were filled with the debris of native depression: the slumped forms of Ree'hd, their possessions and clothes scattered along the streets, drenched in the rain.

As it had been explained to Erlam by many of his Ree'hd friends, there was something inordinately depressing about the rain, and also about the rains that fell in the middle of winter, icy rains, rarely managing to fall as ice itself. Perhaps, thought Erlam, they become closer to their past when it rains. Perhaps, they have never lost their Ree'hdness and when the world falls quiet beneath the torrent of rain, they remember deep in their race-memory how it was to sit along the riverbanks and grow into the world.

Zeitman had once told him that the rain that fell on Ree'hdworld was never pure, that it contained trace chemicals, and often quite complex organic molecules. It had taken very little time to ascertain that the Ree'hd *tasted* the rain, that they tasted, in particular, the other Ree'hd groups, groups that they usually never contacted. Zeitman had called it a pheromone phenomenon.

Kristina came out of the burrows behind Erlam and took his arm. 'I'm sorry Dan. I didn't want to argue with you.'

'Nor me,' said Erlam. They walked down the slope towards the skimmers. A few Ree'hd were crouched outside their burrow entrances on the high ground above the river. They watched Erlam and Erlam waved, but only two waved back. Erlam was still a relative stranger to the burrow complex and the Ree'hd always considered strangers for a long time before reacting positively.

Kristina was obviously thinking of Robert Zeitman. She asked Erlam how much he'd seen of him, and Erlam said – little. He knew that Zeitman had been several times out to the burrows and each time he had been unable to find his wife, or, for that matter, his wife's lover. Kristina said, 'Yes, I know he's been out here. But I can't face talking to him, not when he has such a narrow range of conversation. When I see him coming I hide.'

'I'd call that cowardly,' said Erlam. Could he, he wondered, persuade her to meet and talk with Zeitman again? To have the two of them work together again, but without the emotional involvement of old, would be a real break for the scientific establishment on Ree'hdworld. And it might draw her away from this Ree'hd, Urak.

Erlam smiled at his own thoughts. The experiments were a success, even though the Universe had died.

'Did Robert come running to you after we'd met in the city?'

In the shelter of their two skimmers Erlam's face was quite impassive. 'Running to me?'

'Telling you that I'd tried to kill him.'

Her cropped hair, trying to blow across her face in the breeze, seemed to irritate her. She brushed her scalp impatiently and in her eyes there was an expression of sadness that Erlam could not fathom. She was still interested in Zeitman, that much he could recognize; but was it from motives of vengeance, or from a desire to establish a working relationship with him again? Erlam had a very expressive face and his puzzlement was easy for Kristina to read. After a moment she said, 'I'm sorry, Dan. I shouldn't quizz you.'

'That's all right, Kristina. I have no secrets from my few friends.'

'But Robert is more of a friend than me. I've cut myself off so much . . .'

'Right now I have just five people in my life whom I regard as anywhere near close, and I can't be bothered arranging them in order.' His smile was brief. 'And one of them is now a Ree'hd anyway, and I still can't be bothered giving preference. I wish you felt the same.'

'Oh but I do, Dan. My ex-husband upsets me, yes, but when he stops doing that . . . he's as much a friend as my other human friends. I was angry with him when we met first, a few days back, but I was angry because I thought he was ruining things for me. But he wasn't. He didn't know it, but he gave me the impetus I needed. He made things work for me, Dan. And I'm grateful to him. Believe me.'

'I do,' said Erlam, not believing. 'And I'm glad.'

There was a silence for a moment and Kristina turned to look at the river; then Erlam told her what he knew of Robert Zeitman's reactions to the attack.

It had been quite obvious to Zeitman that Kristina had been responsible for the attempt upon his life. It had been a clumsy attempt, and failed because at the last moment the Ree'hd could not kill. But if it had worked it might well have succeeded in removing Zeitman from the scene without any repercussions. The Rundii menace in the burrows was much too well established as fact for any notions of trickery to have been entertained by the city's Security and Investigation Agency. The one thing that would have fouled the plan, without doubt, would have been the Ree'hd assassin letting the word slip, perhaps when under the influence of drugs.

Obvious though the plan had been, the motivation had remained obscure to Zeitman. He had puzzled long and hard over why his wife (ex-wife) should have so coldly resorted to attempted murder. It fitted no pattern of behaviour that he could have attributed to Kristina, even in her current state of hatred for him. She had threatened to kill him *if* . . . but the attack must have been planned long before, and that suggested that it had always been her intention to rid herself of the burden of her overtly adolescent ex-husband.

In his confusion he had gone to Erlam and he and Erlam had got drunk together, which naturally had helped. He had begun to look back upon that time in the city burrows and laugh at the fool he had made of himself. This, to Erlam, had been a good sign and they had started to sober up, which was not easy, but less easy for the Ree'hd official who was one of Erlam's close colleagues and who had supplied the excuse for the celebration – his terran-style marriage to one of the female Ree'hd in the city. Zeitman seemed to have thrown the bad memories away and was not suffering in consequence. Erlam had patted the depleted flagon of old Irish whiskey and consoled himself at the loss with the fact that it had not let him down. He had finalized arrangements for Susanna to join as Zeitman's assistant, and then told Susanna. She had accepted the job with ill grace but only because Zeitman had left her uncontacted for the whole of the previous day, and she had been lost and alone. Zeitman had seemed pleased at the chance of a challenge; he had set to working on Susanna's affections.

The last Erlam had heard, Zeitman had established friendly exchange.

Kristina seemed fairly pleased. Erlam had emphasized that it had been disappointment and confusion that had sent Zeitman 'running' to him, and not anything malicious. And that was almost certainly the case.

'I notice,' Erlam concluded, changing the subject abruptly. 'That every time a human visits this complex he brings back a report of increasing disdain on the part of the Ree'hd. And they certainly seem hostile to me now.' He glanced at the few Ree'hd who sat outside their burrows and still watched him without moving.

Kristina seemed irritated. 'Dan, I'm not functioning as a

go-between any more. Did you think I was?'

'No.'

'Good. Because I'm not. So what's your point?'

'This bad feeling for the city. Why is it there? This open attacking of tourists. What brought it on? The city has been here for generations. The Ree'hd have only become really agitated in the last year, and the really obvious aggression has only been going on for a few months. Now, something has happened and I want to find out what. Only Zeitman seems to have the magic touch. And you, of course. Why?'

She smiled. 'Zeitman feels.'

'Zeitman feels! What sort of an answer is that?' Erlam, angry, realized that he was too much on edge to get anything really constructive from Kristina. Already, with his shout, she had become solemn and unhappy again. He apologized. Kristina said, 'No apology necessary, Dan. Everyone I meet seems to be jumpy. All I can say is, I feel a part of Ree'hd-world, but I don't understand it. I'll say more. Urak *does*. Every Ree'hd does. Every Ree'hd except those in the city. They don't understand anything, and that is killing the Ree'hd out here and making them angry. I don't know why it has happened so suddenly.

'I understand something else, Dan, and I understand it because I'm not stupid. Something very bad has happened that has upset you and Robert very much. Call it intuition, call it ten out of ten for perception. You're both on edge, both keeping something hidden. At night there are fifty times the usual number of orbiting vessels. That tells me people are running here, running to Ree'hdworld. Running to a second Earth. Is that the answer, Dan? Have they blown the motherworld to smithereens? Is there no longer anywhere all you rootless wonders of map-space can boast to?'

Erlam looked at her in complete astonishment.

'You almost got it,' he said. He turned to his skimmer and opened the underbelly. Just before he climbed inside he paused, looked at Kristina who still stood without expression, watching him. 'Sometimes you frighten me, Kristina. You really do.'

140

'You're only afraid of the alien in me, Dan. And there's really nothing to be frightened of.'

' 'Bye, Kristina.'

'Come back soon, Dan.'

Shortly before dusk the sound of rocket engines, labouring and dying, brought Kristina and all the Ree'hd from their burrows. Heavy black cloud covered the sky, broken to the east where the black was streaked with orange, and the hills there seemed to bask in a yellow light that gave them a semblance of life. The rocket was a small shuttle and it was nosing down to the south west, trailing flame and white smoke.

There was consternation among the Ree'hd, some of whom began to run after the shuttle. Their forms, those who moved, were soon lost in the dimness. The rest, including Kristina, began their slow gathering at the river-side.

Kristina, as she walked from her burrow, waited for what she knew would come. The explosion. It echoed across the still lands, a deep reverberation followed by an ear-shock and then the low moan of winds whipped into a frenzy they had not expected. Bright flames lit the sky to the south west and against that brilliance many Ree'hd said they could observe the silhouetted forms of their kin moving slowly towards the crash. Kristina, with her human restrictions, could see nothing but the light of the flames against the darkening sky.

She sat down on the bank and closed her eyes. After a few minutes the wind character changed, became softer, more intricate. She felt it on her cheeks and opened her mouth as if to drink it. Some of the Ree'hd began to sing, but the great majority remained quiet. Kristina called for Urak and waited.

Urak had taken his leave the previous evening, wandering somewhere to the south. It had been the saddest moment of Kristina's life when he had explained the necessity to go, but she had argued very little, merely nodded and accepted.

She called for him again, but there was nothing. An hour later it was very dark, prematurely so because of the cloud-covering, but her timing was accurate and it was not too long after sundown. Her mind was filled with noise, and when she relaxed a little, the noise grew and she heard the voices of many Ree'hd, talking and singing in their beautiful tongue. She recognized voices of those she knew, and she heard replies from those who were dead, and for a while, to avoid the panic that was growing within her, she followed conversations and prayers.

Here was Kroo-One who had lived in the original burrows over a thousand years before, talking now to Kristina's neighbour, the twisted-backed Ree'hd, Han'a-kree. 'Worry not,' assured the dead One, 'when you join me and my sons, and their sons, and their sons, and your very first Old-kin, then you will find physical perfection again'. What remorse from the broken-backed Han'a-kree! what apology for having prayed so selfishly! And the calm voice across time, so wise, so reasonable.

Adolescent voices joining in a throng, praying for a painless metamorphosis. And a certain lack of response to that; an ancient voice murmuring that such strange things did not happen before the great race died.

Prayers for the recovery of A'mes'ree, who was wandering, and the prayers joined by dead voices, a thousand kin living now beyond the barrier that was still outside Kristina's conception. And the medley of well-wishes carried on the wind, far inland, far form the Ree'hd sphere to where the wanderer tried to find his own personal solution to the life he had lived for thirty-seven Ree'hd years.

Kristina called for Urak again, and narrowed her thoughts until just the singing of the wind was in her awareness; but across it, through it, in it . . . there was no answering call from Urak.

A knotted stomach, a calm reassurance from one of the Ree'hd on the river-bank, spotting her fear, spotting her alien form and saying, 'Listen a while longer, but never feel sadness. If the one is *not* lost, then you may cause him to mourn when he cannot contact home.'

And the realization that suddenly she is accepted as a Ree'hd, and that the natives are no longer hostile towards her.

So she widened her mind and eavesdropped a while longer, and several times she was driven away by mind-voices that were stern, but vaguely amused – as if the voices could identify her humanness and her Ree'hdness, and were tolerant of one, but not of the other. She heard the garble from the past and tried not to think of the implications of what she heard; she thought, momentarily, of Zeitman and of what he would have given to know these facts about the Ree'hd – but in his own time he would come to a full understanding. Her mind bridged time, or maybe it was the voices that covered the centuries . . . or again, perhaps where those voices came from was a place outside time.

The evening before, the first time she had been allowed into the mind-web, Urak had stayed with her and calmed her when she had risen on to her feet and screamed, and soothed her when her mind had tried to rationalize what it heard, and tried to reject it by means of hallucination and hysteria. Through the dusk period Urak had been her guide, allowing her to feel here, and there, to touch this mind and that, helped her to identify the voices of her friends as they were manifested in the whispering world that was the riverside. He showed her the voices of the Pianhmar who still waited, deeper voices, less friendly. He showed her the voices of Rundii, confused voices, waiting for a coherency that Kristina could not imagine.

And then, as she grew accustomed to the strangeness she was experiencing, Urak led her back across the years, to a time when the city of Terming had been just a collection of tents and shacks; back and back, to when there had been no Earthmen on Ree'hdworld, and back . . . to when the sky had roared with the pulse explosions of interstellar drives, and the dust had flown and the vegetation had been overwhelmed and choked by the indifference of the race that lived above it. At that time, on the distant mountains, there had been the sparkle and gleam of sheer metal faces, and at night, above the howl of nature, above the screams and cries of the primitive Ree'hd and Rundii, living in the untouched jungles of the continent, had come the banshee screams of the cities all about, at full production, feeding the nation, fuelling the race that was covering its tracks through the Galaxy as it crept back to its home.

She had left the web and cried, sucked in breath as if, for the past minutes, she had not breathed at all. Urak was there, smiling in his Ree'hd take-off of the human gesture, and his sticky hand reached out and wrapped around her arm. He gently pulled her back to a seated position, and again she closed her eyes.

A Ree'hd called Hans-ree said, hello, and welcomed her, and said that he knew Maguire and that Maguire was a noble Ree'hd and had been noble even when he had been human. And, he said, whatever happens, Maguire is your salvation, always. Whatever he feels himself, he will help you, because I have asked him.

Kristina thanked him, and realized – peripherally – that this was the Hans-ree who had been dead seven hundred years; and he had died, Urak had told her, violently and almost alone. Maguire had prayed over his body, not really understanding what he was doing, and had committed the remains to nature. Maguire could never be forgotten for what he had done, alone and truly blind.

Then, as the Ree'hd had left and night had fallen, and the babble of voices in her mind had lessened, there was Urak, loud and secure, talking to her, though he sat apparently asleep.

Kristina, he had said, *Kristina, you are with us and with everything, and now you can follow me or remain. Whatever happens to me, you will never lose me.*

Why? What could happen?

Tomorrow I am going to leave the sphere. I must go alone. But I shall always be with you, and you will know because I will be in the web.

But none of your kin have died . . . oh, Reems'gaa . . . of course.

Partly Reems'gaa. But I need to wander for a different reason.

Us? What we have talked about? Oh Urak, have I driven you to despair?

His touch was a momentary pressure upon her cool flesh. *Never could I despair with you, Kristina.*

Then don't go.

It's too late. I have gone too far and I have understood too much. I shall leave the sphere in a few hours and I may not come back. But remember . . . I am never gone. You know this now.

I don't want you to die, Urak.

Surely you are not still so human that you cannot accept the basic nature of the Ree'hd?

No.

I'll talk to you at dawn. I will be a long way by then. At dusk you can send your thoughts to me, find me wherever I am.

In the morning, as she sat alone, even before dawn he was a warming presence in her mind. And at dusk she called for him.

Urak, where are you?

And soon panic gripped her. Urak did not reply.

It seemed to Kristina, as she felt hysteria rising in her, that the web became silent. She was watched by many, from the present and from the past, and as she realized this she became ashamed. But a voice that she knew spoke to her, reassured her.

He is not dead, but has decided he will not return.

Then I want to be with him. But where is he?

A second voice spoke to her. *He is in a Rundii sphere, on the same river that you are on. He is still alive. He sits near to where there is a tree-form fallen in the river.*

Kristina rose, leaving the web, and ran for her skimmer.

Rising, wheeling, forward thrust.

The fire passed below and she glanced down, and saw the ripped hull, the shattered vanes, the fire poking explorative fingers through broken observation plates. There were dark

145

shapes scattered on the brilliantly lit ground around. They lay immobile, some burning. Nowhere did a limb twitch, or a crawling figure lift its head to stare into the cold night sky, through flames and soot.

The Ree'hd were shadows, standing motionless and watching the consuming of the craft. What could they do? They watched to remember, so that the world might never forget the destruction of the ship, and the loss of life, whatever its purpose.

Into darkness, through clouds, and the drumbeat of rain. Fighting with stability controls, reading the green and red dials and screens that showed altitude, velocity, wind speed, strain on weak points of hull, internal temperature, life readings . . . many readings, absorbed at a glance, computed without thought.

Mind open, eyes searching darkness for a flicker of movement.

Out of the sphere.

chapter ten

Heading inland.

Mountain ranges and the endless shifting forests, and here the winding shape of a river, choking as a purplish weed clogged its tighter bends; across plains, arid and desolate, crossed by lone animals and the wandering figures of Rundii and Ree'hd, dead creatures, trying to find peace in the parched wastelands. There were buttresses here, and the shadow of the skimmer rippled and distorted across the crags whenever the sun shone through the clouds for a moment. An inland lake, and a commune of Rundii, naked and oblivious of the man-ship passing overhead.

A thousand miles of land. Heading inwards.

*   *   *

Well aware of his weaknesses, Zeitman had long ago lost his fear of self-analysis. Ree'hdworld had always made him lonely. Lonely not for men, but *because* of men. It made him feel that humans were a discord in the Universe, and he disliked discord. He wanted to be alone, and fought for isolation, but in such insularity there lay a certain denial of bodily needs and Zeitman had often felt lonely. It was easy, with any single person, to find an immediate and transient friendship, but his inward direction showed a selfishness not compatible with the keeping of friends.

Of all those that he knew, perhaps only Erlam and Maguire had remained close. Erlam, of course, was equally his own man, equally ill at ease with his fellow race, but was powerful in that he possessed an instinct for direction. He had no particular ambition, but he needed parameters to guide him and, guided, he naturally ended up powerful.

Maguire was different. Friends, he and Zeitman had not really known each other honestly. Maguire had been unforthcoming and Zeitman, unwilling to open up (though not averse to such soul-baring) had found, in Maguire, a purely amicable contact that had pleased him and eased him. If he never knew anything more of the blind man, he would count Maguire as a friend, and it was one of his few lesser worries that perhaps Maguire did not feel a reciprocal emotion.

Maguire did seem to have a basic direction. Certainly he gave no indication of what that direction was, but he moved surely; he seemed to be moving through Ree'hdworld, and meeting with Zeitman and others, in a fashion laid down in a plan. Zeitman wandered. This was his closest link with the Ree'hd, who themselves seemed content to drift through their development. Zeitman's main motivations were a desire for knowledge and for love from two sources: Ree'hdworld and Kristina.

It frightened him to know (and he was sure his knowledge was correct) that Maguire could satiate him as regards *knowledge* of both.

And love?

If Kristina could love an alien in form, he, Zeitman, could

love an alien in emotion. She might no longer think human, and in that way she might no longer *be* human, but by her own philosophy, as he had understood it from Erlam (who had learned much of Kristina's changing life over the last few weeks), that was no barrier to her loving Zeitman. Zeitman needed her, needed her love, needed her help. Physical love he could get elsewhere; that was not important.

He had not put Kristina from his mind. Over the days his reaction to the realization she had tried to kill him had developed into a grudge. He began to suspect that this Ree'hd-worlder, Urak, was instrumental in turning her into a potential murderess. He began to feel great antipathy towards that native. At night, when he dreamed of something other than the fate of Earth, it was of Urak that he dreamed, and there was always anger and fighting, and a great sense of frustration when he woke.

At night Zeitman sat apart from Susanna and Maguire, listening to the two of them talking. Susanna was amusing herself with Maguire's strange sense of sight. She still found it hard to believe that a blind man could see, especially when he claimed to see better than either of his two travelling companions.

'I know I shouldn't say it,' he had said, 'but I keep feeling sympathy for you because you are both blind. I have to tell myself that you are not blind because the word implies a certain sight that has been taken away. You have never had that sight yet, so you can't know of your lack.'

'Who needs to see infra-red? Or ultra-violet?' said Susanna. 'We're all quite content with what we manage to see, thank you.'

'Dan Erlam has good eyes,' said Maguire. 'Most of the thousands of human beings in Terming have good eyes. But you know, Susanna, they are nevertheless blind. They don't see what they're doing, they don't see the consequences of their actions.'

'That's cheating,' said Susanna. 'You're using *blind* in a metaphorical sense. In that way, yes, most of us are blind to all but a fraction of everything.'

'Some things it is not important to be able to see. A few things, that you don't see, it is imperative that you should be able to observe clearly. I pity you all. I can't help it.'

Susanna tested Maguire's 'sight', holding up fingers, objects, making expressions on her face. Maguire found her antics entertaining and answered everything perfectly correctly.

'Well, I don't understand it,' she said at length. 'You need light rays and a retina to see, and you block light rays and probably have no retina worth a damn.'

Maguire laughed. 'You remind me of a Ree'hd I knew, called Hans-ree. He was always inquisitive, always puzzled by how much I could see even though I was blind in the real sense of the word – this was before I gained sight, you understand. I asked him if he could feel the movements of mountains slipping about on their magma underlays; or the rippling of earth? I asked him if he could see the shape of the wind, foaming and bubbling, reaching fingers up and down, and round any object in its way. He couldn't, of course, and he was not totally convinced that I could. But of course I could. I could see it with every sense but sight. I didn't miss much in those days, and these days . . . I miss nothing.'

Sunrise and the mountain world erupted into life. Susanna awoke suddenly, found Zeitman and Maguire gone and followed them out on to the slopes. She had to shield her eyes against the brilliance of the sun that was creeping above the horizon.

'Where's Maguire?' she asked, seeing Zeitman standing alone. He glanced at her and smiled. 'Got fed up travelling conventionally. He must have gone during the night. I expect we'll see him again before too long.'

Barren though their temporary camp-site had seemed at night, now, at dawn, it was crawling with life. The rocks themselves seemed to move, and cascades of dust and earth tumbled downwards as multipedal forms, green and purple, and some shining black, scattered and scurried and hunted.

'Look there.'

A biology lesson for Susanna. She followed Zeitman's

pointing finger and saw a huge, undulating form drifting across the interlocked branches of the giant flora in the valley, three or four miles distant.

'That thing must be more than two hundred yards across!'

'One of Ree'hdworld's more exotic life-forms. It's called a *broo`kk* – remember that Ree'hd we met at the landing station?'

'She was attacked by one of them? My God!'

'It's feeding on the tiny homeotherms that live in the foliage.' He watched the *broo'kk* as it moved across the tree-forms, rippling as it adjusted to the irregularities of the surface that it regarded as land.

'No birds,' said Susanna staring into the empty skies. 'No, wait . . . what's that?' She pointed to a small black shape soaring vertically in a tight spiral.

Zeitman shook his head. 'Not birds. The air was never conquered on Ree'hdworld. Or if it was, it was not a conquest that survived.' With the powerful winds it was a complete incongruity to Zeitman that there were no winged animals. More so because, as Susanna was noticing, there were creatures that used the air for transport quite a lot. Vortex-risers, as they had been termed early on – creatures with membraneous extensions of their bodies with which they caught the up-currents and spiralled away high into the sky to fall back some way removed. With this as a beginning, powered flight was but an evolutionary shuffle away. But it had not been a beginning. For as far back as the fossil record went there were vortex-risers, but nothing that could have been the remains of a flyer. Powered flight had never come into its own.

'Look at the wind down there,' said Susanna. 'It's blowing a gale.'

The stillness, the gentleness of the wind at their camp-site, was an incongruity; but Zeitman knew that this was the way things worked – at dawn, when the lowlands bent to breaking point before the screaming blast, much of the highlands was still. During the day and night the highlands felt the fury of the wind, whereas the lowlands, large tracts at least, fell quiet.

Now that they had a full day to travel Zeitman decided to abandon the proposed return to Terming for supplies and instead move on a straight course for the temperate lands where Maguire had said Kawashima was to be found.

They skimmed over the mountain range and into the wild country beyond, and had gone only a short way when the gleam of metal caught Susanna's eye. Zeitman spiralled for a moment as he searched the rocky terrain to the east, and then he too saw the unmistakable sparkle of a machine upon the dull earth.

In minutes the skimmer was circling the wreck, and Zeitman had the alpha-scanner set wide, looking for survivors. The ship was a fifty-person, low-orbit shuttle and it had been knocked from the sky by a missile, but the blow had been a glancing one, quite obviously, and though the belly had been ripped out of the craft, there was no reason why, with competent handling – and this ship had been brought down competently – a few persons should not have survived.

Zeitman's first thoughts were for survivors, but in a matter of seconds the implication of the forced landing was hitting him. This might be the first . . . What if all the ships that were orbiting Ree'hdworld tried to come in for a forced landing? Zeitman could imagine this valley gutted and cleared, and the huts and the roads being built, and the driving back of the wild Rundii, and the push to the sea . . .

Why had the missile not been more effective? What good was a killing-machine if it only maimed? Damn the installation for not taking more care of what it owned!

But for the moment, since the missile had not destroyed completely, the responsibility was on Zeitman to make contact with the survivors (if any) and see to their well-being. Zeitman himself was not a killer.

The alpha-scanner picked up a low reading some way distant, where the land was carved in deep gashes and the flora was beginning to thicken. But Susanna, without any machine-aid, spotted the group of humans at a distance of a mile.

Zeitman raced the skimmer, low over the ground, and hovered above them. Twenty-one humans, seated in a large circle about a central fire which was now cold and black. They were all clothed in overcoats improvised from blankets, and they huddled with heads down as if in prayer.

They made no sign of recognition as the air-jets of the skimmer set the dead fire into a flurry of carbon ash, and moved the thin mat covering in the clearing into a frenzy of activity.

'There's something wrong,' Zeitman spoke softly and then, as if he refused to accept what the alpha-scanner was telling him, he keyed the hailer and called down to the group. No response. Susanna said, 'They're dead. They have to be.'

Zeitman knew she was right and he tapped the alpha-scanner which was registering a tiny reading, but not anywhere near high enough. He landed the skimmer a short way from the ring of humans and left Susanna sitting inside the cramped cabin while he took a closer look.

She watched him walk towards them, and she looked again at the dial on the sensor, now registering slightly higher as Zeitman walked into its range of view. For a reason unknown even to herself she felt very sad.

When Susanna left the skimmer, later, and walked across to where Zeitman sat outside the circle of dead humans, she knew there was someone alive somewhere and told Zeitman of the increasing reading on the alpha-scanner.

She walked round the circle and looked at the dead. They were all squatting, their heads were bowed upon their chests, and their arms hung straight down by their sides, palms flat upon the ground. When Susanna touched one, a girl of maybe eighteen, the body toppled sideways. It was stiff, but not stiff enough to make it totally rigid. The girl's yellow hair covered her face and Susanna bent down and smoothed it back to look at the pallid skin.

'She looks peaceful.'

'They all look peaceful,' said Zeitman.

'And they died . . . ?'

Zeitman didn't move. He was thinking of a terrible hour, now more than ten Ree'hd years in his past . . .

*　　　*　　　*

A rough hand shaking him awake, the stale breath of an unclean Ree'hd, the close face, unblinking eyes, the moisture on song lips, the heat radiating from the skin of the breast . . . a Ree'hd in distress.

'Joe . . .'

Guttural. The Ree'hd – a retarded creature, a community member of very low intelligence – in human terms, a moron. Zeitman was awake in an instant, sitting up on his rough bed. The Ree'hd crouched by him and looked him straight in the eye. Kristina, his girlfriend, was not beside him and he glanced at his collar-watch and saw it was well past noon. He had had too much to drink in the city, the night before, and presumably Kristina had let him sleep.

Again the Ree'hd said, 'Joe . . .'

This time Zeitman caught the full implication. He reacted as if someone had shot him, but for a few moments he kept on living and breathing, reacting normally. Then he blacked out and when he came to he felt himself being dragged towards the exit of the burrow, and the Ree'hd was screeching.

Zeitman screamed and twisted out of the Ree'hd's grip, climbed to his feet and ran to the river in panic. Joe wasn't there, and then he saw him, sitting on the rocks a few hundred yards from the rushing waters.

Sighing with relief Zeitman walked towards him. He had been so afraid for that moment . . . The retarded Ree'hd was older than Zeitman, but with its juvenile mentality it found pleasure in the childish playing of the ten-year-old that Zeitman was caring for while the boy's parents lay ill in a Terming hospital.

Zeitman and Kristina had brought the boy to these burrows for a few days, and when this particular Ree'hd had become attached to him Zeitman had felt a little anxious, but had not disallowed the contact. His fear had been that, being so near the river, the retarded Ree'hd would cause the boy to drown.

Zeitman came closer to Joe, and called to him. Joe sat on the rocky ledge looking at his feet.

There was something about the boy's attitude, the way the

head was bowed, the hands, palm flat upon the ground . . .

'JOE!'

Tripping as he ran, Zeitman reached the hunched figure and for a long moment there was only the feel of the boy's body as he clutched it against his own, and the racing of blood through his head, and the scream that he fought against until he was physically sick and, dropping the body, he vomited across the rocks and the cowed form of the retarded Ree'hd.

'Accident . . . accident . . .' murmured the Ree'hd. And Zeitman had felt the pressure of the creature's mind, and knew, without thinking, that the backward native had found his ability to mind-kill – so long denied him – and he had not been able to control it. At terrible cost.

It came back to Zeitman with unexpected suddenness as he looked at the squatting forms of the twenty-one humans. He remembered that the Ree'hd, those long years back, had himself arranged the limbs of the boy into what he regarded as the proper death attitude for a human.

Now it was occurring to Zeitman that there were no Ree'hd this far inland to have so arranged the human bodies; and the Rundii, though they moved unexpectedly, were not known to inhabit this particular sector of the continent. And if they did . . . where had they learned the Ree'hd habit of death arrangement?

There were no marks upon any body, though Zeitman searched hard. Susanna watched him, sensing in his urgency some of the uneasiness that Zeitman was feeling. Zeitman, were he to trouble to document his emotion, might have found that he was not so much afraid of finding a sign of Rundii interference, as he was of finding a sign of the Pianhmar. To his uncertain knowledge the Pianhmar had not been credited with the ability to mind-kill; but what did that mean? Who could say anything about the Pianhmar that was not wholly subjective?

In the stillness following his final efforts to locate a mark of violence, the flora behind Zeitman parted and a fearsome-looking man appeared.

Susanna had already stooped behind one of the squatting corpses, and Zeitman rose and glanced at her to make sure that she was relatively safe before he turned to face the stranger: a man of short stature, with clotted blood in his close-cut beard, and his spacer's uniform in rags. He had wrapped a luxury quilt around himself, and on his head, set uncomfortably upon his uncombed hair, he wore the cap of an officer. He stood for a moment staring at Zeitman, his eyes, behind slightly tinted goggles, wide. He seemed to be shivering.

Then he walked towards Zeitman and extended his hand. 'My name's Ballantyne. I imagine that I'm dying.'

'We can probably help you,' said Zeitman, recognizing a certain finality in the man's attitude. 'The city of Terming isn't far away and you don't look too bad . . .'

Ballantyne shook his head. 'I didn't get my drugs. There was no time.' He looked at the circle of corpses. 'They didn't either, but they didn't die from what's killing me. What killed them? Animals? No . . . they were talking about ghosts . . .'

Zeitman was taken by surprise. Ballantyne noticed and said, 'Ghosts? Does that mean something?'

Yes, thought Zeitman, it means something! It means everything. What about that, Susanna? What about the ghostly Pianhmar now?

He looked over his shoulder and couldn't help smiling. Susanna seemed very afraid. She said, 'Robert, there were ghosts in Terming, weren't there? Didn't Erlam say something about ghosts?'

'Yes,' said Zeitman. He was thinking: why did they kill? And will they kill us?

To Ballantyne he said, 'My guess is these people died of exposure. The nights are bitter at this time of the spring.'

Ballantyne shivered more obviously and drew the quilt tighter about his shoulder. 'I know. I nearly died last night as well. I have no cataphrak.'

'We have a spare in the skimmer. How long have you been down?'

'Since yesterday. The ship was struck by a missile. I guess

the natives aren't too friendly. I jumped with the delicate machinery we thought we'd need, just before impact. I underestimated the time to impact and landed a long way from the ship. Most of the equipment was out of service, though not unrescuable, but I made contact over my suit short-wave. They were babbling about ghosts in the jungle, and then after a few hours there was just silence. It took me a day to catch up with the group and by the time I got here Hernandez and the rest were like this. I was frightened and I went back down the valley a way, but when I saw your ship I came back.'

'Hernandez was the shuttle captain?' asked Zeitman.

Ballantyne pointed to the only spacer in the group of dead. 'He was master of the *Grantham*, not just the shuttle. I was communications officer. As you can see, the ship was pretty well gutted. There's an auto-survival unit that should have functioned but obviously didn't, but worse, the core was exposed. They had to move away. Couldn't even use the hulk as a shelter.'

'If the core had been exposed,' said Zeitman, 'it would have registered when I scanned the wreck. There was no radiation of any sort.'

Ballantyne eased off his small pack and withdrew a narrow-angle counter which he held pointed at the distant shuttle. He stared at it for a moment, then shook the gadget, turned it over and back, and stared again. 'I don't understand . . . there was a burning rad when I looked before. Somebody covered it up . . .'

Very powerful ghosts, thought Zeitman, and wondered what Maguire could tell him about it.

With the bodies sealed back in the shuttle Ballantyne visibly relaxed. He cleaned his skin wounds and shaved the beard from his face, leaving just a thin moustache. Washed, and warm as the cataphrak he had put on started to make efficient use of his own body heat, he became less convinced that he was dying; but Zeitman, without the other's knowledge, had run a diagnostat across his back and it was a depressing report that Zeitman filed in his mind.

Ballantyne was harbouring a blood organism known in Terming as Ree'hdworld Scurvy. It was a simple unicell harboured quite safely by the Ree'hd. In humans, however, its toxins were precipitated on the walls of blood vessels and made them weak. Hence easy bruising, and since the favoured site of deposition was, for some reason, the brain, Ballantyne's ultimate fate was death by massive cerebral haemorrhage. And the installation had no remedy, except prayer.

Saying nothing of his diagnosis, Zeitman listened to Ballantyne's fears and regrets, expressed as they sealed the bodies away for ever.

Ballantyne stood back from the sealed airlock of the shuttle and watched the red heat fade to dull silver grey. He seemed fatalistic and turned to Zeitman and shrugged. 'They were big-headed bastards, but I felt very close to Hernandez. I think he only went along with the notion because he felt empty without Earth and didn't want to miss the chance to live out his days in comfort.'

'What notion?' asked Susanna as they walked across the rough ground back to the skimmer.

'The Saved. Most colonies become intensely God-fearing for the first few decades of their existence and it was only natural, I suppose, that when those colonies got to hear that Earth had been hit by Fear they should imagine themselves to have been saved in some way. God's chosen few.' Ballantyne chuckled. 'There were plenty of them, the *chosen few*. That's what I mean – big-headed.'

Ballantyne and Hernandez had been two of a five man crew who had assisted with the evacuation of colonists from New Villefranche, a high-G. world of Bianco's Star. With the stellar mother showing a little too much variability for security a massive lift from the three colonized worlds had been organized, and this was part of the first shipment. The news from Earth had reached the colony before the arrival of Hernandez and his ship and by that time any panic had been quelled. Fear, the colony leaders had told them, is a God-given cross to mankind, and he has punished humanity by eliminating the homeworld. Most of the colony were robed in red, smiling, full of their own importance, all convinced that they had been saved, and that now they were to range far and wide and spread the love of the Saviour. Earth – they had rationalized – had been the final resting ground for the evil of the race and God had selected his chosen few to colonise certain worlds where they might escape the effects of his wrath.

It had, thought Zeitman, the essential beauty that it eliminated depression at the loss of the motherworld.

Rene Hernandez coming under the influence of one of the younger females among the Saved, had moved slightly to the way of thinking of what Ballantyne regarded as a group of clinically insane. It amused him that their first decision had been to hit an Earth-type world to start their good work of weeding out those few black souls who had escaped God's wrath. Ballantyne, whose life had been threatened twice by the fanatic who led the group, paradoxically had been the only survivor, and that because he had chuted from the crashing shuttle seconds before impact and in some way had avoided observation by the avenging forces that had struck the rest soon after.

'Space is filled with nuts at the moment,' he concluded, 'all putting a different interpretation on what has happened on Earth. Everyone is rationalizing their panic, but that's what it is, pure and simple. Thousands of people have left colony worlds where there is no Fear, has been no Fear, and might never be any Fear – but they leave, anyway, to get as far away as possible from the stricken sectors, and what they don't realize is that they're probably carrying the disease with them anyway.' Changing the subject abruptly, and pointing to the sealed shuttle, 'Shall we pray for them? Do you believe in that sort of thing?'

Susanna said, 'I had you down as an agnostic . . .'

'Oh no. I was brought up to believe in the Universal God, He who has no shape and becomes the True God of all shapes and forms, colours and cultural developments. I worshipped Thor, and Vishnu, and the Father of Christ, and Star Brother, and Dru'iss whose atoms are the dust that fills space. I saw them all, with a little prompting from a neuro-jammer. Star

Brother was everything a friend should be, only when I grew a little older my Rationalist weeded out a latent homosexual tendency in me and I recognized a certain physical wish-fulfillment in the form of Star Brother . . .'

'Which wouldn't contradict your doctrine,' pointed out Susanna.

Ballantyne didn't disagree with her. 'It made me feel a little sick, though. I decided gods were for those who had an unconscious realization that their own ideal would never be found. To be completely honest, the only god I found any sort of sense in was Himself, who died on the Cross in one form. You know who I mean, don't you?'

Susanna looked thoughtful for a moment, then shook her head.

'Oh well, it doesn't matter.'

They stood in silence for a few minutes, Zeitman and Susanna exchanging weary glances, all three of them huddled against the biting wind. After a while Ballantyne turned away from the shuttle and they walked back towards the skimmer.

'We already had a ship load of evacuees when the news came,' he said as they sat in the cramped cabin of the skimmer, sipping coffee. 'Most of them are still in orbit. We felt a responsibility towards them and the decision was taken first to dump them where they wanted to be, and then to decide our individual plans and make sure each crew man got his wish.

'I was for getting to a cosy world, such as Ree'hdworld, and so was Hernandez. My cabin-mate, a girl I was very fond of, was for running, heading for the deep, getting as far away from planets as she could. If Fear was grabbing for worlds, she said, then space was the safest place to be. She figured on going three or four thousand light years into intergee and closing down bodily systems for a thousand years or so. Then coming back and starting again. I said, what if the Galaxy is gone? A chance she would take. My way, she said, I was giving up because the chances were that the spread of Fear indicated the approaching death of the Universe – the intelligent Universe. And that, she figured, meant the Ree'hd would go

159

too, eventually. And if I was with the Ree'hd, then maybe I'd go to a Ree'hd heaven, by mistake. Or worse, a Ree'hd hell.

'That struck us as very funny, but deep down Vivienne believed it. She didn't wait for us to get rid of our cargo – she stole a shuttle and she's out there now, speeding towards the deep, with a complete seed-bank – including some of me – a veritable ark. If man survives she'll come back in a thousand years to find herself a relic.'

Her and how many others, wondered Zeitman. Aloud he said, 'When this group decided to come to Ree'hdworld, didn't anyone stop to consider the intelligence on this world? Didn't it seem unfair to you to risk this race for your own skin?'

Ballantyne smiled narrowly and said, 'Zeitman, I'm a spacer, not a scientist. To me a planet is plus or minus G., high or low oxygen, classified on a six-point scale for ease of survival. Intelligent creatures are beyond my experience. I didn't know what to do or say when the suggestion was made that we should come to Ree'hdworld. I thought of what I remembered about the planet from school books, namely that the natives live at the coast and only at the coast—'

'Wrong.'

'Well, don't tell me, tell the education authorities on two hundred and twenty-two fifth-generation worlds. We learn that there are only two intelligent races in the Universe, us and the Ree'hd, and the Ree'hd are at a stage of development about equivalent to stone-age man.'

'A little inaccurate,' said Susanna. 'What do you say, Robert?'

Zeitman said, 'Just a little. The Ree'hd could well be at a very advanced stage of development.'

Ballantyne looked from one to the other of them, a half-smile on his face. 'That's starshit. They have nothing that could classify them as advanced.'

'They have no need of it,' said Zeitman softly. 'That's more advanced than us, isn't it?'

'Do you really believe that? I don't think you do. I don't think anybody does. It's an axiom, isn't it? Self-awareness leads to self-expression, and any positive move like that is easier with machinery.'

'That sounds like school-book philosophy,' said Susanna. She grinned at Zeitman who shrugged and irritated her by saying, 'I think he could be right.'

Ballantyne laughed. 'It makes sense doesn't it? Machines, however simple, are a sign of civilization and the Ree'hd don't have them.'

Imbecile, thought Zeitman, suddenly disliking Ballantyne intensely. Aloud he said, 'What constitutes a machine, though? And at what stage of development is it necessary to have them to prove intelligence . . . or rather, civilization? Early? Late? Is civilization merely the developing of systems that can do without machinery, or vice versa? Just because Earth took one alternative, doesn't mean to say it's the *only* way.'

'That philosophy,' said Ballantyne dryly, 'sounds home-grown. I'll stick to text books. They're authoritative.'

'And think human.' It was almost as tedious as arguing with Susanna, thought Zeitman. But he could expect no different. Spacers were not necessarily without sensitivities, but more often than not they were.

Susanna, Zeitman noticed, was still annoyed that her attempt to defend him had met with his rebuff. What did she know anyway? She referred to a Ree'hd as 'it', and was far more intent on becoming Zeitman's constant companion than she was in understanding the planet that she was now effectively exiled upon.

There was too much of importance to Zeitman (by his own standards) for him to concern himself with Susanna, how-ever. There were lights in the night sky that were a threat to natural processes on Ree'hdworld, and if there was just one spacer on each with an attitude as well trained in ignorance as Ballantyne's, then the next few weeks could see a constant rain of wreckage and survivors scattered across the two con-tinents.

More worrying, perhaps, assuming that the fugitives in

orbit made it down and claimed rights of survival (and assuming that they survived whatever had killed the first twenty-one) what attitudes might they hold concerning the survival rights of the natives?

People who wanted to land and then commit an honourable suicide (if there were such) would be welcome, but missionaries, seeing in the Ree'hd some sort of primitive and malleable culture, would have to be removed quietly and permanently from the scene.

They remained seated in the skimmer in silence, and the hours slipped by. Zeitman was conscious of time going by, but he felt that Ballantyne – for all that he represented to Zeitman – should give the word to leave his dead companion behind; it seemed to Zeitman that the spacer was growing accustomed to having lost the only person (apart from the unknown Vivienne) that he had felt close to. When he had buried Hernandez completely, they could move on towards the Pianhmar sphere and (on Ballantyne's insistence) to the excavation site.

chapter eleven

There was very little daylight left by the time the alpha-scanner picked up the archaeological site. For nearly an hour the skimmer had been shaken by mountain winds and sleeting rain, driving across the tangled, colourful land below. Ballantyne was fascinated by the jungle and repeatedly pointed out the bulky forms that moved within and across the vegetation. From the skimmer it was impossible to tell which of the meat-eating animals each passing shape was, but to Zeitman there was a passing interest merely in the fact of their presence. It was only the second time he had journeyed into this most violent of the continent's spheres.

Susanna pointed to the flickering scanner and Zeitman turned the skimmer to fly low over the jungle to where steeply sloping cliffs rose above the land. A gorge through the cliffs, a hair-raising run of the gauntlet through up-draughts and between waving plants that slapped and grasped at the tiny vehicle as if they were aware of its passing and were reaching for food. And then they were out and into the start of a deep valley that shimmered purple and red as the rain evaporated and the filtered sun set the air alight.

Only the specifically human-life readings told Zeitman where to look for the camp, and even as they hovered above the site it was impossible to distinguish any human or artificial features below. The whole site was covered by a cryptic water-proofing beneath which, presumably, Kawashima was still digging.

Zeitman touched down at the edge of the tangled undergrowth that formed a sudden and uninviting wall behind and around the clearing. As he switched off the motor he saw a figure appearing from beneath the tent. He was muddy and half naked, a short, fat man, and for a moment Zeitman didn't recognize Kawashima. When he realized who it was he was glad that the man had a smile on his face.

Kawashima waved as Zeitman stepped from the skimmer, then looked up into the sky. He turned back and called something that Zeitman didn't catch. A moment later the canvas covering retracted silently and the work-site was exposed.

It was a shallow excavation but Zeitman saw that this was because much of the excavated earth had been pushed back into the hole. Three impassive Ree'hd squatted by the pit, idly rubbing the dirt from their limbs. They were adolescents and were probably a far more effective excavation machine than the compact robot that Zeitman might have used. Seeing them made Zeitman uneasy, for it was an indication of how callous the Ree'hd from Terming had become. Zeitman knew of no Ree'hd from any commune who could have been induced to come to this sphere, let alone excavate for a sign of the dead. It wasn't necessarily fear on their part, it was respect.

Then Zeitman's attention was taken by the tarpaulin-covered object nearly a man's height, placed a short distance away. Kawashima turned to follow Zeitman's gaze and his grin grew even broader. 'Will this make me famous, Zeitman?' he shouted.

'I imagine,' said Zeitman. 'It's certainly the discovery of the millenium.'

Kawashima bowed, then extended his hand which Zeitman grasped briefly. They looked at each other for a moment, and Kawashima said, 'I guess I owe you an apology. I feel bounteous today! I apologize for my behaviour. Forget it ever happened.'

'It never happened,' said Zeitman, with a laugh. Kawashima's manner amused him. 'You seem to have been expecting us.'

'I was. You know the man without eyes? Maguire? He said he would tell you to come. I was grateful. I wanted a man who shares my love and belief in the Pianhmar to be here with me. I'm glad you've come.'

It was difficult to tell whether Kawashima was playing false. Did he really value nothing but the fame of being the discoverer of the first Pianhmar artifact? If so it was certainly not 'love' that he shared in common with Zeitman.

Behind him Ballantyne coughed, not by way of a hint, but a genuine racking cough, and Zeitman turned to see him staring at blood on the palm of his hand. He wiped the trace on his trouser leg and looked at Zeitman with an expression of despair. Not knowing what to say, Zeitman introduced him to Kawashima, and then presented Susanna.

Kawashima seemed delighted with the girl, and she with him. 'Are you oriental?' he asked. Susanna shook her head. 'Dominion.'

'Ah. Shame. You look oriental . . . I thought you might have been from Japan, from Earth.' He let go of her hand and looked at the covered statue. 'Wait until they hear this on Earth, Zeitman. A university post for sure! What I have always dreamed about.'

So Kawashima was not yet aware of the situation. Zeitman glanced at Ballantyne, wondering how to let the man know to keep quiet, but Ballantyne had interpreted the situation and indicated that he understood.

They walked towards the excavation. 'It's been raining a lot,' said Kawashima. 'Makes things difficult. The water seeps along the top of the soil, though it doesn't seem to penetrate downwards too far. That makes things nice for digging, but how it drains I don't know. Anyway, soil water or no, this statue is in remarkably good condition. As far as I can see it might have been buried yesterday. Hope it wasn't,' he added with a laugh.

They had gathered about the covered statue and now Kawashima unveiled it with a dramatic gesture. Susanna's surprise was the only surprise that registered, but all Zeitman could hear was the stammering of his heart; he stared back through time at a Pianhmar.

The statue was indeed undamaged by its centuries of immersion in the clay-like soil of this part of the continent. There were still patches where the clinging matrix had not been washed away, but the details were there for Zeitman's eager eyes to distinguish.

It would have been larger than a Ree'hd, when standing. Physically it was almost the same, but there was a cranial ridge running from left to right, and the lateral eyes were far more dorsal. The song lips were not lips at all, rather they seemed to have been horny ridges surrounding a tiny gash that would have been difficult to manipulate into many shapes. Probably, then, the Pianhmar had been less dependent upon song and sound. Zeitman had heard from more than one Ree'hd that the Pianhmar had communicated by thoughts, but like all the facts he heard from the Ree'hd he had to ask how did they know? And they only said, *they knew*.

But they may well have been right on this point. In which case the mind-arts were better developed on Ree'hdworld than even the mind-killing ability. And perhaps the Ree'hd were latent (or disguised) telepaths themselves.

It was impossible to tell the colouring of the body, of course, though Zeitman, as he scrutinized the statue closely, imagined he could tell there was a wider and narrower sexual skin than the Ree'hd possessed. The legs seemed the same, but there were ridges of the contractile tissue that showed a different patterning to the ridges of a Ree'hd. By the signs, difficult to interpret as they were, the Pianhmar had been bandier than the Ree'hd, but had been able to crouch with far more comfort; and possibly they could have moved sideways with speed, though if there were any advantage in this Zeitman didn't know it.

He walked around the statue and ran his fingers down the horny knobs that covered the back. Another difference. But it was quite apparent that the Ree'hd and the beasts that this stone idol had been fashioned after were the same stock.

So three species had arisen in the millions of years the Ree'hd claimed they had been in existence, and perhaps among the scanty fossils that lay in the museum in Terming were, in fact, many more relics of Pianhmar, wrongly classified as Ree'hd or Rundii. Perhaps. But *three* species was what fascinated Zeitman. The Pianhmar, rising to great heights culturally, scientifically, and then vanishing, and during all this time (according, again, to the fossil record) the Ree'hd and the Rundii were eking out their existence as wild animals. Relating it anthropomorphically, which Zeitman liked to do, though only for fun, it was as if Cro-Magnon man had existed alongside twenty-second century man for a thousand years, untouched, unchanged, and not just for the few hundred that in fact they *had* existed (until the novelty of primitive man in the twentieth and twenty-first centuries had become too much to resist). Man had eliminated living pre-history, which was no reason the Pianhmar should have done the same. They had existed contemporaneously for many millenia. And that was an astonishing bit of alien demography.

Susanna was now fully converted to the Pianhmar. She also seemed converted to Kawashima and asked him pointed and perceptive questions, and generally pleased him greatly. She was helping scrub the mud from his back, something he was obviously enjoying very much, and Zeitman noticed Ballantyne standing a little way away, watching, seeming sick and unhappy. There was a great blue shadow over the man's left cheek where he had banged his face leaving the skimmer. Zeitman felt a great sympathy for the man, who knew he was dying and knew that it wouldn't be long.

Zeitman led Ballantyne into the large tent that Kawashima had erected for living quarters. Ballantyne stretched out on a soft mattress and sighed with relief. He closed his eyes and smiled, lifted a hand and signalled thanks.

Outside, Kawashima was clean and dry, and robed warmly in a blue gown. He watched Zeitman approach and looked past him to the tent. 'He all right?'

'He won't live through the night,' said Zeitman. 'And I think he knows it.'

'I'm sorry,' said Kawashima, glancing at Susanna who was pale and solemn. 'A good friend?'

She shook her head. 'A survivor we picked up on our way here. His ship crashed.'

'He was trying to land illegally,' deduced Kawashima instantly.

Changing the subject Zeitman said loudly, 'A triumph, Kawashima. A triumph.'

Kawashima bowed and smiled. 'For all of us, Zeitman. For all of us.'

Zeitman took Susanna's arm and led her back to the statue. 'I hope you're a confirmed believer in the Pianhmar now?'

She smiled, and nodded. 'I'm totally converted. Harry was telling me that this was probably buried in the individual's favourite spot. There aren't any remains below.'

'In this soil wouldn't they have decayed completely anyway?'

'No, no.' Kawashima knelt and reached up a handful of the light-brown dirt. 'We've dug Ree'hd remains out of this type of soil. They're very brittle and crystalline, but they seem to survive. I don't understand the chemical reactions, but I think the calcium in their "bones" forms a harder crystal with the minerals in the soil around. But we've found no bones, and I don't think we will. It's like the life-holes of the coastal Ree'hd. They chip a depression in a rock, usually below sea level, and that's *all* they do. The body can be dropped off somewhere for convenience, but the important remains are the depression in the rock, and the memory. I think it's lovely. But frustrating.'

'Very,' agreed Zeitman. 'And what about tools? Any around?'

Kawashima shook his head. There had been nothing but the statue. They all turned again to look at it. All eyes closed, it seemed very much at peace. In this way it differed slightly from the miniature versions that the Ree'hd left in their deserted burrows.

'It could almost be asleep,' said Susanna. 'It's very realistic.'

Kawashima said, 'Do you believe in Universal Axioms, Zeitman?'

Zeitman considered the question for a moment, then said, 'Some.'

'So do I,' Kawashima continued.

'Forgive my ignorance,' said Susanna politely, 'But . . . Universal Axiom?'

'It's a bit of a joke, really,' said Kawashima. 'A Universal Axiom is a cultural ethic that seems to hold true of primitive species anywhere in the Universe. Since Man, Ree'hd and Rundii are the only real intelligences after the dolphins of Earth vanished into extinction it isn't hard to find ethics in common. People write deliberately ridiculous papers on these Axioms, but often there is a considerable amount of truth in what is written.

'The point I was going to make was that there's an Axiom I believe in thoroughly, but it can't be proved. I think technologically advanced beings lose so much identity that their self-presentations either become unconsciously blurred, or laboriously detailed. Art forms during man's technological renaissance contradicted their own ethic. Hand paintings showed, and show, an increasing tendency towards "essence"; at the same time there was, and is, a huge craze for photography, for capturing oneself in explicit detail. I mean, look at the holodyne things – *moving* photographs.

'The Axiom might be true, but the reasoning I've given might not be. Here . . . this statue, I think, represents the work of a race that has lost its self-identity. It needs to present itself in detail to assure a correct after-life. The Ree'hd, fascinating creatures, are exactly the opposite. When they are creating for a positive purpose, such as protecting spirits, they go for detail, yes. But in presenting themselves to history . . . well, a hole in the ground. They seem to be quite satisfied that memory of each individual will last for all time without pictures or statues. It's an opposing ethic to the Pianhmar.'

'How about the Rundii?' asked Susanna. Susanna's conversion to real interest in Ree'hdworld was satisfying to Zeitman in a selfish sort of way; she now represented a potentially far stronger prop for him during the next few weeks.

'The Rundii,' said Kawashima, 'present a problem. They have no real cultural development, but they understand fire and I have seen them use it. They have no obvious self-expression and I . . I still doubt that they are truly self-aware.'

'But they have a language, they talk . . .' said Susanna.

'They talk *at* people. It's often a defensive reaction – highly specialized, yes, but unprovoked communication is what is necessary for it to be used as a criterion of intelligence and self-awareness.'

Zeitman was a little confused by Kawishima's insistence on an old idea. 'What about the curiosity you mentioned?'

'I'm not convinced.'

'What about the Rundii language – the real language, they have.'

'Signs, sounds – basic, primitive. A cat has as much.'

Should he mention his encounter with the Rundii? The feeling of confusion, of awareness he had received from them? No. Kawashima would argue – he was not the sort of man to put any faith in 'feelings'.

Zeitman remained silent, watching dusk fall, waiting for

the wind and wondering whether it would come to this vantage point in the mountains.

Maguire had certainly started something! A change of thinking and attitude in Terming was a foregone conclusion now, and the Pianhmar statue would cause a great upheaval when they showed it for the first time. A legend dispelled, and a new history required.

Maguire had shown the way to that and he seemed to be intent on doing a lot of way-showing. It couldn't be (could it?) that he was in some way involved with what was happening on Ree'hdworld? No. If anything Maguire was a consequence of what was happening ...

The Pianhmar active suddenly for the first time in hundreds of years; the Ree'hd becoming angry with the human presence on their world; the Rundii becoming aware – all at the same time, all in a very *short* time. Coincidence was impossible – there was a link, and Maguire was close to that link.

Where *was* Maguire? And why wouldn't he be still for more than a few hours?

chapter twelve

There, where the river made a sudden turn to the south, a tree-form, sprawled across the water, lifeless. And a few yards from the river's edge, a fire, burning fiercely: a beacon.

The land was in almost total darkness and the fire, small and obviously to be short-lived, burned bright in her eyes. She could see a stooped figure quite close by, and it seemed that he looked up towards her, the firelight making his lateral eyes shine. She could tell it was not Urak, but she couldn't recognize the Ree'hd at all. A feeling of apprehension overwhelmed her relief and she circled lower.

She landed badly, with the left vane caught on some high vegetation, preventing the skimmer from lying flat on the ground. Hardly aware of this she made her way to the fire, looking into the darkness all about for a sign of movement. The Ree'hd was gone when she arrived, and a small pile of dried husks suggested that the creature had stayed merely to feed the inadequate fire.

She was cold despite her layers of clothing. Her body felt dead, in a metabolic trough. It was a few hours from sunrise and she needed to close her eyes and sleep. Crouching near the fire she absorbed some of its heat, but this close to the crackling blaze she could not hear if anything was in the bush around her. And here, in the Rundii sphere that lay closest to the Ree'hd community, there were night creatures that might attack in panic or because they were hungry. The fear-of-stranger instinct had long since passed from these lands.

Where did she start to search for Urak? With her belt-light at full illumination she could only see a distance of thirty yards or so; thereafter everything was a two dimensional vision of black and grey, a frightening wall of indistinct features. The river was a noisy gushing some way to the east, but there was no moonlight sparkle; there were too many clouds.

Crouching by the fire Kristina opened her mind and called Urak. Nothing came to her that she could construe as a reply, and she opened her eyes and stared into the greyness.

She had never before felt so helpless. All ingenuity seemed to have vapourized, all intuition deserted her. She realized that she was counting on Urak appearing from the darkness and taking her in his arms, leading her from the darkness to a place of warmth and light where she could look at him again, and see that he was *not* going to sacrifice his life, and that he had decided to stay with her in the world they both knew . . .

Her eyes began to close. She jerked awake at some subconscious sound and shivered. After nearly an hour the isolation grew intolerable and she walked back to the skimmer. Through a break in the clouds Dollar Moon was throwing light upon the river and with every shadow that passed across the shining surface, her heart jumped and her awareness desperately tried to fashion a Ree'hd shape from what she secretly knew was just a moving animal, or a piece of floating vegetation.

She curled up on the floor of the skimmer and closed her eyes.

During the night she dreamed she rose and walked to the water's edge, and crouched by the river with her fingers trailing in the peripheral currents. Dollar Moon was high and everywhere was glowing with a blue light, and she let her gaze wander about her, searching the shadows. Urak floated by in the water and his body, face up, seemed to smile. As the body passed, it rolled in the water and in the instant before the dead face was submerged, the song lips parted and spoke her name.

She screamed and plunged into the river, reaching for Urak, but he had slipped on into the darkness and her fingers found only an icy grip.

Strong hands took her by the shoulders and pulled her back to the bank, and laid her out upon the cold turf. Warm lips pressed to hers and she gagged and twisted away, and staring upwards saw Zeitman, grinning hugely and bending over her to kiss her again.

'Kristina,' he said. 'It's just you and me again, like it was, like it was. I killed him and there's just the two of us, like it was.'

'NO!'

She twisted from him but he was over her and as his hands tore her clothes from her shivering body she saw, as she lay face down, staring into the brush, the grinning features of Maguire as he squatted like a Ree'hd and waved to her.

'Help me,' she screamed, and felt Zeitman penetrate her and she screamed louder, and Urak walked in front of her and she screamed louder, and Urak walked in front of her, squatted and watched her and his song lips moved, and the words spoke in her mind, 'Physical love is irrelevant, Kristina. You can give Zeitman what *he* wants at no loss to what *we* want.'

She felt water over her head and her feet reached down to try and find the bottom of the river, but there was no bottom and she was carried rapidly downstream, with the pain of Zeitman's rape affecting her whole body. She went below the surface and water filled her mouth and nose and she thrashed wildly and popped back to the surface, screaming and crying and when she opened her eyes there was Urak's dead face rolling over in the water, the eyes staring blindly at her, the lips stretched into a human grin, and as she watched so his arm came out and pulled her under and she felt icy water in her lungs, and Zeitman was laughing somewhere, and his laugh turned into the crying of some lumbering beast . . .

Waking, Kristina found she was lying in her own vomit. The taste in her mouth was enough to make her retch again and she crawled to the medical locker at the back of the skimmer and took out a bulb of mouth-wash.

She could still hear the awful laughing sound that had been the last thing she had heard in her dream. Only now it was coming from outside the skimmer, and looking up she realized that the sky was brightening.

It was nearly dawn, and by the swirling ashes of the fire a huge, grey shape was standing and staring at the human artifact that had invaded its territory. Grotesque, yet comically so, with air-sacs pulsating outside its body, and horizontally slit eyes staring from an enormous mound of a head. When it cried it opened a mouth that split its head from east to west, and three rows of razor-sharp cutting plates sparkled and flashed.

Rubbing her eyes Kristina shuddered as the details of her dream refused to slip away quietly; worse, the details blurred and she was left with the sensations of fear and despair that had predominated in her nightmare. She felt very depressed. Because it was not Ree'hd-like she refused her system the luxury of a nuro-stim tablet. She would overcome the depression by will-power.

As the depression passed, one thought refused to leave her. Perhaps Urak had died during the night and she had dreamed of his body as it really had been, floating silently and sadly down the river. It was an unbearable thought and as she changed her clothes for cleaner garments and tried not to think of what she must look like, she put it from her mind by fussing about her appearance. She felt so messy, so dishevelled, that her greatest personal desire at the moment was to brush her hair through and paint out the signs of strain from her face. But there was no time, and it was too human a reaction anyway. She tried to feel ashamed of herself and succeeded.

When she stepped from the skimmer the wind hit her like a sudden explosion, and the creature by the dead fire bellowed and shuffled forward two paces. She sent the ashes of the fire scattering spectacularly with a well placed burst of her vaze, and the aggressor fled into the undergrowth in total silence. She listened to its crashing departure and when she thought it was safely gone she walked straight to the river and listened for Urak.

After a while her mind became filled with the noises of the voice-network, songs and prayers, jumbled and indecipherable. Nowhere was there any coherence, but she narrowed and widened her mind as she searched for the one voice above all that she desired to hear.

When a voice did speak to her, it was not Urak's.

Kristina . . . stay completely still. Do not open your eyes. Listen.

Who is that? Maguire? Is that you Maguire?

A hand touched her shoulder and she began to move, half opening her eyes and turning her head, but Maguire's voice was urgent and demanding. *You must remain blind. Please, Kristina.*

She turned her head away and closed her eyes tightly. But she reached up a hand and touched Maguire's as it rested on her shoulder. There was something very reassuring about the touch, and she had a feeling that soon she would need re-assurance.

Where's Urak?

He's right here, Kristina – no! eyes shut, body still.

I don't understand.

She felt uneasy. She could hear only Maguire's breathing. There was no sound as of a Ree'hd, or any other being. Maguire's grip was tight and she took courage from the pressure of the blind man's fingers. But inside her closed eyes she was seeing hellish visions and experiencing the visual beginnings of a faint.

Kristina, you must not look at Urak. Do you promise?

I promise.

There was a moment's quiet, Kristina's mind searching, every nerve in her body seemed to be on edge, waiting to respond to Urak's voice.

You shouldn't have followed me.

So calm, so gentle. In her mind the slight trembling of his voice when speaking interLing did not register. It was Urak, and Kristina felt immense relief.

Why can't I look at you, Urak?

I'm wandering, Kristina. When a Ree'hd wanders he changes, sometimes. I have changed a little . . .

It's of no importance. You're so ugly any change is for the better.

Perhaps the change would not upset you, but I would prefer that you did not look at me. I would feel that you were taking from me and I might make a wrong decision.

That sounded decidedly phoney, Kristina couldn't help thinking, but she tried not to let the thought surface too much.

To Urak she said, *'Why should understanding love make you so afraid? I don't understand that Urak. I thought that what we had learned as fact was something wonderful.*

Wonderful, echoed Urak. Was he angry? *Kristina, in your human mind I detect something, a feeling that all alienness must be complicated and unfathomable. Faced with the Ree'hd who seem simple and uncomplicated you cannot accept that this is the case. It may make things difficult that the complex truths, searched for by one race, should be the normal adolescent discoveries of another, but that is no reason for the one to be laughed at and for the process of understanding to be prematurely concluded. This is what I fear the most, Kristina. Not only my own revelations, small as they are, but what your ex-race will reveal because of their insensitivity. For generations, Kristina, the Ree'hd have forced a greater simplicity upon themselves, have been very unforthcoming about themselves and the past, and they had every reason to do that. It would have been so easy for a small team of scientists from your world to examine us, consider us, and interpret us. And if that happened, we would be finished. A few gave evidence that they could be trusted. Yourself, which is why you are now a Ree'hd. And the man you were once with. But even he has not been able to penetrate fully our essential simplicity.*

Kristina was confused. A sharp reminder from Maguire kept her eyes closed, but she shook her head vigorously.

Are you saying that the Ree'hd have a positive destiny – one that is simple by our standards – and to know it before time is to destroy the Ree'hd?

This is what we believe.

And when is time?

When we discover it as a race, for ourselves. Is that not simplicity itself? And really, it isn't very much to ask.

So there was a greater fear among the Ree'hd than the fear of what a vast number of humans might do to the natural history of the place. They feared the questioning few, the curious handful who, with the best of intentions, might cause them to jump the evolutionary gun.

I fear humans for every reason, said Urak, perhaps having followed Kristina's reflection. *For discovery, and for destruction, for their lack of destiny, and their insularity. Your ex-race is a frightening phenomenon, Kristina.*

Kristina thought hard. More and more she was coming to realize that something was very wrong with Urak, that if she opened her eyes she would be very shocked, very hurt, perhaps saddened to the point of her own destruction. What had

Urak meant when he referred to the Ree'hd destiny? Had he meant the evolutionary process that would one day bring them into space, in the tracks of the Pianhmar? Somehow that seemed too gross, too terrestrial. Did he mean the slow process of devolution? The return to the natural spheres of the world? Was that the great destiny of the Ree'hd?

I know very little. But I feel I know too much. I have told no other Ree'hd than you that I feel I have learned more than I should. You, like me, must die with that knowledge. Do you promise?

I do, Urak. Of course I do. But apart from our love, I know of nothing that could have upset you. Is the Ree'hd destiny to understand love?

Partly, perhaps. To understand nature and the forces that direct it. To become a part of nature in every way. To achieve total awareness of nothing but nature. This is how we are motivated and it may be our destiny. Does it sound simple?

Yes.

What is simple then?

There is no yearning in it. There is no direction outwards. There is no striving for new frontiers, for expanding to extremes.

A primitive trait, laughed Urak. *And you're right. We have no inclination to go beyond our burrows. Our purpose is understanding. The Pianhmar were the great explorers. Everything they learned is with us. Everything they saw can be seen by us. Why should we repeat ourselves?*

Kristina said nothing. In her mind there was a vision, a pattern, and she became fascinated by it, and with what it told her. Perhaps Urak had put it there because eventually she realized that he was gone.

She called for him, her eyes still shut, but there was no reply. Eventually Maguire said aloud, 'You can open your eyes.'

The sun was just above the hills, a faint orange disc seen through thickening clouds. The wind had dropped away to a whisper. Looking round, Kristina saw Maguire sitting immediately behind her, his blind eyes not quite meeting hers, a faint smile on his lips. Of Urak there was no sign.

'Where is he? Was he really here?'

'He still is. Every Ree'hd is everywhere that is occupied by a Ree'hd, and you are one, remember?'

'Was he here physically, though?' she asked. She was sad, felt very quiet, almost on the point of despair. Maguire laughed and put his arm around her shoulder. 'Is it so important to you? Can't you be satisfied with closing your eyes and having him with you in your mind, in your soul? Must his grotesque body be squatting above yours, sticky tendrils touching your chubby pink fingers, lateral eyes twisted forward and gazing rapturously at your oval face?'

'He wasn't here . . . all that about Ree'hd changing when they wander, it was all to stop me opening my eyes and seeing he wasn't here.' She hunched forward. 'I feel empty, Maguire. Bloody empty.'

'Then you're no Ree'hd,' said Maguire irritably.

'I can't help it!' She suddenly twisted and stared fully at Maguire, and in her face there was such urgency that Maguire was taken aback and all warmth was lost from his smile. 'What is it, Kristina . . . ?'

'Where is he, Maguire? Where's his body?'

Maguire sat motionless for a long time, as around them the world came alive, and the river seemed to flow a little more briskly. Kristina continued to beg for Maguire to take her to Urak.

Continually Maguire said, he's here, right by you.

At length they rose to their feet and Kristina led the blind man to her skimmer. The vessel shot into the air and then flew low over the land as they headed back into the Ree'hd sphere, following the flow of the river. They left the Rundii sphere.

All the time Kristina searched the ground and the waters below for a sign of the Ree'hd she had lost. All the time Maguire reproached her for being so human when she had adopted a native nationality. But perhaps he saw, in her depression, a dogmatic determination to satisfy, perhaps for the last time in her life, a human whim.

'There, in the rocks . . .'

Below, where the river widened and became shallower, there was an outcropping of crystalline rocks, rising above the water, and sparkling green. Urak lay between two boulders, his limbs trailing in the currents and moving gently. His face was down and there was a gruesome pallor to his skin.

Landing the skimmer at the nearest possible point to the body, Kristina ran along the river-bank and waded into the water to kneel by her lover.

From the edge of the bush Maguire watched her and gradually, for the first time, peered deep into her mind, and what he saw there made him stand, suddenly, in shock, and he shouted, 'No . . . not yet, Kristina! Oh no!'

And as Kristina sobbed over the Ree'hd body she held in her arms, Maguire was gone.

chapter thirteen

During the night, as they lay in the security of the double tent and listened to the movements of the sphere outside, Ballantyne became very ill. He retained consciousness and his sense of humour, but eventually resigned himself to death. Susanna sat beside him and talked to him, and from his body-sack, Zeitman watched and listened. Her voice was a whisper and Ballantyne's a monotonous murmuring, interspersed with his forced laughter. Kawashima slept noisily and talked in his sleep in the incomprehensible language of his father, a crude distillation of the most difficult aspects of Japanese and the most illogical aspects of centauran slang.

By morning Ballantyne's skin was a mass of purple blotches. His mouth was flecked with foam which he tried to wipe away with hands that trembled violently. Susanna had her arm around him and her half-closed eyes testified to her lack of sleep.

Zeitman rolled up his sack and crossed to where Ballantyne was obviously on his way out. 'Any pain?'

'No, thank God. Just a feeling of finality.' The eyes that stared at Zeitman were dilated, almost sightless. 'Is there nothing . . . ?'

'A lingering death, or a quick one. They're your two choices.'

Ballantyne's eyes closed and he nodded imperceptibly. Susanna withdrew her arm from around the spacer and stood up. She walked outside to where the wind had dropped and the first rain of the day was beginning to fall. Kawashima reached into the underbelly of his skimmer, which formed half the roof of their tent, and withdrew a small box. He took out a skin-pad and passed it to Ballantyne who stripped off the covering layer with fingers that were suddenly very steady. Applying the pad to his arm he lay back and waved to the Japanese. Zeitman and Kawashima looked at each other and left the tent.

They washed in the rain (an anomalously warm rain) and Kawashima, without modesty, urinated on to the purplish turf. Zeitman spent a while staring at the Pianhmar statue, its serenity reflecting sleep with uncanny reality. Two of the Ree'hd diggers were some way distant, walking towards the camp and carrying several small animals in their arms. Since an adolescent Ree'hd was unable to mind-kill, they had used their skill with throwing discs. As they came into the camp and dropped their catch, Zeitman, as a matter of instinct, tried to classify the animals and realized that he couldn't. They were variations he had not met before. The Ree'hd stretched their song lips to make human smiles. 'They're good,' said one.

Kawashima glanced at the catch. 'I've eaten them every damn day we've been here. They're passable. Nutritionally useless.'

'As everything,' said Zeitman, more to himself than to Kawashima. The two Ree'hd went below the canopy by the work-site and began to cook breakfast.

The solid forest in the valley was now broken as the tree-forms had spread out and lifted their branches so that the rain would fall into the ground below. Susanna was walking through the 'treeline', two or three hundred yards from where the site was set on higher ground. As she walked, apparently in deep thought, so the life-forms seemed to shuffle away from her. Her red uniform was soon indistinguishable in the brown and blue colouring of the bush.

'Is it safe to walk there?'

'It's not safe anywhere round here, Zeitman,' said Kawashima. 'I nearly lost one of my Ree'hd diggers within hours of setting up camp. Carnivorous giants, completely brainless. They live either on the higher ground in the caves and spend their days scattered about hunting, or in the jungle down in the valley and migrate up here during the day. I can't decide which.'

'These are what the Ree'hd call *Kr'oom*?'

'Variations on the same. Twice the size of a man, with six legs, naturally, the middle pair functioning as arms when moving on front and back legs. They use the top pair when attacking. A very comical beast, Zeitman, except for its ferocity. For a while they were frightened of humans . . .'

'Yes,' said Zeitman. 'I know. The fear of a stranger phenomenon. They've grown out of that for the last two hundred years.'

Kawashima shook his head. 'Not up here they haven't. Not completely. I get the feeling that there's a lot of population movement between the various spheres . . . you know that there are no Ree'hd-killing animals in the Ree'hd spheres, but in the Rundii spheres and up here, the land is infested with *K'room* – blood eaters – and fifty other types. Sure, the *K'room* in the lowlands soon learned that man was edible, and that knowledge has reached *some* of the population up here. But not all, and that means . . . unpredictability. They could be fearless migrants and attack, or fearful locals and run. We haven't had much trouble to be honest. But at night there's a lot of movement outside.'

'Yes, I noticed.'

Foremost in Zeitman's mind now was whether to tell Kawashima that all the fashioned artifacts in the various Federation museums were likely to have been Pianhmar. Kawashima would certainly find out in time, but Zeitman would have preferred not to have been the imparter of that particular information. He was still unsure as to whether or not the Japanese needed the acclaim at being the first to discover an undeniably Pianhmar object. If that *was* the case then, since the man's ego was so formidable, he might find it easy work discrediting any claim that off-Ree'hdworld artifacts belonged to the same race. And that would not do at all.

'I feel,' said Kawashima as they stood in the rain and soaked in the feeling of the place, 'that this valley was once very important to the Pianhmar. I have no evidence for that, of course, but there's an aura about the place. Don't you think?'

Just a valley, wide-bottomed and steep-sloped, with sparkling black and white rocks above the jungle line, and a fairly solid canopy of blue for as far as the eye could see. A sparse area of bush between the dense tangle in the valley and the steeper, exposed slopes of the hills, but a bush layer that was deep and rich. And here, too, were the gentler, soil-covered slopes which Kawashima (with Maguire's hint to deep-ray in the area) had made his find. The whole area seemed to gleam, too brightly for colour to be anything other than a blur. The rain was a solid veil between camp-site and the farther reaches of the valley. There was, as Zeitman concentrated, something enormously peaceful about the place. The rain was a monotonous beating, and all other sound was dead. A clatter from the camp told of breakfast in preparation, but the sound was muted in the stillness. A strange sensation, the more so for being on a world where it was almost never still.

'I don't know,' said Zeitman. 'It looks too natural, too undisturbed . . .'

'It could be as much as three thousand years since the

Pianhmar last lived here. That's plenty of time for the whole sphere to overgrow.'

'Have you searched the valley? The caves?'

'I haven't searched the valley at all. I've been too busy up here, besides which it looks damn difficult getting down there. I looked in a few of the caves, up behind the site, but no, nothing. No concealed stacks of machinery, or give-away chisel marks. They covered their tracks well.'

Covered their tracks, repeated Zeitman to himself; and therein, he thought, lies a history of a whole Universe for man to unravel. Had they not wanted to be remembered? And how could a race vanish so completely, so utterly? How could the metals and plastics of a high technology just become absorbed? Where had everything gone?

To Kawashima (the Japanese went on to say) the obvious place to look, it had seemed, was Wooburren, the smaller continent. Zeitman agreed. He had spent over two years on Wooburren himself and had found nothing but plants, high winds, banshee screams (related to certain flora) and the un-canny sensation that he was being watched, which was a human and very natural reaction to being isolated in a deser-ted world. He said as much to Kawashima who confirmed that he too, within months of arriving on Ree'hdworld, had gone with Kristina to the other continent and systematically searched the place. Zeitman could not imagine why Kristina would have wanted to go again. She, more than Zeitman him-self, had found that land mass more frightening than any nightmare. Towards the end of their time there, certainly, she had begun to feel more at ease, almost finding the place ex-citing. They had left by mutual agreement, and had talked no more of going back.

Telling this to Kawashima evoked a protective response from the man. 'We didn't go alone. We had a Ree'hd with us. Urak? Yes, Urak.'

It was too obvious for words! Or was it? It was not for many months after this that Kristina and Urak had become 'lovers', in Kristina's sense of the word. So Kristina had said, at least. Had she lied? Did their mutual interest go back to a time only months after Zeitman had left?

Kawashima continued, 'She felt close to the world, she said. Closer than any other human. And she said she felt closest when on Wooburren. We spent very little time there, had a difference of opinion which was my fault because I became lonely and searched for some unscientific loving, and was not unnaturally rejected. I hope that doesn't offend you, Zeitman.' Not at all, thought Zeitman. 'The two of them,' Kawashima went on, 'spent many hours alone and out of contact with me and the tiny installation there. Urak, it seemed to me, grew increasingly uncomfortable being on the continent. He hadn't really wanted to come in the first place. It wasn't the eeriness of the place . . . I think he felt he had no right to be there. They were always talking about "understanding". Understanding the planet, or the race . . . I'm not totally sure which. Urak was very disturbed by this because he was understanding too much, with Kristina's help, and again he thought that was wrong. Very queer. They left without me, quite suddenly. We had a robo-skimmer, so I wasn't stranded, but I'm afraid a certain antipathy had arisen between myself and Kristina, and after that – all this time – we have hardly been in contact. She's losing her humanity.'

'I know,' said Zeitman. Losing?

Lost!

Kawashima suddenly shivered. He was wearing only his cataphrak which left his feet uncovered, and he was probably getting a chill. Zeitman, more prudently, had a wetskin over his clothes, but his hair was drenched. As they walked back to the canopy Zeitman spotted movement up on the rocky slopes. Several *K'room* were up there, moving furtively towards the camp. Kawashima noticed them too, but shrugged. 'They're always there. They haven't been any trouble for five days, I don't see why they should start now.'

Zeitman, nevertheless, felt uneasy about Susanna being alone and out of sight. He was pulling on his headgear, and watching as a Ree'hd checked a vaze for him, when she reappeared, walking slowly and without interest towards the camp. Zeitman relaxed.

Kawashima, already eating, pointed to her. 'You say she wasn't a good friend of Ballantyne's?'

'No. I don't know why it should have taken her so badly.'

'Death gets to some people. She's a nice girl, but how can she be your assistant when she knows so little about the situation here?'

'A position of convenience. Her family paid a lot of money to send her to Ree'hdworld. I think they wanted to get rid of her, to be honest. They couldn't . . .' He had been about to say 'they couldn't stop her landing here'. 'They couldn't refuse her, really. I took her on to get her out of harm's way. She's shaping up into a valuable companion.' He hoped that was true.

Susanna walked up to the double tent and looked inside for a moment. She let the flap fall back into place and joined Zeitman and Kawashima under the open canopy, drying her hair with a towel proffered by one of the Ree'hd. She looked at the meat sizzling in the pan and grimaced. Kawashima reached into his suit pouch and found a cheap and nasty nutropak but she declined that too. 'I'm not hungry. And you look obscene.'

Kawashima was still in just his web, which was not very concealing even if it was warm. He pulled his headgear from the pile of clothes beside him and placed it on his lap. 'Better?'

Susanna buried her head in the towel and massaged her scalp vigorously. With a smile at Kawashima, Zeitman reached across to the cooked meat and helped himself liberally. 'Dan Erlam gave me the impression that you've found out a lot more about Ree'hdworld since I left – apart from the Rundii, I mean.'

Kawashima was thoughtfully silent for a few seconds. 'Yes,' he said. 'It was reading your own reports that got me interested. I have no proof for my idea, just intuition . . .'

'Right. Same with me. I felt there was something wrong the first time I got here, years ago now.'

'It's not . . . it's not that it's wrong – it's just, well, too convenient.'

'I agree. What's your conclusion?'

A moment's silence, the fall of rain on the canopy top, and the crackle of fat in the pan. A look between them, an unspoken recognition that each was right. Susanna's drying action stopped. The world around them seemed to listen.

'It's all engineered,' said Kawashima softly. 'We've been sitting in the biggest alien artifact in the galaxy and we haven't recognized it.'

Zeitman could only nod his head. After a while in which no words were passed between them and they did nothing but stare at the slowly cooking meat, Zeitman said, 'Everything worked out for the Ree'hd to save them from perishing. Everything. On their own, without help, they couldn't survive. It's not obvious, and I wouldn't formalize the idea, but I think it has to be that way.'

There was, for example, mind-killing. Kawashima had spent a long time pinning down the generations when mind-killing had first appeared. It had appeared, not slowly, not as a gradually spreading quirk of nature, but suddenly, all at once. It had been a gift – that was the only logical explanation. There was a flaw in that argument, of course, namely that this was Ree'hdworld and not Earth, that evolution here was not towards survival of the fittest, but survival of the most useful. Competition did not work to eliminate the less successfully adapted, but to enhance that which made adaptation for others easier. And that was very different to Earth. Nevertheless, traits did not suddenly appear, and mind-killing as far as Kawashima could determine from yards of burrow records, *had*. And to corroborate his idea, the Ree'hd themselves had spoken of the first generation that had mind-killed, (and that was something that Zeitman had never heard).

Like mind-killing, the specialized digging forelimb of the adolescent Ree'hd appeared to have come into Ree'hd biology quite suddenly. At the same time the Ree'hd were beginning their burrow existence, digging shallow chambers out of the softer rocks and soil of their spheres. Did way of life necessitate form? Or form permit way of life?

And in the environment, too, there was anomaly. 'Silver fish' which contained, in their metabolic network, everything a Ree'hd required, even though, as Zeitman had proved to himself five times at least, there was more to a 'silver fish' than the fish itself needed. Earth that shifted upwards to preserve the softness and richness of the Pianhmar spheres. It was a function of the lower mobile flora, carrying the earth, and it enabled statues to be buried on mountain slopes, despite a soil of clay-like consistency that would have been more logically found on the lower part of the gradient.

Zeitman's personal clincher was the 'coding' of the treeforms, the shuffling, whistling plants that scoured the top-soil with roots that could be retracted in an instant, and which wandered Ree'hdworld as if they owned the place. On both continents an identical tree-form flourished. On the uninhabited one the ten code-cells of each plant showed a single cluster of coding protein. On this continent, however, the cell plasm of each of those ten units contained five clusters of coding proteins, and four were manifestly docile, unused ... waiting.

This, at least, was Zeitman's interpretation. Waiting for what he didn't know; but he was convinced that it was an unnatural possession.

It was engineering!

When he had finished eating Kawashima began to talk about his future. The first thing to do, he declared, was to take the statue to Earth, hold the biggest exhibition in the history of the Galaxy, and draw so much attention to the great history of Ree'hdworld that the grip of InterSystems Biochemicals would be forced from the planet by popular demand!

He talked on, but Zeitman ceased to listen. Kawashima would have to be told that no such idea could ever be achieved – he would have to know the truth; but when? And how?

The Japanese, as Zeitman understood it, had far stronger links with Earth than he himself had. Both Kawashima's parents had returned to Earth when their son had come to live on Ree'hdworld. When he learned of what had happened he would feel a tremendous loss. Zeitman's parents were also on Earth, and yet he felt no such grief. Perhaps because, once he had discovered Ree'hdworld and all that it could mean to him, his parents had slipped from his immediate sphere of love. It was as if they had died many years ago and he returned, on occasion, merely to look at a photograph collection, an emotionless and dissatisfying pursuit.

'You're not listening, Zeitman,' Kawashima snapped suddenly.

'No – I'm sorry, I have something on my mind.'

'Like what?'

And without thinking any more about it Zeitman told Kawashima that Fear had been carried to Earth and was causing the slow death of the world, and that he could never go back.

Kawashima listened without a word, staring at Zeitman all the time, and eventually shaking his head as if what he heard was something he could not or would not believe. He stood up suddenly and walked away from the shelter of the canopy, down towards the valley and out of sight.

Zeitman followed after a few minutes, and found him sitting on the saturated ground, staring through the veil of driving rain towards the gorge that connected this valley with the open jungle beyond.

'I shouldn't have told you yet. I'm sorry.'

'Damn right!' snapped Kawashima miserably. 'I could bust into you, Zeitman! You could have waited. You could have let me enjoy my triumph a while longer. You could have let me dream my dream a few days more. But no. You've shattered me. I feel shattered, Zeitman. And you've done it. Phase out. I need to think.'

Sitting down beside him Zeitman said, 'I'm sorry I had to tell you now, but I couldn't risk telling you back in Terming where you might have run off and spooked the whole installation. The whole of Ree'hdworld is existing in ignorance, except for one or two people, Susanna and myself, and yourself, and the city fathers. You can understand why the rest of the population is unaware of the facts, can't you? You can understand why we have to get everyone off-planet who shouldn't be here, and then stop any further landing at all. It only takes one hysterical Japanese running through the streets and suddenly we have ten thousand applications for survival status. And we certainly don't want that.'

'Okay, Zeitman, you've made your point. And I agree. Of course I agree. Jesus, what a thing! What a terrible thing!'

They sat in silence, water pouring down their faces, off their hands. Suddenly Kawashima pointed towards the gorge. 'You know what they're called, these hills? Hellgate mountains. That gorge, the one you came through, that's hell-gate. It's a Ree'hd term. I suppose in the past a Ree'hd could have wandered here. The hellgate mountains have been carried in their language for a long time. They said they were the centre of the Pianhmar spheres, and that's partly what sent me up here looking.' He seemed reluctant to credit Maguire with any help, thought Zeitman. It was easy to understand what a blow to the man's ego the news had been. 'It never occurred to me at the time,' Kawashima continued, 'to think what the name implied about the Ree'hd, that they have a conception of a dark place.'

'Their dark place is the place where the lost go. Limbo would be more appropriate.'

'Limbogate mountains? Not so impressive. Here we are, Zeitman, in hell. We've lost our chance now. We're out in the cold. Forgotten people. Remnants. You know what? I think there's a common God and he has grown tired of humans. So he's ended them. He brings an end to Earth and knows that every human being who isn't on Earth will die thereafter. There's something about Earth that keeps man driving away from it, but if they lose touch with it . . . they come running back. It's an adolescent reaction, Zeitman. "Look how far we can go" . . . but always in eyeshot.

'We invaded this world and have interrupted a process of evolution, and if we go on interrupting it then this planet will never again spawn fully intelligent beings. They'll never have a chance at getting between worlds, of proving their technology, of benefiting from a Universal knowledge. We'll never know if the Pianhmar made it into space, but I suspect that they didn't. And here we all are, frustrating the planet's second attempt . . .'

Zeitman thought of how wrong Kawashima was, and yet how right!

Here was a world that had given one race to the stars, and was now preparing to give its second. In the same way, perhaps, Earth might one day produce a second civilization, and a third – to match the Rundii? – and a fourth and a fifth. Perhaps that was the way of things in the Galaxy. There were only a few worlds with the potential to produce intelligent beings, and they would try and try again until eventually they would produce the correct formula of intelligence and compassion. Perhaps Earth was too hard, and had ended of its own accord following some genetic blueprint that had been built into man from the beginning.

And therein lay a thought too staggering to take in all at once. Something came into Zeitman's mind, a thought, a memory of a conversation with Ballantyne – What they don't realize (Ballantyne had said) is that they're probably carrying the disease with them. And if it was some strange virus disease, then yes, the panic-stricken refugees may well have been carrying Fear with them wherever they went. But man carried more than parasites as passengers – he carried his own destiny, the basic elements of his own eventual destruction.

On Ree'hdworld, in the space of a few months, several things had begun to happen – if Zeitman were to be honest with himself, it would be impossible to deny his feeling that a trigger had been squeezed, and a set of evolutionary mechanisms started up – perhaps the next in a sequence of events that had been triggered one after another since life on Ree'hdworld began.

But how did *Homo sapiens,* and the trouble that *he* was undergoing, fit into the scheme?

What if man had such a trigger within him? Not in the individual form that he assumed, but in the single entity that was the human race. What if, for the past years, a new process of evolution had been gearing into operation, unrecognized except by its tragic side effect – the neurotic disability that had come to be known as Fear?

The Pianhmar had evolved and devolved, they had lived and died, to make way for a second race. Was man at the beginning of his devolution? Was his ensuing death just part of the natural process of life and not the result of a freak disease?

And if the two sequences of change were not coincidental in their timing, was there perhaps a trigger, a plan of events coded in the whole Galaxy? Triggers in the human race and the alien race being squeezed together . . . evolution and devolution on a cosmic scale . . .

His thoughts were interrupted by Kawashima's loud and despairing voice. 'We've killed this world, Zeitman. There's no way we can undo what we've done, and there's no way we can reduce the continuing effect. We've split the race of the Ree'hd and for some reason they can't be split. There's something about them that requires they all live the same, that they all develop the same.'

'I know,' said Zeitman.

'We've been punished. There's nothing left now.'

'There's still understanding . . .'

'Oh shit, Zeitman! I'm so tired of that word!'

'Tired? Or afraid? Look, Kawashima, you've got the first ever definite Pianhmar remains. The Pianhmar are no longer myth, they're fact. In the last few days we've learned as much about Ree'hdworld as in the previous two hundred years! That's a lot of understanding, Kawashima, and a large stride towards becoming a part of the world. Think of that!'

Kawashima shook his head. He wiped the rain from his eyes. 'No. No, we're human beings and we wouldn't fit in a world manufactured for the Ree'hd.'

'You're wrong,' said Zeitman flatly. 'You're so wrong. With understanding comes belonging. Kristina is already a Ree'hd. She is human in form, but she exists in the Ree'hd sphere, and she is part of the world. That's all that is important to her, and to the Ree'hd who have accepted her. We can do the same, all of us who care. But we have to throw off all our human needs, such as human company.'

'And there are too many humans on Ree'hdworld to make that possible.'

That much was true. There were far too many.

'For a few of us,' he said, 'There is an end more worthwhile than any terrestrial death . . .'

Zeitman looked inwards for a moment and wondered if he was being too patronizing. Where was the cynical streak Kristina had always accused him of having? And why had he not noticed its passing?

'Don't give up,' he went on. Kawashima was silent. 'Don't give up. Keep fighting, keep understanding.'

'Why?' Kawashima shouted suddenly. 'For God's sake why? Who's going to know? Who's going to applaud?' Angry, now, Kawashima began to reflect his true nature. 'This would have made my name, Zeitman. It would have put me on the map. I needed that fame – we all need it, and I was close to getting it! Christ! What a thing to happen . . .'

'In the face of death all you can think of is yourself? I can hardly—'

'Fuck off, Zeitman! Bust out! Leave me alone!'

From anger to melancholy again – a heavy silence, the monotonous sound of rain washing across the earth.

Zeitman hesitated. He could detect, in Kawashima's depression and anger, a stronger death-wish than Ballantyne's. He reached out a hand to touch the Japanese, and Kawashima looked up at him. It was a terribly empty gaze, and Zeitman felt instantly afraid . . .

Susanna screamed.

Zeitman ran through the rain, only half aware that Kawashima had remained seated. When he arrived at the canopy he found the three adolescent Ree'hd lying dead before the statue, and Susanna, on her knees, hands over her mouth, staring at the statue with an expression on her face that was unmistakably terror.

Zeitman turned to look at the statue, and as he did so he took an involuntary step backwards.

The statue's forward eyes were open and watching him.

Clay was falling from the creature's joints as its arms straightened fractionally.

Reaching out, Zeitman pulled Susanna to her feet and without letting his eyes leave those of the Pianhmar, he pulled her away from the creature. A hand touched his shoulder and he struck out, panicking, and sent Kevin Maguire sprawling to the turf.

'Where the hell did you come from?' Zeitman shouted.

'Take it easy,' cried Maguire, and Zeitman stopped. Maguire stood up and Zeitman saw he was trembling. 'I didn't understand, Zeitman, I didn't understand . . .' He began to cry, the tears lost in the rain that covered his face. ' . . . I just hadn't realized fully . . . I'm sorry, Zeitman.'

'What? What is it? What hadn't you realized?'

'Kristina . . . she . . . I didn't understand!'

He turned and ran, and before he reached the beginning of the bush he vanished. Zeitman screamed his name twice but the sound was lost in the downpour and Maguire did not reappear.

Susanna was sobbing. 'It's alive, Robert. It's alive. It killed those three Ree'hd. It *thought* them dead, and then it started to kill me. It was horrible. I was completely paralysed for a moment, and then it stopped . . .'

Kristina – the Pianhmar – Zeitman turned from valley to canopy, his mind in total turmoil. Was Kristina in danger? Was the Pianhmar really alive? – What should he do first? – What was more important? – Kristina – Pianhmar . . .

Susanna trembled in his arms.

Beneath the canopy the Pianhmar closed its eyes.

chapter fourteen

At the burrows, near dawn. Zeitman was haggard and drenched with sweat. Susanna was little better. They had flown all day and through most of the night to reach this place from the Hellgate mountains.

They had hardly spoken a word to each other during the long hours fighting against time. Zeitman had deliberately put all thought of the Pianhmar statue from his mind; he was terrified of feeling regret at having left the site. But if the Pianhmar, assuming it to be a living creature and not an animated representation, had allowed itself to be contacted once, it would allow it again. Kristina's unknown danger seemed, to Zeitman, to be of more immediate importance.

He ran into Kristina's burrow, but it was empty. He stood for a moment and listened to his heart, urging himself to calm, but there was no calm within him. On the walls he saw the graffiti of ages, and forced himself not to look at the pin-woman sign he had seen a few days ago, the first time he had fruitlessly driven to these burrows.

Walking outside again he stood in the darkness and watched a group of Ree'hd making their way towards the river. It was too early for them to be gathering for their dawn ritual. He walked after them and stopped them. 'Where's Kristina?'

One of them made a sound indicating anger. 'That tells me nothing!' shouted Zeitman. 'Where has she gone?'

'With Urak,' said the Ree'hd, and again the sound of anger. They tried to walk on, around Zeitman, but he reached out and stopped them, looked at each of them in turn. 'I need her. Where has she gone?'

'That is theirs to know,' said a young female. 'We are without a One. We are even without the One's kin. They have both deserted. This community will decay. Humans!'

They walked past Zeitman who stood quite motionless and felt anger rise within him. Susanna stood twenty yards away and watched.

The Ree'hd has taken her, then, run off with her!

He felt a fury he had never known, and decided, without conscious effort, that he would kill Urak . . . he would *have* to kill the Ree'hd.

By the water's edge the group of Ree'hd were squatting and mind-killing 'silver fish'. That was strange; it was not the season for catching those animals for food. There was plenty of game to be had on the lowlands around the burrows.

One of the Ree'hd was half immersed in the icy water, picking the dead animals from the river-bed and placing them on the bank. The whole group seemed despondent. They paid Zeitman not the slightest attention.

He followed them down and watched them for a while, able to make out the slightly phosphorescent bodies of the fish, and the dull grey shapes of the Ree'hd. The sun was an hour from rising.

'Why did they go?' he asked. 'For God's sake tell me.'

'To die,' said the female Ree'hd. His cry of anguish was so sudden that it frightened the Ree'hd in the river and he lost his balance and had to swim rapidly against the current.

Zeitman cried her name over and over and the sound carried away through the night. 'Where have they gone?' he shouted. The city, to the burrows there, to the deep place. Would she be so foolish as to go there, knowing that Zeitman would be sure to look? He thought she might. The place had an individual meaning to them both and she may well have thought that Urak should share that meaning with her.

He ran for his skimmer, determined to hunt them down and kill the Ree'hd. Susanna stopped him as he ran towards his machine, and she pointed towards Terming. Following her gaze Zeitman saw what she had noticed and he had not.

The horizon was glowing.

The city was burning. Zeitman, running through the streets towards where he would find Erlam, found himself suddenly moving against a tide of panicked human beings, for the most part screaming their anguish.

He was nearly at the central sector of the city and he could see flames licking high into the sky ahead of him. He could see the tall building that contained Erlam's office. It was not yet extensively on fire, but the building next to it was burning furiously and fingers of grey-red flame were reaching across the gap. Without Erlam to authorize it he doubted if he could get into the burrows from the only direction he could cope with, the museum entrance. It was an uncomfortable thought that Erlam might have been among the running crowds.

Zeitman stumbled over a body, a young man, his face burned away by a vaze. For a moment he was stunned, then he found himself surrounded by screaming people again, some falling, some clutching burns, some dying before his eyes.

He ran to the side of the road and tried to see where the blasts were coming from. There seemed to be two assassins on every roof-top he looked at, and in several windows and doorways too he could see the blue flashes of vaze beams, taking a terrible toll of life.

Not understanding, not wanting to understand, Zeitman crouched low and ran away from them, doubled back and came into the same street some yards behind the area of carnage. Without more than a second's glance at the killers he raced towards Erlam's office.

The streets were filled with dead, and in only a few places were the automatic fire-fighters putting out anything like a combative gush of foam. In those streets bodies seemed to float on a river of white as it rolled slowly between the deserted, burning buildings. It was a sight unpleasant in the extreme and Zeitman kept running, wading, thrashing through the foam, never wanting to stop.

A firebrand floated towards him, touched to a building and spread its fire across the wall. For a second or two Zeitman failed to comprehend that there was anything strange about it; then he stopped.

When he looked again he saw the shape behind the brand,

Ree'hd-like, yet not a Ree'hd. He recognized it immediately. All around him was the crackle of flame and the shrieking of humans, sounds that were carried and distorted by the rising wind, yet this noise seemed to fade as he looked at the shimmering grey figure. Through its form he could see the city beyond it, and in that city he could see more of the ghostly grey shapes, setting fire to each and every building in the sector. The wind fanned the flames and the fire jumped swiftly between blocks carrying its destruction in a rapidly widening circle.

The Pianhmar waved its firebrand again and vanished from Zeitman's sight. Where it had been it left a burning block.

Zeitman left the area and continued inwards, hardly daring to think of what he had seen – a ghost – an avenging angel, setting fire to the cancer that was not yet too deeply rooted in its world.

The building where Erlam lived was beginning to burn when he reached it. Finding his way through flames into the foyer he discovered that the fire-fighting jets were weeping mere dribbles and he smashed through the nozzles so that a great belch of foam covered the floor and the flame. Satisfied that this room at least would remain fire-free for a few minutes, he began the long run up the stairwell.

Erlam's office and extensive living apartment were both deserted, but did not give the impression of having been hastily evacuated. From the window of the office Zeitman had a clear view of the city and could see the extent of the fire. It was extensive. The fiercest flames were to the north where by now most of the buildings were gutted and ruined, and there was a circle of darkness in the spreading inferno. Within that circle there was a shape that was familiar to Zeitman. A large freighter, buckled and burned, lying across nearly a quarter of a mile of city. A large ship with an enormous fuel capacity. Had her Master tried to land in the city? Or had he been trying to land just outside and been hit by one of the installation's ill-aimed missiles? Whatever the reason, it seemed quite obvious to Zeitman that, however much the Pianhmar were assisting the spread of the fire,

Terming had been effectively destroyed by that particular refugee, and was now belching her own refugees into the surrounding lands where the damage they might cause would be irretrievable. Already he could see the flash and scatter of air-sleds taking off across the roof tops. How far would they get, he wondered? How far . . . ?

Behind him the door opened and Zeitman turned. Erlam stood there, face black with smoke, clothes filthy. He held a vaze in his hand pointed at Zeitman, but when he saw who the intruder was he let his arm fall and came into the room, taking a deep breath and wiping a hand across his eyes.

'Zeitman . . . you turn up at the most inconvenient of moments.'

Zeitman stared at his friend, and at the vaze he still clutched. 'You were among them, Dan? You were out there killing those people?'

Erlam tossed the weapon on to his desk. 'Why the hell not? Someone's got to stop them.'

Cold-blooded murder against the survival of the Ree'hd – there was really no question as to where Zeitman's sympathies should lie, but because it was not an expedient to which he himself would have resorted he found it difficult to accept the casual slaughter of his own kind.

He turned away from Erlam and looked down at the wrecked ship. 'What happened Dan? That freighter?'

'That damn freighter. I don't know if it was a missile or bad navigation. It doesn't matter now. What matters is that most people crammed inside it survived. The ship blew out within minutes of crashing down, but by that time Terming had received its first and last consignment of hysterical, angry refugees from Alcayd, a very unpleasant world crawling with crabs where they had no inclination to remain. It took precisely one hour for the news they carried to spread from ship to the edges of Terming. By that time the fire had spread phenomenally fast, and there was no one willing to fight it. They were all too busy running. They reacted in every way I hoped they wouldn't. They completely panicked. A lot of them wanted to get to the landing-site and get a ship home – those that came from nice worlds in this sector, who had least reason to feel they needed to move to safer lodgings in the Galaxy. A few of them may have made it off-world. I doubt it. They evacuated Terming like gas into a vacuum. Christ only knows how many are out there in the surrounding lands now.

'It seemed the right thing to do, Robert. Can you believe that? It seemed the right thing to do, to go out there and kill them. And I wasn't the only one.'

'If you were so convinced of your extermination rights, why stop? Why leave off?'

'Too many of them. Anyway, it's all pointless now. We've not only destroyed ourselves, we've destroyed the Ree'hd, the whole bit.'

'You can't know that for a fact, Dan,' said Zeitman. He was thinking of a circle of dead humans up in the highlands. He was thinking of a Pianhmar 'statue' that had thought-killed three city Ree'hd. The creature might still be sitting there, beneath its canopy. Complacent, eyes closed, wondering, perhaps, why Robert Zeitman had run from it when it had allowed him to live.

He felt angry at himself, and perhaps there was bitterness too, but he shook the feeling off and told Erlam about the humans that he and Susanna had come across in the Pianhmar sphere, and he told him, too, about the humans he had seen as he had flown into Terming, an hour or so before. It had been difficult to see in the darkness, even with the reddish glow cast across everything by the brighter flames, but he had seen, he was sure, hundreds of human shapes, squatting on the ground, motionless. 'If I were you Dan, I'd take a look outside the city walls before you start jumping to too many conclusions.'

'Conclusions!' snapped Erlam. He sat down behind his desk and picked up the vaze. 'Conclusions,' he repeated. Looking up at Zeitman he said, 'This is the conclusion, Robert. And what a lousy end. I had hoped . . . I really had hoped that we could have had orderly withdrawal from Ree'hdworld over the span of several years. I would have really pushed for that.'

'I know,' said Zeitman.

'Times change,' said Erlam, sinking deeper into melancholy. 'I hated every damn human in the city this morning. I hated with my heart, with my guts, a real gut hate. When I went out there, in the darkness with those others, shooting with total indiscrimination into those panicking imbeciles, I had only one thought. Get as many as possible now so we have fewer to hunt down later. Robert, I don't *care* about the people on this world. There are too many of us. I *do* care about me, and I care about the planet. Since I myself have no future I'm directing my talent for orderliness towards the total elimination of human life from Ree'hdworld.'

There was nothing to say and Zeitman found himself staring at his old friend, searching for some sign of the real Dan Erlam, the youthful extrovert, the self-centred man who had conducted affairs in Terming with raised voice and forceful personality. All he saw, as he searched, was an ageing, tired man, fallen and defeated.

'By the time any Federation high command arrive they'll find a gutted city,' continued Erlam. 'A gutted city and a lot of bodies, and just a very few of us waiting to be removed because one thing I'm sure of is that after this there will be no humans on Ree'hdworld for a long time to come.'

'No humans, perhaps, but Ree'hd . . .'

Erlam waved him to silence. 'I know what you're going to say, Robert. Kristina is a friend of mine too, remember? That is . . . yes, that is a way out, I suppose. But not for me. For you, perhaps, for Kristina . . . but not for me.'

The large window of the office cracked, loudly and suddenly. Both men were taken by surprise and turned to look to where thick black smoke had built up to obscure all sight of the city below. Flames darted across the front of the window and as they stared at them so the window cracked again, and fragments of the material dropped to the floor of the office.

'Let's get out of here, Dan.'

Erlam made no effort to move. 'That was supposed to be fireproof . . .'

'Never mind that, Dan. This place will go up at any moment; let's get the hell out of here.'

'I'll stay a while. Go and find Kristina.'

Yes, Kristina. That was why he was here after all. 'Where is she, Dan? In the burrows?'

'Happy, wherever she is. You're close to this Maguire . . . and Maguire is a Ree'hd too. You might be able to find the easy way out.'

'You too, Dan. And Kawashima, and all the others who are closer to Ree'hdworld than to any other.' Fleetingly, he thought of Kawashima, and of the convincing he had tried to do there, and he realized that he was doing a lot of reasoning lately, and getting very little response. And yet he was right. There was no need for the few of them to ever leave Ree'hdworld, and it was that thought that was driving Erlam to obvious despair. They all belonged. Maguire had said so!

'I don't belong and you know it. I'm human and I'm an administrator – I order, I *make* order. There's no law in biology, no sense of orderliness in a random group of random creatures behaving randomly. I couldn't stand it, Robert. I'm not made that way.

'Leave me, will you? I want to think.'

Like Kawashima. Death-wish.

'Dan, there are Pianhmar in the city – I've seen them. Like ghosts. They're burning buildings and mind-killing indiscriminately.'

Erlam did not seem surprised. 'Total chaos,' he said. 'Total bloody chaos.'

'But don't you see? The chaos will be short-lived, Dan. Think about that. A day of panic, and then the remnants will pick themselves up and need a guiding force. Think about it.'

Zeitman straightened up and as he did so, flames burst into the office through the shattered window. Zeitman glanced down at Erlam who stared back and raised a hand in salute; no smile, no sign of inner warmth.

Zeitman turned and ran from the office. Behind him the fire roared louder. See you in hell, Dan, he thought.

Around him there was only fire. The streets were littered with dead, and the buildings grew dark as flame consumed them. Zeitman was an arrogant figure, standing in the square, his face turned to where the grey storm clouds refused to let loose upon the burning city. He screamed for Maguire, over and over. His voice was lost in the crackle and roar of flame and the crash and destruction of masonry. A few figures moved past him, stooped and grey: Ree'hd, moving from the city, out beyond this dying outpost of humanity to where the Ree'hd burrows waited.

Zeitman shouted again. 'Maguire! Where are you? For God's sake, I need you.'

Kristina had not been in the special burrows. There had been only a few huddled people down there, cold and fearful, waiting for the fires to die down. They were still alive, but they would soon die.

Zeitman felt alone. Very alone. Maguire did not answer and Zeitman was at a loss as to what to do.

Through the flames, running and hiding her head beneath spread fingers, came Susanna. She stopped a few yards from Zeitman and stared at him. There were tears in her eyes. 'They're all dead, Robert. All of them.'

Zeitman walked over to her and she stood, motionless, as he wrapped his arms around her and held her tight. She was distressed and he tried to soothe her, but the heat was too fierce, the smoke too choking, for them to linger long.

He led her back through the burning city, to the cooler streets and beyond. He could see the skimmer, half a mile away, and he could see the death toll. It was many hundreds. They sat in the death position with palms flat on the ground and bodies slightly bowed. All eyes were closed and they seemed at peace.

Without touching any of them, Zeitman walked across the hard ground to the skimmer. From its cockpit he could see that there were many more human forms lined up along the river-shore, all crouched as if praying. They had come into the country in the dark hours preceding dawn and had not seen that their precursors were finding a premature and permanent resting-place so close to the city. They had died themselves, then, and in the darkness had been unnoticed as the crowds had continued to flood from the installation.

At dawn they made a bizarre spectacle.

'Who did it? Was it the Ree'hd?'

'The Pianhmar,' said Zeitman. Susanna said nothing. After a while, as they skipped low across a hill and came into sight of the Ree'hd burrows, she said, 'Why would they do it? Why would they kill?'

'Protection. Obviously. But they have a certain compassion; they are respectful of the dead. And they also preserve those who feel for them.'

Susanna looked at him. She was grimy and wet, but there was life in her face, and an almost childish expression of dependency. 'Us? Are we people who feel for them?'

'That's right.' Zeitman smiled, glanced at her.

'But I didn't believe in them before.'

'Nor did I for a long time. Perhaps they spared you because you're close to me.'

She turned away. 'But you still want Kristina. She's been haunting you since we first met.'

He couldn't argue with that. 'I want to find her for many reasons. I want to know how to become the sort of human Ree'hd that she and Maguire have become.' He didn't really think there was anything to know. He couldn't, he knew, be as Kristina, totally isolated from humans and from human motivations. But he could go a long way along those lines. What he really needed was Maguire and Kristina with him, so that together they could survive on this world, and if it had to be, they could wander and die together. Zeitman missed the company of those others who were closest to the world.

Susanna said, 'No, Robert. You want her. You can't be anything without her, and you're nursing a grievance against that Ree'hd, Urak. If she's dead you'll die. If she's alive, but refuses you, you'll do something stupid, and perhaps die anyway.'

'Perhaps you're right,' said Zeitman angrily. He swore loudly as the skimmer landed side first, and span round on the ground, throwing its two occupants out of their seats. He climbed out of the machine and rubbed his bruised shoulder. Susanna came after him. 'Do you want to stay here?' he asked. 'On Ree'hdworld, I mean. Stay and try and find some sort of peace . . . ?'

She shook her head. 'I find no feeling for this place at all. I have no feeling for the Pianhmar, or the Ree'hd, or . . . or even you, Robert. I have no feeling for you at all.'

'You did have . . .'

She looked at him sharply, 'All that death! All those dead people, Robert. It didn't do anything to you. It didn't upset you, or depress you, or worry you . . . it was . . . it was just fact, to you. An event, an occurrence. It was done, and you've forgotten it. I'll never forget it; I'll never understand it, Robert. This is a horrible world, a callous place. I have no wish to stay here, no wish at all.'

She walked past him towards the Ree'hd burrows to ask for shelter for a while. Zeitman watched her go, wondering how she thought she would leave Ree'hdworld. She would probably manage it. There were shuttles at the landing-station, and they were probably still there, and she would escape Ree'hdworld somehow, Zeitman was sure of it.

He went to Kristina's burrow. She was still not there and he stood in the dimness and stared at the pin-woman on the wall. After a moment he drew his vaze and obliterated that section of the wall, and feeling contempt for his own anger he went outside and climbed back into his skimmer.

He had only one idea left. To follow the river until it began, and hope that somewhere along its length he would find her, and Urak, and perhaps Maguire as well.

chapter fifteen

He's coming.

I know. I feel sorry for him, in a way.

I'm sorry too. For misunderstanding everything.

It wasn't your fault, Maguire.

Ignorance is no excuse. I'm naive, Kristina. I just never caught up with my thwarted development.

Don't worry.

But I'm so stupid.

A little naive, as you said. And only as a human.

I was shattered when I saw inside your mind and saw your determination to die. I'd forgotten that you could not lose your humanity completely before you passed on. I don't know, somehow I felt sure you'd get back with Robert, and I thought I'd help things along. I even told him not to worry . . .

I know what you were doing. I forgive you. You weren't to know how committed I was, since you weren't reading me.

Imagine me, a re-matchmaker.

Nice try.

He's landing. He's seen you. He's on his own, no Susanna to be seen. She was nice. Not his type, though.

Obviously not Robert's type.

He's running towards you. Now he's slowed. He hasn't seen me yet. My God, I can sense him crying. He's really crying.

Zeitman approached and knelt beside her. She didn't look at him, but her eyes were open and staring across the water. Here the river was wide and its bed rose to break the water's surface with several boulders; beyond the boulders the river swirled and rushed. Zeitman would have liked to have swum in that turmoil of icy liquid.

The ground below him was wet. He looked about and saw tall, stooping tree-forms, their branches digging deeply into the turf, reaching perhaps through the soil to the river itself.

They were purple-leaved and heavy, and would soon divide. They seemed to listen to the tranquillity.

Across the river the bank was littered with craggy rocks and fan shaped plants that reflected the sparse light in a multitude of colours. Behind them the land rose steeply and to the south was a very high hill, its sheer cliffs presented to the observer from Zeitman's position. From that hill there would be an unsurpassed view of this part of the river valley.

'You've picked a good spot to die,' said Zeitman, hardly able to keep the emotion from his voice. 'Kristina, why do it? Why?'

She didn't smile, didn't flinch. 'I feel it's right.'

'That's what the Ree'hd always say: "I feel it's right." And maybe it is right, maybe it is the correct thing to do, but if you die now, Kristina, I'll never find out. I need you with me as I find out . . . as I find out for myself if it's *right*.'

'Robert, your trouble is, you have no courage, not deep down where it counts. Strip away the outer layers of Robert Zeitman and you find an intelligent man with no strength. A weak man who will spend his life looking for a prop, looking for someone to hold his hand. And what sickens me, Robert, is that even if you know this now, you've only known it for about a week. If you'd recognized it twenty years ago . . .' she looked at him, just briefly. There was contempt in her eyes, and something else . . . a shadow, a hint of pity. She didn't finish the sentence but let her gaze drift back to the flowing river.

She was right, of course, as Erlam had been. There were too many questions he had not asked or had not pursued – and all the time it had been his emotional infatuation that had weakened his approach and clouded his judgement. He was on the verge of redundancy. But there was nothing he could do about it except acknowledge the weaknesses that others had accused him of.

He turned back to Kristina.

'If it's right to die, then why haven't you died already? Why are you lingering like this?'

'I'm afraid of water.' Now she smiled, just a little. 'It's so silly isn't it? I want to join Urak, but I'm afraid of water. When I die I want it to be peacefully, but if I step below that water surface I shall die in agony. I don't know what to do. I've been sitting here for over a day trying to find the courage. Trying to find the sort of strength that you *do* have, Robert. I'd ask you to help me, but . . .'

'No!'

'No, I thought not.'

Confusion and helplessness seemed to be the order of the day, thought Zeitman coldly. 'Where's Maguire?'

'Over the river.'

Zeitman scanned the rocks and profuse plant life on the slopes rising up across the river and eventually saw Maguire, crouched in a small recess, almost completely in darkness. Light flashed from the rings he wore as he lifted a hand in acknowledgement. He was watching them intensely, perhaps himself confused and helpless. 'I needed him earlier. He didn't come.'

'He's been there a long time. When I die he'll spend some time with you.'

It was all so stupid, thought Zeitman. Here, a human woman whom he loved, dying because she thought she was an alien. And not only dying, but forcing herself to die in a manner that was abhorrent to her.

'I don't understand this desire for death. Urak's too. Why does he want to die? Is it me? Does he feel he has done wrong?'

'Urak is already dead. Did he feel wrong? No, he felt he had done everything right. His death, and mine, are for different reasons.'

'Please tell me.'

'We know too much. As a human what I know is of interest, scientific fascination if you will. But as a Ree'hd – which I now am – it is too much knowledge for the stage at which we exist. I must follow Urak into . . . into nature, if you like.'

'Back to the biosphere . . .'

'Ashes to ashes, as they used to say.'

'The "stage" at which you exist,' echoed Zeitman. He thought about that for a while, and about a world where there was much that had been programmed by a greater race than now ruled, and how 'programming' and 'stage-by-stage development' went together in a neat package of cause and effect . . .

Tell him.

Why? You can tell him later.

From you it will give him an idea of why you want to die. It will help him accept the need for your death. Tell him.

She said, 'Three nights ago I joined the Ree'hd in their dusk song for the first time. I felt very strange at first, and shocked, too. They're fantastically well developed telepaths.'

'I suspected that,' murmured Zeitman. He had been right! They *had* been concealing their true nature.

'They're not individually telepathic, but have a mind web, an open channel, if you like, allowing them total communication. They communicate with both the living and the dead. Does that surprise you?'

Yes, thought Zeitman. Yes indeed! So many surprises, in such short order . . .

Kristina went on, 'There is no death on this world, of course. Well, anyway, plants die, animals die, but the Ree'hd and the Rundii and the Pianhmar . . . they don't *really* die.

'Urak didn't understand the mechanism, or the purpose. All natural Ree'hd are aware that they pass between the stages of physical evolution. They all know that their physical destiny is to become a Rundii. They have no individual memory of their lives as Pianhmar, but they all seem aware that the knowledge and skills of the Pianhmar exist with them. They will carry it all forward.'

Zeitman exhaled slowly, trying to cope with the visual images he was putting up to help understand what Kristina was saying. How often they had talked about an after-life for the Ree'hd, and of reincarnation among the Ree'hd population. How near they had been, and yet how far.

'And when a Rundii dies?'

'The completed life process seems to end with the death of

the Rundii form and the Ree'hdworlder then goes to a waiting-place.'

'Wooburren? It was spooky enough.'

'Yes. Urak sensed it. It truly frightened him to be there. Whether or not such prematurely formed Ree'hdworlders have missed their chance of participating in the final great rise to civilization I don't know. I suspect the final manifestation of life on this world will be more metaphysical than physical.'

'How do you know all this?' asked Zeitman. 'Urak?'

'I saw the pattern shortly after he left. He spoke to me of the function of the Ree'hd, and I realized that each race had a different purpose. Maguire filled in the gaps later.'

Zeitman saw the pattern too. It was so alien it frightened him. Not bizarre, just – unhuman. The Pianhmar became masters of technology, and then, in the space of a few centuries, they devolved, and the world became the Ree'hd's, and they became . . . what? Close to nature? Kristina explained it to him as far as she herself understood it: the search for true empathy with other individuals, and how the seemingly obvious truth that love can transcend species, being important only between self-aware creatures of any shape or form, how that might have been one of the 'deep' understandings that the Ree'hd searched for. She had realized the same as part of her own development and had scared Urak when she explained it to him because Urak recognized that he was becoming ahead of his time.

'So what is the Rundii function?'

Kristina shrugged. 'It could be anything. Who can tell? It's still the day of the Ree'hd, and the Rundii have thousands of years of primitivism to live through before the scene is theirs.'

'What does Maguire think?'

'He thinks theirs is to be the final expression of what the two preceding races have learned. The Rundii may well be greater than the Pianhmar seem to have been. But that will not be for an age and a half, and in the meantime there will be a steady accumulation of completed life-forms – they have to mean something to the process of evolution.' She looked round at Zeitman. 'I'm going to stay around and find out exactly what. From the inside.'

Fascinating, thought Robert Zeitman the scientist. An intelligent being with three physical forms, spread through time, and through which it must pass to evolve fully. There would be those that had been Pianhmar at the height of the civilization, and which then became Ree'hd at the beginning of their self-awareness. Others, perhaps, that were Pianhmar in their early stages and which, still waiting, might come to the Ree'hd when the Ree'hd were preparing to make way for the Rundii.

He remembered the gathering place of souls in the old burrows; perhaps it was just a symbol, but it had had more meaning than either he or Kristina had realized. And on the wind, perhaps, came the forms or voices of the waiting lives, and in a sense the past and the present were physically interlocked. And every individual was important because the whole Ree'hd race had to advance together, and achieve its particular understanding together, and devolve together.

Zeitman looked at the ash ingrained in his hands, and thought of Erlam, perhaps a cinder on a cracking street – and the loss was not too great. Not by any means.

He said to Kristina, 'Where do you fit into this developmental pattern? How can you say you're a Ree'hd?'

'I don't know, Robert. I only know that I can. I shall not remember being human, and perhaps I'll make a very poor Rundii. Perhaps we all would if we went together. But it's a wonderful progression, isn't it?'

In his heart Zeitman thought that it was.

Zeitman felt a great emptiness and was conscious of a feeling of loss. It was the feeling he had always feared, that aching loneliness when the mind can picture clearly what it would be like if things had worked out better. Zeitman left Kristina and tried not to imagine her slumped form, short black hair glistening with dampness, body moulded to the ruddy turf. He walked for a long time, thinking about Ree'hdworld, about Earth, about mechanisms of control that spanned millenia.

He began to climb the steep hill and edged around until he was on a narrow ledge leading across the sheer drop that he had seen from the river-side. Here there was a good silence, save for the wind and the clatter of falling stones.

He was only half aware of the increasing height, and the way the land stretched out below him, the distant mountains coming more into view, white-capped and magical.

Tiny cliff-dwelling animals raced vertically up the sedimentary rock-face, and vanished into holes and cracks in the crumbling surface. Others peered at him from their own vantage points. Occasionally a shrill cry split the silence and a bigger creature withdrew its body as Zeitman edged past, holding hard against the cliff and picking his steps with care.

Stopping, he looked back and down and saw the meandering shape of the river with its even width suddenly widening out. He could see Kristina, a small huddle at the edge of the bush.

Sitting tightly against the cliff-face, the tips of his toes just an inch or two away from the drop-away of the ledge, Zeitman closed his eyes and let his whole body soak in the mournful wailing of the wind. It was a good sound because it complemented Zeitman's mood.

He was, there was no denying, a shameful example of a rational thinking man. He had asked the right questions, but in the end he had turned to others for the answers. Although that wasn't completely true; he had figured out the engineered nature of Ree'hdworld – a vestige of what he had once been had allowed him that last insight. He was grateful for that.

So much had happened in so short a time, and the extremes were staggering. He had arrived on Ree'hdworld hoping to spend the rest of his days in the scientific establishment at Terming, and in less than a week he had seen that city burned to the ground. He had come back hoping to find a new relationship with his wife, and he had found a woman shrugging off the last vestiges of her humanity. He had come back to a world of legend and found the legend to be fact with the Pianhmar, now participating so actively in the reassertion of

Ree'hdworlder control of the planet, spreading fire in the city and terminating the lives of those humans they could see were likely to be detrimental to the Ree'hd.

The Pianhmar had assisted the Ree'hd before. They were – truly – guardian angels. Zeitman wondered if, by engineering the environment as they probably had done, they might have negated much of the point of the Ree'hd phase of their existence. He ran the question over and over in his head, wondering if he was missing a point somewhere . . .

He sank into a semi-doze – his body's reaction to its own chill. The wind was very cold and blew in his face. He felt his hair moving, followed the ripples of sensation across his face, sank deeper into sleep . . .

Water filled his lungs!

He came up choking and screaming, and then a more ferocious sensation hit him – pain, deep in his chest, spreading through his whole body, numbing his legs and arms.

'Kristina!' he screamed, coming to his feet and staring down into the river-valley as the killing pain ebbed his strength away.

He saw her in the water, a slim shape vanishing beneath the surface, and in that moment he went completely limp and felt the cliff leave him, was vaguely aware of his fall, and the painless impact that drove his senses from him.

chapter sixteen

There was no sensation of time passing. Still shocked at the death of his wife, Zeitman returned to awareness, but the lingering emotion of that instant on the cliff passed rapidly from his system.

'I can't move.'

'Don't try.' Maguire's voice.

'And it's dark. Are my eyes open? Is it night? I'm in bandages, is that it?'

'Keep calm, Robert. You're in good hands.'

He fought against the darkness. It was a terrifying sensation and he fought it with all his will. He knew, without knowing, that his eyes were open, that the sun was trying to shine, that there were no bandages hiding his eyes.

He was blind. Totally. And he could not move.

'The fall . . .'

'It was a long fall and you were lucky to survive. But you have me and I'm not going to leave you.'

'Maguire.' Zeitman reached out and felt for Maguire and realized that he had not moved. He couldn't move; his limbs refused to twitch. He felt confined, as if he were bound in some metal strait-jacket and could not even blink his eyes.

Maguire told him they were nearly a hundred miles from where he had fallen. Zeitman tried to monitor the sensation coming from his touch receptors and gradually became aware of some girding restraint. When he asked about it Maguire explained that he was strapped and secured to a stretcher.

'Are you taking me somewhere?'

'Into a Pianhmar sphere. I would have jumped with you in short jumps, but I found I couldn't manage it. We have to do it the hard way.'

'And you're pulling me all the way to the Hellgate mountains?'

'No. I enlisted the aid of four Rundii.'

Now Zeitman heard the laboured breathing all around of creatures of Ree'hdworld. 'But, how . . . ?'

'Communication,' said Maguire. 'Communication of my need. They understand more than your human friends gave them credit for . . .'

He lay calm in the darkness and tried to imagine it as night, or in a darkened room. When panic began to creep into the pit of his stomach he fought it back. He felt a lurching movement and realized that he had regained consciousness during a brief respite. Now the group wound on through the river-valley, climbing, Maguire said, to come over the hills at their lowest point. Beyond the hills was another river where there was much for Maguire to remember.

They reached this place within a day and Zeitman listened to the water and the winds, and he heard the Rundii murmuring in their guttural language, and he heard Maguire murmuring his thoughts.

At length Maguire reached out a hand and touched Zeitman's face. 'Are you awake?'

'Yes,' said Zeitman. In the last few hours he had realized that not even his lips could move. When he spoke, then, he was speaking without sound, although all the cranial sensations of vocalization were there. Maguire had affirmed that they were not talking aloud. 'But don't worry,' he said. 'You are already mending and the Pianhmar will finish mending you completely.'

'Thank God. I couldn't bear this darkness for very long.'

Maguire was conspicuous by his silence. Zeitman said, 'What is it? What about my blindness? They *can* fix me, can't they?'

'I don't know,' said Maguire. 'They may choose not to. I can't tell.'

Oh God, thought Zeitman. Oh sweet Saviour, I'm blind for life. I'll stare into blackness until I die. 'Why?' he demanded. 'Why should they choose not to mend my sight?'

Maguire said, 'Don't think about it, Robert. You'll only distress yourself. Listen, do you know what this place is? This is the place that my old friend Hans-ree left his physical life. He was attacked by a *K'room* and it dismembered him and scattered him in front of me. Horrifying moment. In those days I was as blind as you, sightwise. But I looked across the river and saw a mountain, and felt that mountain move, and felt it by sensing the pattern of the winds, and the movements of sound from its slopes and crags. Can you see that mountain Robert? Can you feel it? It's there, a beautiful mountain, all purple plants and blue and silver rocks. I feel very at home with that mountain.'

Zeitman said nothing. He tried to imagine what Maguire

was looking at with every sense . . . with every sense except sight itself. He tried to imagine what it was going to be like never seeing again, never experiencing a sunrise . . . except by feeling how it affected the wind!

It distressed him and he withdrew for a long time.

They moved on. Days. Long days and Maguire talked very little. He poured water and liquid food between Zeitman's lips and massaged his body vigorously every day. After a while Zeitman felt sensation of movement returning to his limbs. He felt the satisfying twitch of muscle as he exerted his willpower. Maguire said, 'Good. Good. You're twitching like it's all there is to live for. Keep trying.'

One day, after Zeitman had slept long and soundly, they came to the Hellgate mountains and found the remains of the excavation that had brought Kawashima to his own sought-after heights.

By now Zeitman could move his hands, and he could appreciate touch and temperature on most of his body surface. But he was still substantially paralysed. He could blink, and when he blinked he imagined he could see lights, but they were meaningless. He could move his lips and make swallowing motions.

'Is it still there?' he asked Maguire.

'The Pianhmar? Yes, he's still here. You'll see him again. Soon, I hope. And you'll see more.'

'How much more?'

'You'll see the valley. You'll see a sight that may frighten you, but I doubt that it will.'

Impatient to see again, but not daring to ask how Maguire could be so sure now that he would, he said, 'What's in the valley? Describe it.'

'Pianhmar. Millions of them. The ghost forms, of course – they've all left their bodies behind a long time ago. They are the Pianhmar who have not yet passed into the Ree'hd form, and they fill this valley, and all the valleys behind.'

Zeitman lay in silence, trying to imagine what Maguire was seeing, a forest-filled valley seething with life-forms from another age. 'I was here. I looked down that valley with Kawashima, and we saw nothing.'

'That doesn't surprise you, does it?' asked Maguire. 'They're not going to let themselves be seen.'

Zeitman listened hard for some sound that would tell of the gathering Pianhmar, but there were only natural sounds.

Maguire said, 'When I first came to this valley it was filled with what I thought were statues. I sat on them, scraped them, leaned against them, and you can imagine how startled I was when I was told that these "burial" statues were in fact the Pianhmar themselves.'

'Not just animated statues, then, but living creatures . . .'

'Almost right . . . they are Pianhmar in stasis, and whether or not that constitutes living . . . well, you're the biologist. They adopt the static form before they die, living in a sort of suspended animation for hundreds and hundreds of years, gradually becoming buried. They *can* come out of stasis since mentally they are still active and aware. The few that I met when I first came up here had done so and they stayed with me for a long time. They helped me to understand what was going on, and all the time they were eaten up with grief at my blindness. They hated to be looked at directly, which is why I had been sent in the first place, but meeting an intelligent creature with no visual sense hit a heart chord somewhere in them and they took me under their wing.'

'And stayed with you for seven hundred years.'

'Sort of. I suppose their physical forms returned to the soil. The whole race was devolving, as you put it. Fading out. In those last few hundred years there was a sense of conservation of life force, and life force was draining into the world, or could be taken by seeing creatures – strange, Robert, isn't it? A race as advanced as the Pianhmar adopting such a primitive trait at the end. But they weren't primitive by any means. They took me across the Galaxy. A first look for a blind man. A last look for the Pianhmar themselves. You know what? I still don't know what form or shape or size I was. We visited places that had been important to them, worlds where they had once lived in great numbers. On some there were humans, but they never seemed to see us.

'Then they became agitated. I didn't understand why until I got back and found that the Rundii were rising fast, and that a bloody great alien city was set in the middle of the continent and acting as a very efficient thorn, worrying away at the Ree'hd.'

Zeitman interrupted him. 'Something I don't understand – why did they take you like that? What did they hope to gain . . . .?'

Maguire shook his head. 'It's difficult to say, even now. Perhaps compassion for a blind man who had worked so hard to find them . . . but also, I think, there was a moment of panic – a long moment of panic when the realization of their dying clashed with . . . what can one say? . . . the fact of their achievements. Pride, perhaps, an unwillingness to become totally eclipsed without just *one* outside intelligence having seen a fragment of their work.'

'The pride before the fall,' said Zeitman.

'Yes.' Maguire was sad. 'Yes, I suppose so.' After a silence lasting several seconds he went on, 'The Pianhmar left me, on a world where there was a human city set – though they didn't know it – upon a Pianhmar city of twenty thousand years before. I shipped back to Ree'hdworld as soon as I could – I couldn't use my special talent to travel that far, not without their help. Soon after that I made the acquaintance of Robert Zeitman, and Kristina Schriock, and Harry Kawashima.'

'Kawashima. Where is he?'

Maguire was silent, but on Zeitman's insistence he finally said, 'He could have become a part of things, but he was too much the glory-hunter. He couldn't overcome his depression. A great loss.'

'And Erlam?'

Maguire laughed. 'I think he saw reason. The last I saw of him he was busy organizing the reduction of Terming to a rubble. They've erected a tent-city, just like the one that I came to for the first time.'

For a moment Zeitman felt a great cheerfulness; he had thought Erlam dead for sure, and he was relieved to know that the man had survived his fit of melancholy.

It began to rain, hard and cold; Zeitman felt it on his body and loved it. The rain was driving down the valley, from the direction of the gorge he had navigated with Susanna not so long ago.

He heard the shuffling and complaining of the Rundii, running for the shelter of Kawashima's canopy, still in place. He felt his stretcher being pulled and Maguire's laboured breathing told of the struggle the blind man was having.

'No. Don't move me . . . I like it.'

The motion stopped and Zeitman heard Maguire come to squat beside him, and the rain drenched them, soaked them to the skin.

There was a strange sensation behind Zeitman's eyes, not of colour but of movement. As he stared blindly across the valley, so form and definition came to the movement and he saw them then – thousands, perhaps millions as Maguire had said. They covered the hills and the boulder and forest-strewn valley bottom, and there were many who sat quite close to Zeitman and watched him.

'You've seen before,' said Maguire. 'Imagine what it was like for me, experiencing sight for the first time.'

'Whose eyes am I seeing through?'

'Theirs. There is a Pianhmar with you now, and he will remain with you until you die. There's one with me, always has been. Unconscious, unintrusive. You'll see better than any human because you see an object in whatever way you want to. Infra-red, it's there at a thought; ultra-violet, the same thing. The Pianhmar have a very expansive visual sense – even in the ghost-form. They won't return your own sight, but you'll find that's no loss. They need you, and they need you with as much sensory perfection as is possible.'

Zeitman continued to stare at the gathered masses of the Pianhmar. There were so many . . . and they needed him . . .

Then Maguire's words registered and he asked what he had

meant. How could they need a man who was crippled? What could *he* do?'

'You won't be crippled long,' said Maguire. 'And what can you do? Perhaps nothing. Perhaps a lot. During the next few years there has got to be much change on Ree'hdworld. What's left of the Federation must be fully acquainted with the situation here and the final decision to isolate the planet must be based on knowledge and reason, not on fear. You may become a very active contact man.'

'You and me both, I hope,' said Zeitman.

Maguire was quiet for a moment. 'Not me, Robert. I'm too old. The Pianhmar will patch you up as good as new, but for my part, it's time I acknowledged the fact that I'm long past my second childhood.'

He was gone, then, and Zeitman was alone. He watched the Pianhmar and the Pianhmar watched him, and after a while he realized that he was no longer afraid.

OTHER TITLES AVAILABLE FROM
VGSF

The prices shown below were correct at the time
of going to press (January 1987)

☐	03995 7	WITCH WORLD	*Andre Norton*	£2.50
☐	03990 6	THE MASKS OF TIME	*Robert Silverberg*	£2.95
☐	04008 4	HEGIRA	*Greg Bear*	£2.95
☐	04032 7	THE FACELESS MAN	*Jack Vance*	£2.50
☐	03987 6	NIGHT WALK	*Bob Shaw*	£2.50
☐	04009 2	ANGEL WITH THE SWORD	*C.J. Cherryh*	£2.95
☐	04022 X	MISSION OF GRAVITY	*Hal Clement*	£2.50
☐	03988 4	THE OTHER SIDE OF THE SKY		
			Arthur C. Clarke	£2.95
☐	03996 5	WEB OF THE WITCH WORLD	*Andre Norton*	£2.50
☐	04010 6	EYE AMONG THE BLIND	*Robert Holdstock*	£2.50

Available July 1987

☐	04007 6	STAR GATE	*Andre Norton*	£2.50
☐	03989 2	TO LIVE AGAIN	*Robert Silverberg*	£2.95

Available August 1987

☐	03999 X	YEAR OF THE UNICORN	*Andre Norton*	£2.50
☐	04053 X	THE BRAVE FREE MEN	*Jack Vance*	£2.50

Also available: GOLLANCZ CLASSIC SF

☐	03819 5	THE SIRENS OF TITAN	*Kurt Vonnegut*	£3.50
☐	03821 7	MORE THAN HUMAN	*Theodore Sturgeon*	£2.95
☐	03820 9	A TIME OF CHANGES	*Robert Silverberg*	£2.95
☐	03818 7	NOVA	*Samuel R. Delany*	£2.95
☐	03849 7	THE CITY AND THE STARS	*Arthur C. Clarke*	£2.95
☐	03850 0	THE DOOR INTO SUMMER	*Robert Heinlein*	£2.95
☐	03852 7	WOLFBANE	*Frederik Pohl & C.M. Kornbluth*	£2.95
☐	03851 9	THE REPRODUCTIVE SYSTEM	*John Sladek*	£2.95
☐	03978 7	A FALL OF MOONDUST	*Arthur C. Clarke*	£3.50
☐	03980 9	A WREATH OF STARS	*Bob Shaw*	£2.95
☐	03979 5	ROGUE MOON	*Algis Budrys*	£2.95
☐	03981 7	MAN PLUS	*Frederik Pohl*	£3.50
☐	03993 0	INVERTED WORLD	*Christopher Priest*	£3.50
☐	04061 0	FLOWERS FOR ALGERNON	*Daniel Keyes*	£3.50

All these books are available at your shop or newsagent or can be
ordered direct from the publisher. Just tick the titles you want and fill
in the form overleaf.

VGSF, Cash Sales Department, PO Box 11, Falmouth, Cornwall.

Please send cheque or postal order, no currency.

Please allow cost of book(s) plus the following for postage and packing:

UK customers – Allow 60p for the first book, 25p for the second book plus 15p for each additional book ordered, to a maximum charge of £1.90.

BFPO – Allow 60p for the first book, 25p for the second book plus 15p per copy for the next seven books, thereafter 9p per book.

Overseas customers including Eire – Allow £1.25 for the first book, 75p for the second book plus 28p for each additional book ordered.

NAME *(Block letters)* ....

ADDRESS...

....

....